HITLER'S BOMB

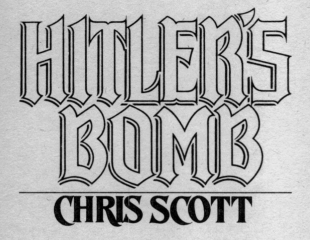

CHRIS SCOTT

STEIN AND DAY / *Publishers* / New York

The principal characters in this book are fictitious and are not derivative of anyone living or dead. Some of the people and organizations referred to exist or existed, but any words, actions, or attitudes attributed to them are entirely the product of the author's imagination.

FIRST STEIN AND DAY PAPERBACK EDITION MAY 1986
Hitler's Bomb was originally published in hardcover
by Stein and Day/*Publishers*.

STEIN AND DAY/*Publishers*
Scarborough House
Briarcliff Manor, N.Y. 10510
ISBN 0-8128-8240-7

For Heather Sherratt

Author's Note

The true story of the Nazi atom bomb project is told in David Irving's *The Virus House* (London: William Kimber, 1967), to which book the author acknowledges a large debt. The American side of the story is covered by *The Secret History of the Atomic Bomb*, edited by Anthony Cave Brown and Charles B. MacDonald (New York: Delta, 1977); and the subject is examined from the point of view of British scientific intelligence by R. V. Jones's *Most Secret War* (London: Hamish Hamilton, 1978).

Chris Scott
McDonald's Corners, Ontario, 1985

Beware the Jabberwock, my son!
The jaws that bite, the claws
that catch!
Beware the Jubjub bird, and shun
The frumious Bandersnatch!

—Lewis Carroll
Through the Looking Glass

HITLER'S BOMB

PROLOGUE

Carlo Peat met Johnson in the lobby of the Hotel Metropole, Lugano, on the afternoon of August 28, 1982. Carlo had aged, the reporter thought, since their last meeting six or seven years ago. How old was he now? Seventy-one or -two? But he still had that baby-faced look about him, the look of an old baby born too late, a Victorian antiquary long incubating in time's womb.

They went up to Carlo's room, a room with a view overlooking the lake. Johnson talked about Piltdown Man and the deathbed confession of a Cambridge professor that exonerated Charles Dawson, the Sussex solicitor who had found the bones.

"I think it was that French priest who did it," Carlo said. "What's the man's name?"

"Teilhard de Chardin." Johnson said it. "Why him?"

"Because he had a theory that fitted in with the bones," Carlo said. "Because he was there when they were found, and so had opportunity as well as motive; because he was a priest, and therefore beyond suspicion; and because he had a sense of humor, and was human. It seems obvious to me." Carlo sounded bored.

Artfully, Johnson turned the conversation to an art historian unknighted, and another, more well-known historian who had resigned from the British Academy to protest the persecution of gentlemen spies. It wasn't what the reporter wanted to talk about, but it would do.

"Ah, the fickle majesty of princes," Carlo said. "The vorpal blade goes snicker-snack. So very British. No wonder the rest of the world finds it hard to understand us. Soon there'll be nothing left to resign

13

from, and that will be the end of that. Do you know the story about Philby?"

"Which one?"

"In Moscow. Philby hears they're going to make a film about him. 'F-f-fine,' he says. 'Who's playing me?' They tell him Michael Caine. 'Oh, no,' says Philby, 'not a f-f-fellow like that. He couldn't play me. Not a cockney. No class.'"

Johnson smiled. "Did Philby have class?"

"He had, I think, what the Greeks called *aristeia*. He was very good with women and brigadiers."

"You used to call him Harold, didn't you?"

"Still do. It's his name. I called him other things, too."

"But never Kim?"

"Too Kiplingesque. I was an intelligence officer. Too practical to be seduced by anything resembling an idea." Carlo's eyes twinkled. They were merry and very blue, and Johnson knew that look of old.

"Tell me about the German atomic bomb," he said.

"There wasn't one."

"It's odd you chose this hotel," Johnson said. "A man called Dorf stayed here in February 1945—Generaloberst Wilhelm Friederich Dorf."

Carlo got up and walked over to the balcony overlooking the blue sweep of the lake. "Would you like a sherry, Mr. Johnson?"

"Findlater's," Johnson said, a ritual drink with Carlo. He watched Carlo pour and went on: "Dorf was on the board of Degussa, the parent company of Auer Gesellschaft, the chemical company that refined the uranium at Oranienburg concentration camp. Degussa is one of those acronyms the Germans were so very fond of. It stands for the *Deutsche Gold und Silber Scheideanstalt,* the German Gold and Silver Refining Company. They're still in business, still in the *same* business—separating U^{235} for Bonn's nuclear generating plants, read plutonium for the American military. Colonel General Dorf met Miles Cavendish here on the seventeenth of February 1945, a Saturday. Cavendish was one of your agents."

"I forget," said Carlo obtusely.

"Balthazar," Johnson said, "that's what you used to call him. You hadn't forgotten him the last time we met."

"Oh, but he's dead, Mr. Johnson. He was dead then and that must mean he's dead now. So few of us come back to life, you know." Carlo handed the reporter a sherry. "You must have such a different perspective on things," he said, "having grown up with the bomb, I mean. Obviously, we didn't. Let me tell you a story. I knew this man once—call him Brown. He was from Tube Alloys, which was sort of like our version of the Manhattan Project before we threw our lot in with the Americans—the tubular man, I called him. At the beginning of the war, the tubular man was the recipient of one of Churchill's 'prayers.' This one went something like this: 'Pray tell me, what is the likelihood of German atomic bombs raining down on London?' That shows you how ignorant we were, you see."

"You mean Churchill used the plural?"

"Exactly. One bomb would have been enough. We had no real idea of what we were dealing with. Even at the beginning of 1945, although the Manhattan Project was well under way, Trinity—the first actual test of the bomb—was still several months off. That was in, ah, July, I think, if memory serves me correctly. Then, of course, with all the secret weapons and everything, we began to wonder whether the Germans really had beaten us to the post. We had such a good source, you know. Bandersnatch—Philby's source. Everything had to go through Philby, or not through him—depending on the case. If Philby didn't like something, he could sit on it. Like the July Plot. He was head of the German section, you see, and controlled all our games with the enemy."

The reporter nodded; Carlo sat down and sipped at his drink. "Even the scientists were at sixes and sevens," Carlo added. "The tubular man came unstuck with the PM, by the way. In 1941 he pooh-poohed the notion of Nazi atom bombs raining down on London and four years later he had to admit that one bomb might be enough to do the job."

"I imagine that spoiled his chances for postwar preferment," said Johnson.

Carlo smiled. "And then there were the Webers," he said. "Herr Professor Weber saying one thing and his daughter the opposite."

"Tell me about them," the reporter urged.

"It was such an incredibly brilliant provocation," Carlo mused.

"Wasn't she a Nazi who realized that the war was lost and that she'd better take her business elsewhere?" asked Johnson.

"Oh, no, Mr. Johnson." Carlo contrived to look quite shocked, the reporter thought. "In her case I don't believe politics entered into it at all. Love, perhaps, various kinds of. As simple as that."

"Or as complex?"

Carlo signified assent by waving his free hand. "Mind you," he conceded, "there may have been something of what you say in her father, but he was moved by personal and professional considerations—as indeed was Katherina, though with somewhat different effects. There's no denying that she was a very courageous person. By the way, when I said just now that there wasn't a German atomic bomb, that doesn't mean there wasn't any research effort. They had one of the best theoretical physicists in the world, Werner Heisenberg, who won the Nobel prize in '33. You should remember that it was the victors who wrote the history, and to the victors, the spoils—in this case most of the German nuclear scientists."

"As well as the rocket people," Johnson said.

Carlo nodded. "Naturally, that worried us the most: the possibility of a nuclear device in one of their V-2 rockets, though as it happened things didn't quite turn out that way. . . ."

The reporter waited patiently.

"What I remember most is a box of matches, the name of an inn, and the Greek word for olive grove," said Carlo, wondering how much, if any, Greek the reporter knew.

"It's *Alsos*," Carlo began.

1: SOURCE

> *"High treason is high treason."*
> —General Gehlen, *Memoirs*

Memo to: H.C.P.
From: H.A.R.P.
December 21, 1944

ULTRA SECRET

Source BANDERSNATCH reports évacuation of Kaiser-Wilhelm Institute for Chemistry to HECHINGEN, a small town forty kilometers southwest of Stuttgart, last February. Same source reports completed evacuation of KWI for Physics to south Germany at the end of last month (July). Among scientists reported moving south, or about to move, are Werner HEISENBERG, Otto HAHN, Karl von WEIZSÄCKER, Karl WIRZ, and Hugo and Katherina WEBER. Professor GERLACH of Munich has suggested site at HAIGERLOCH, fifty kilometers southwest of Stuttgart, for Berlin VIRUS HOUSE pile B VIII. Site understood to be wine cellar of Swan Inn has been requisitioned by the Reichsforschungsrat, the Reich Research Council, under code name SPELEOLOGICAL RESEARCH UNIT. Source reports deliveries of coke and electrical generating equipment to HAIGERLOCH, but no heavy water or *Spezialmetall*.

"Precisely the point, of course," Kim Philby remarked. He was hunched forward in a swivel chair, his jaws clenched on an unlit pipe. A tin of Balkan Sobranie, unopened, sat on his desk. He was very English—tweedy, with a cultivated stutter. Before the war he had been a member of the Anglo-German Fellowship. Because of his connections, Philby had to do with all things German at Broadway. The Friends, in their clubby way, knew him by the sobriquet Kim, after the hero of Kipling's novel, a man with two sides to his head. To his face Carlo had never called him anything but Harold. Harold Philby. So prosaic. Carlo was like that.

"Is it?" he asked, knowing that Harold loved mysteries. Light streamed in through the window, a mellow December morning though the forecast called for snow and the gas fire stuttered in Harold's grate, a poisonous blue.

"*Spezialmetall.* U^{235}."

"Why saddle me with this, Harold?" Outside the relatively specialized world of disinformation, Carlo allowed himself few diversions, and nuclear physics was not one of them. A classicist by training, he had written a book on the Manichaeans—*Mani: Father of Grandeurs and Prince of Darkness.* The book was an indulgence, angelology another (his father had been a Church of England clergyman), along with Chinese domestic well architecture of the Fifth Han Dynasty, on which subject he was an authority. "I know nothing at all about nuclear physics," he complained, adding to make himself perfectly clear: "Absolutely. Nuts and kernels. Democritus. All bosh. Matter doesn't interest me. In any case this memo is way out of date. It says July here and it'll soon be Christmas. How do you make water heavy, Harold? I suppose you're going to tell me they've got the uranium, and that this is all part of Werewolf and the Alpine Redoubt?"

"Haigerloch is in the B-b-black Forest, actually."

"Sorry." Carlo waved aside Harold's objection. "I never was much good at geography, either. Bandersnatch, isn't that from *Alice in Wonderland?*"

"*Through the Looking Glass*—'The Jabberwocky,' you know."

"Ah." Carlo knew. It suited him if Harold felt superior.

"We've had nothing but first-class scientific intelligence from this source ever since the assassination attempt against Hitler," Harold

18

went on. "So much so that we thought he—or she—had to be a scientist. I know this doesn't really concern you, Carlo, but Bandersnatch is very special—special enough to be kept from the Americans. Ever since last November they've been sending out field missions to gather nuclear intelligence of their own. Well, that's their business, but we don't want them to know about Bandersnatch. You should know, by the way, that they've code-named their teams *Alsos*—"

"Grove."

"What?"

"It's Greek for grove—*Alsos*."

"So it is," Harold reflected. He reached for the Sobranie tin and began filling his pipe with the dark, rich-smelling mixture. Methodically he searched his pockets, finding a box of Swan Vestas. The Swan was the name of the inn mentioned in Harold's memo. Carlo wondered what it was all about. Why is he telling me this; why is he telling me this now?

Carlo concentrated his gaze innocently on the pinkish sandpaper strip along the edge of the Vestas box. Fascinated, he watched Harold Philby probe the box with an index finger. He had never noticed before what spatulate fingers Harold had. They seemed ill-suited to the task of extracting a match from the box, doubly so since the box was in fact empty. Carlo believed that small things often reveal much of a man: Harold's finger went on probing inside the box long after his brain must have known that it was empty. Carlo wondered why.

Years later he would remember this incident. He would recall then that the military director of the Los Alamos project was a General Leslie Groves, a fact unknown to him at the time but not to Harold, who had smiled oddly, sheepishly.

"Fascinating," Philby said at length, arranging the half-open matchbox on top of the tin and laying his pipe down beside it, "but hardly the point. I've been thinking, you know, that we ought to have a team of our own, lest we get left out of the pickings."

Carlo agreed that this sounded like a good idea. "But I still don't see what this has to do with me, Harold."

"No?" Philby had used his most charming smile. "Well, it's like this, Carlo. We bagged the Webers last week. They crossed into

Switzerland and the Swiss let us have them. Good, we thought, splendid—one of them must be B-b-bandersnatch. Not so, Carlo. The girl denies it and her father is off his head. As mad as a hatter. Tried to kill himself by sawing at his wrists with a table knife, so naturally we had to put him in hospital. You know what I mean, straitjacket and all that. Anyway, I thought the business would be just up your street, especially since if we do decide to go ahead with our own *Alsos* team, independently of the Americans, any action we take must inevitably be based on intelligence from Bandersnatch—past, present, or future." Harold fiddled with his pipe and directed a level, appealing gaze at Carlo.

"I take it your source is still active, then?"

"Oh, yes. Indeed."

"Where is he—Weber?"

"The Retreat, you know. York. Nice out-of-the-way place. Not London, I mean. Run by Quakers on Heslington Road. Can't miss it. A G-g-gothic sort of pile."

"I had planned to spend Christmas in Norwich with mother," Carlo complained. "Still . . ." The national interest, as so often before, had intervened to lighten this domestic burden.

"I knew you'd do it."

"What makes you think I can get any sense out of him?"

"Angels," Harold said. "Professor Doctor Weber has been talking to angels."

"And what have they told him?" asked Carlo.

"How to make an atomic bomb," answered Harold, striking a match that he selected from his desk drawer. "An emergency supply," he said, smiling.

20

2: RUDOLF STENGEL

June 17, 1944, was not a good day for Standartenführer Rudolf Stengel, who, as head of the SD's Frontier Intelligence Service, just happened to be present when the V-1 headed for London turned around and landed explosively, north of Soissons, on top of the bunker housing Adolf Hitler and his generals. Fortunately this happened after lunch, otherwise Stengel wouldn't have eaten at all that day.

First Rundstedt, then Rommel, had spent the morning telling Hitler that the war was as good as lost unless the German armies in Normandy could be pulled back to the line of the Orne. *"Starre Verteidigung!"* was the answer to that. "Stand fast!" When enemy fighter-bombers forced a retreat to the bunker, Rommel announced that, without air cover, the situation was hopeless—and that in his opinion the eastern front was also on the verge of collapse. "Therefore I urgently request that this war be brought to an end, *mein Führer.*"

"Don't you worry your head about that issue," Hitler smirked. "You look to your own invasion front. You talk to me of making peace, Herr Generalfeldmarschall, yet it is I who have the means at hand to force the British into making peace. Is that not so, Stengel?"

The Standartenführer looked the very model of corpse-like obedience, gaunt, sallow, crop-headed—a heel-clicking machine. Looks can be deceptive; Stengel had perfected his. He was fifty years of age, a veteran of Verdun.

"Jawohl, mein Führer!" was his answer.

"Even before the war," Hitler continued, "German science had solved the riddle of the atom. Soon, very soon, I shall have a revolutionary new warhead for the V-2 rocket—a warhead many thousands of times more powerful than the most powerful conventional explosive. But in the meantime, even without nuclear weapons, Flakgruppe Wachtel has more than four hundred V-1 launching sites ready—each site capable of launching one bomb every twenty minutes."

Stengel wondered where Hitler was getting his information from. As soon as Wachtel built a new site it was blasted out of existence by the enemy air forces. The Great Concreter, he was called in Germany.

As usual, the Führer had all the facts at his fingertips. "Think of it, gentlemen. One bomb every twenty minutes from four hundred sites equals twenty-eight thousand eight hundred bombs a day. Since each bomb has an eight hundred and sixteen-kilogram warhead, that's more than twenty-three and a half million kilos of high explosives raining down on the enemy's capital every day!"

"In that case, *mein Führer*," asked Rommel, "why not use these weapons against the enemy's beachheads?"

"Or the invasion ports?" Rundstedt put in.

"Because, you see, they must be used against a political target!" the Führer declared triumphantly. Which was when the V-1 struck overhead, shaking the bunker and its inhabitants.

They suffered no physical harm.

Stengel did not see Hitler again until December, after the Webers' defection. He was summoned to the Führerbunker in Berlin and received the order with some trepidation. Terrible rumors, some of them, it was true, inspired by the Reichsführer SS himself, swept Himmler's security service about the mental and physical condition of the man in the bunker. Stengel, descending the snow-drifted steps in the Reich Chancellery gardens, was struck by the thought that Hitler had promised, after his accession to power, that it would take him only ten years to make Berlin unrecognizable. That promise, like others, he had yet to fulfill completely. The center of Berlin was still quite recognizable.

Elsewhere, only Spandau in the west end had escaped the worst of the bombing. Whole city blocks had been eradicated in the *Terrorbomber* raids of the preceding winter. Sometimes only a single apartment building still stood, its walls and floors anatomically exposed, teetering like a giant doll's house on the brink of collapse. One thousand acres had been wiped out in a single night, block on rubble-strewn block reminding Stengel of the mountainous *glacis* of the Verdun forts. Jagged ruins filled the horizon with all the fossilized frenzy of a catastrophe that had occurred long ago, for although the bombers returned nightly they came in nothing like the numbers of that last winter. These were nuisance raids, nothing more. The bombers had left their work half-done, moving on to other battles, other cities; had left this one like a partially defleshed carcass, its silver sinews, the rivers, raw and bloodied—a recognizable corpse, a corpse whose brain, after a fashion, still functioned.

Even at this eleventh hour that brain was still actively plotting victory. The Ardennes offensive had opened on the sixteenth, and Hitler was buoyed by news of early successes. Even so Stengel was surprised at the changes in the man since their last meeting. The Führer's eyes were sunken behind his glasses yet his eyeballs were curiously protuberant, his cheeks hollow, and his complexion ashen. That famous mustache now was flecked with gray, and Stengel noted the stipple of dried saliva at the corners of Hitler's mouth.

As he rose to shake the Standartenführer by the hand, the Führer had difficulty keeping his balance. His left hand and the whole of his left side trembled convulsively, forcing Stengel to recall those rumors of Parkinson's disease and terminal syphilis. His handshake was limp, and Stengel, almost recoiling from the damp, cool touch of that hand, which reminded him of lizard flesh, could not help but notice that an orderly had to guide the Führer into his chair at the head of the conference table. He was like a decrepit old man, senile in body if not in mind.

"So, the Webers are gone, *ja?*" he rasped.

Stengel said that they were, and the Führer nodded curtly.

"Weber is afraid and will do as I have asked," said Stengel. "The girl may be more difficult, but I am ready for that, you may rest assured, *mein Führer*."

"Then everything is prepared. Now you see the reason—for this." Hitler made a stab at the map on the table before him. "By attacking here in the direction of Antwerp we shall draw American reinforcements away from the south. Later, we shall attack in the south, hence safeguarding the lower Rhineland—which means, of course, our nuclear-research facilities in Württemburg. Germany must have time, Stengel. Time—that is her secret weapon now, and only I, the Führer, possess the unshakeable will to lead the German people to total victory!

"Gentlemen," Hitler addressed the assembled staff officers, who listened, Stengel thought, with practiced politeness, "this attack, in which I know you have so little confidence, will buy time for the Reich. In three months—by March or April at the latest—my scientists have promised me the atomic bomb. Then we shall strike with unprecedented ferocity against our enemies, whoever they may be, wherever they may be!"

This threat drained the Führer. His head nodded and he peered across the room from under hooded lids. Stengel watched in amazement as a brown eminence, leaping from his chair by the wall, shooed the officers through the double doors like a mother hen her brood. This was Reichsleiter Martin Bormann.

"That will be all, Frau Junge," Hitler said to his stenographer.

She, too, left through the double doors, and as Stengel watched her go he saw Bormann, about to close the doors from the outside, looking up at him with an extraordinary expression. At once ingratiating and supercilious, it was a look of sheer animal malice, Stengel thought, except of course no animal could look like that, with the possible exception of a dog. And then the doors closed and Bormann was gone, leaving Stengel alone with the Führer.

3: HUGO WEBER

Collinson led Carlo past a roomful of old men who stared out at the grounds as if on to a great green ocean.

Leaving behind the smell of urine and floor polish, the two men entered a long glass tunnel. "This is the original building we're coming to," the psychiatrist remarked. "It was built at the beginning of the last century by a chocolate manufacturer. Nowadays it's used for day patients or for special cases like Weber. I have a flat there."

Carlo heard a peal of distant bells through the glass. "The minster," Collinson said. He had a lean, angular, animated face that exuded confidence. This man was good at his job. Carlo liked him.

A harsher, more resonant yet distinctly human peal came to Carlo's ear. "That's Ding-dong Bell," the psychiatrist explained. "Every afternoon at four he tolls the bells for his dead mum." Collinson did not look at his watch. Overconfident, Carlo supposed. Or was it the natural, human assumption that even in this limbo of lost and distressed souls some things run like clockwork? Carlo put the psychiatrist's assertiveness down to the postmeridinal tolling of the bells—human or ecclesiastic. The same thing happening in the same place every day at the same time—wasn't that a species of operant conditioning? It was enough to drive you gaga anyway, and Carlo searched Collinson's face for symptoms of loopiness. He found none, only the next assertion rising:

"By the way, we have another patient who might interest you."

"Yes?"

"This one hears voices from aircraft."

The psychiatrist had a sense of humor at least. Carlo was reassured.

25

They met Robey, the head nurse, a moment later. Robey, Carlo saw at once, did not have a sense of humor. He was loitering by a green baize notice board in the lobby of the old building. A fussy little man in a pin-striped suit, he might have been a solicitor's clerk—definitely not the sort of person you would associate with a madhouse, Carlo thought.

"A first-class psychopath, Weber," Robey declared. He had that just-you-wait-and-see tone that schoolmasters use to refer to their least-favorite pupils.

Carlo said: "I would like to see him alone, if that's possible."

"Certainly it's possible," Robey acknowledged.

"But unwise, you think?"

"That depends on your definition of wisdom," the little man sniped. Carlo turned to Collinson, but the psychiatrist simply had a quizzical look on his face.

"You've read the notes?" asked Robey.

"Yes," said Carlo.

"Angels," Robey said, with a sudden bitterness that surprised Carlo. "There aren't any angels." Robey seemed personally offended.

"Here we are," Collinson said.

There was a sentry at the door of Weber's room, which was locked. Carlo tapped lightly on the door, but there was no answer from within.

"You ight as well unlock it," Collinson said to Robey, then turned to Carlo: "You were looking at me most curiously a moment ago. I wondered why."

"I was practicing," Carlo said.

Robey unlocked the door. Carlo left the two men in the corridor, closing the door behind him.

Inside, the physicist and first-class psychopath was sitting on his bed with his legs drawn up in a fetal crouch. Hugo Weber was in his late fifties. He was dressed in "strong" clothing—straitjacket and three-ply canvas trousers. His arms, belted at the shoulders and wrists, were tied in front of him so that he looked oddly put together, stuffed like a scarecrow, the pink and gray collar of his pajama top sticking out from under the straitjacket. Hugo Weber's hair was gray like the stubble on his chin, the same color as his clothing. He was a study in grays and pinks, his face scribbled over with tiny red veins, dark shadows under his eyes like pools of lead.

"Professor Weber," Carlo said, "my name is Harland Caisho Peat, and I'm an officer in British intelligence."

Weber returned a sullen stare. According to the case notes, Hugo Weber had slashed his wrists again two days ago with a piece of glass from a broken tumbler. Carlo gave him credit for persistence, and wondered how long it would take to bleed to death like that. Forever. There had to be a more efficient means of dispatching yourself; Weber could have gone for the jugular, for example, or swallowed the glass. But this was assuming he had wanted to die and, further, that his wish had been rational. Yet even irrational suicides succeed without too much difficulty, Carlo reflected, provided they're determined enough, and Hugo Weber did not lack determination. Therefore, he had not wanted to die, Carlo concluded.

Carlo's gaze flicked around the room. The only things in it, apart from the failed suicide on the bed, were a sink and a Victorian writing desk such as might have belonged to a child of the chocolate manufacturer. Its feet were bolted to the ground; the windows were barred on the outside and covered by a heavy mesh screen on the inside, and the single electric light bulb on the ceiling was similarly caged. There were no curtains for Weber to hang himself with, and his keepers had taken away the bed sheets.

Carlo lifted the lid of the writing desk and looked inside. Empty. "Do they not let you have writing materials?" he asked sympathetically.

The straitjacketed Weber gave a kind of shrug. It was an eloquent gesture.

"Forgive me," Carlo said, "but you have the remedy to that in your own hands." He decided to talk about something that had been troubling him for some time. "This place reminds me of somewhere, somewhere else. I've been wondering what it was all morning. You gave me the answer just now, quite unintentionally. It was a little country hospital in Norfolk in the year 1918, Armistice Day as a matter of fact. My father committed suicide, you see, when I was a boy.

He was a vicar, you know, and he gave a sermon about the peace, then went out and hanged himself. Just like that, or not quite, not exactly. He left a note—Horace's ode, you must know it. *Dulce et decorum,* and all that. . . . Many of his generation were killed, and I suppose he felt left out. What a waste, everything he stood for was such a waste."

Carlo finished his speech, which drew fire from the professor: "And so they sent you here, an expert on suicides, to see me?" Weber's English was unaccented, which was no surprise to Carlo. The professor had spent enough time at the Cavendish Laboratories before the war.

"I'm certainly no expert on nuclear physics," Carlo rejoined.

"It scarcely matters," Hugo Weber said wearily.

"Do you mind if I sit down?"

"Be my guest."

Carlo clambered on to the desk top and planted his feet on the bench. "Tell me about the Virus House," he said, facing Weber.

"You must know the story by now; you must know everything about me. That I'm crazy, for example. That I see angels."

"Lots of people do," Carlo said. "Anyway, it is often so much more interesting—and useful—if you can hear these things from the person concerned. Wouldn't you agree?"

"Very well," Hugo Weber conceded. "So you want to know about the Virus House? There's not much to say. It was built by Dr. Karl Wirz in October 1940 in the grounds of the Institute of Biology and Research, next door to the Institute of Physics. It was housed inside a wooden barracks, with the reactor pit in the floor. Dangerous? Very. We called it the Virus House to keep people away, because of their health not because we were afraid of spies. Later, toward the end of 1943 when the bombing became really bad, work began on a bunker. So you can see the Allied air offensive improved our safety precautions, if not our security."

"It was slack then?"

"Ah, so that is what interests you? My dear Herr Peat, one nuclear scientist in Germany can hardly take another seriously, so why should the authorities? We are a fractious crowd, you know. The Reichsmarschall's Plenipotentiary for Nuclear Physics is listed in the Berlin phone book. When Heisenberg had a fire in his laboratory at Leipzig, the fire chief congratulated him on this convincing display of atomic power! Let me tell you about German nuclear science. The truth is that theoretical physics in Germany is light-years ahead of that in England or America. We have the greatest theoretical physicist in the world, next to Einstein—I mean Heisenberg himself—but the man is totally impractical, no administrator, and certainly no experimenter. We have some excellent chemists, I would say the best in the world, and if they wish to work on Buna or synthetic gasoline, all well and good—they are given every facility. But if they express so much as an interest in, say, the problems of gaseous diffusion of uranium isotopes, then they are threatened with the concentration camp. For the most part German nuclear science is starved of funds. And no wonder! My colleagues are happy to live in cloud-cuckoo-land. No clear direction, no central control, every man for himself, agency competing against agency, lab against lab. Terrible! Or it was until recently."

Carlo was fascinated. "Did you mention this to anyone else?" he asked. "My predecessors, I mean."

"What? No. There were several people came to see me but they took me for a madman, a lunatic. I am sick of life, maybe," Weber declared, "but not insane."

Carlo ignored this. "You said 'until recently' just now. It's the recently that interests me. Does this go back to the Haigerloch acquisition, for example? Perhaps you would care to tell me about that."

"The Haigerloch acquisition was an emergency measure in case things got too hot in Berlin even with the bunker. Gerlach spent a holiday there before the war. He said it was like a stage setting for *Götterdämmerung*, with the river cleaving the village and the old chapel set atop one of the cliffs. Gerlach had stayed at the Swan Inn and remembered the wine cellar, a natural cave in the cliff underneath the church. He thought about it when the Institute for Chemistry was being moved to Hechingen, about ten kilometers away, but I think it was July or August before he did anything about it. There were great plans for the whole region, but I do not think they will amount to much. Germany is finished."

Carlo changed the subject: "How did you get out?"

Weber was ready with an answer, and Carlo thought he saw the slightest smile tug at the physicist's face. It was a subcutaneous smile, hidden beneath the surface, perhaps only a nervous tic, but Carlo made a note of it.

Weber wanted to talk and he wanted to be believed. Carlo wondered about his predecessors. Whom had Harold sent—the Plods from Five? That would be like showing Weber the instruments of torture. Whoever they had been, they had botched the interrogation, precipitating the second suicide attempt. Had it been an attention-getting device, then? Carlo didn't know.

"I was to go and see a colleague in Bern," Weber said. "His name is Dukas, but this also concerns Heisenberg. Heisenberg, you see, is obsessed with the ratio between the internal multiplication of neutrons in an atomic pile and their surface release. What this means is that if you bombard an atom of hydrogen with a neutron source, then in the ensuing reaction only a certain proportion of the liberated neutrons will split other nuclei of hydrogen. It's like trying to build up the national population: you have to prevent emigration and solve infant mortality. Heisenberg concentrated on the former to the exclusion of the latter. He was convinced that if you could stop free neutrons leaving the pile, then the population within it would automatically go up until a self-sustaining chain reaction was achieved. This, by the way, led him to overestimate the mass needed to make an atomic bomb. But I'll come to that later—you asked me how I escaped. Well, with Heisenberg obsessed with this Cabalistic ratio of his, I told him that Dukas in Bern had the magic formula for a material that would reflect free neutrons back into U^{235}, the isotope we were using in Berlin. I demanded that Katherina and I be allowed to go to Bern to talk with Dukas. It was as simple as that."

"Demanded?"

"Yes. Obviously you have no idea of my importance." Hugo Weber bridled. "Besides, I am not blind. Stengel, who was then often at the Virus House, did nothing to prevent our escape. There, Katherina's influence was paramount. What have you done with her by the way? Where is Katherina?"

"She is well and sends her regards," Carlo replied, hesitating for a moment. "Stengel—who is he?"

"A security man. Not atomic security, you understand. Frontier security."

Which covered a multitude of evils, Carlo reflected. He was very circumspect: "And his hobby was nuclear physics?"

"His hobby was my daughter," Weber said bluntly.

"You mentioned none of this to the people who came before," Carlo said.

"It is something I have thought about in retrospect," Hugo Weber said stiffly. "Also, I would not like people to run away with the wrong idea."

"Which is?"

"You know what I mean, Herr Peat. And if you do not, I suggest you confer with your colleagues on the subject."

The Plods—had to be, Carlo thought, surprised to find himself thinking and sounding like one: "Supposing that Stengel was influenced by 'unprofessional calculations'—I think we can live with that theory. Doesn't it strike you as strange that he should let Katherina out of his clutches, so to speak?"

"Maybe." Under stress Hugo Weber whitened. Small white blotches mottled his pink complexion. Carlo put the phenomenon down to constriction of the blood vessels. He had scored a point, but he was none too happy about it. "Looking at it from the outside," Hugo Weber said, "I don't know." He was very uncomfortable. "I am not Stengel's keeper. How should I know what was on his mind?"

"And what about Katherina's?"

"An unworthy insinuation, if I follow you, Herr Peat." Weber had thought the thing through. "If Stengel had asked Katherina to spy for him, she would have told me."

Like a dutiful German daughter, Carlo thought. He said: "Which she didn't, of course?"

"Most definitely not."

"Is this something you've thought about in retrospect, too?"

"Yes, to be frank, a great deal. At the time also."

"But you didn't say anything to her?"

"No. Why should I have? Is a father supposed to ask his daughter if she is a spy?"

"Not if it compromises her," Carlo said. Or him, he thought. This untoward turn in the questioning distressed Carlo, who had been inclined to believe that Weber was telling the truth, at least what the physicist thought was the truth. Now Carlo was unsure what to believe.

Blinking owlishly, he flourished a large handkerchief and blew his nose. The Herr Professor gave him a disapproving look as he inspected the contents. Inspired, Carlo said: "Tell me about the heavy water shipments to Haigerloch."

"There weren't any!" Hugo Weber looked at Carlo as if he were an idiot. "That's just it. Don't you understand? We had trouble enough gathering the stuff at the Virus House. It was worth more than its weight in gold, and just as jealously guarded. Supplies from the Norsk hydro plant were severely limited, what with sabotage, bombing raids, passive resistance, one thing and another. The Norwegians were never very cooperative. So to overcome this problem I proposed that another pile be built in some safe place such as Haigerloch, this time using graphite as a moderator instead of heavy water. I suggested coke as a source of the graphite, and there is no shortage of that even in Germany today. At the same time I also suggested using plutonium as the fissile material for the bomb. We could obtain a ready supply of that, I believed, from a graphite-moderated pile. This was in response to Heisenberg, who was making all sorts of difficulties. We can use graphite, he said, but only as a reflector, not as a moderator. It was the neutron escape again, you see. Heisenberg believed that we could turn the neutrons back on the pile core and initiate the reaction that way. He'd also calculated that we would have to assemble forty tons of U^{235} before we could explode a device. Imagine that! Forty tons of the isotope! Absolutely beyond our refining capacity! But when I put forward my plan, Heisenberg and von Weizsäcker wouldn't listen to me, and so we had to go on scrounging heavy water from whatever source we could find—Italy, Belgium, France, all over the Reich. We were collecting it in minute quantities—kilograms!—and you can have no idea how difficult transportation became as time went on. Here I speak not just of the damage done by the bombing but the obstructionism of German officials!"

"Where is it now?" asked Carlo.

"Still in Berlin, as far as I know."

"How much?"

"About a ton and a half imperial. Do you know what I think, Herr Peat?" Hugo Weber went on distractedly. "I think those two were not seriously interested in making a German bomb. Von Weizsäcker, especially, knew that I was right about the plutonium, but he would always defer to the master. Naturally! He was Heisenberg's research student, and his father was Reichminister of something-or-other, actually First Secretary at the Foreign Office. And so I was out of the picture altogether!"

Carlo understood. "Is that why you decided to take your business elsewhere?" he asked.

"Exactly!" The physicist seemed relieved. "I could not have put it better myself. I decided to take my business elsewhere. Yes, that is it exactly."

"Then you won't mind my asking what, apart from professional calculations, moved you to take this decision?"

Hugo Weber looked slightly puzzled.

"Was it for reasons of humanity?" Carlo prompted. "Dislike of the regime, perhaps? Or—forgive me—were you persuaded out of intelligent self-interest? You knew that the war was lost, and you also knew the price of failure. Therefore you decided to remove yourself, and Katherina, from personal danger." This time the mention of his daughter drew no response from Hugo Weber. The same slightly puzzled look remained on his pink and gray features. It was uncanny, Carlo thought, but the physicist's expression was as blank as if someone had thrown a switch in his head.

"Professor Weber?"

"I am sorry." Weber's gaze cleared. "It is evidently not a matter to which I have given sufficient thought."

The lie was so palpable that Carlo smiled openly. But not for long. What, in God's name, if Weber was telling the truth?

A new idea struck Carlo: "Your wife, Professor Weber—?"

"Oh, a cerebral hemorrhage."

"Dead?"

"No, but not alive and certainly beyond harm's reach. She is in Germany, where it suits her, a human vegetable."

Carlo was aghast. "Then do you mean to tell me"—he was very civil nevertheless—"that you cannot give me one reason why, apart from certain differences with your colleagues, in the middle of this struggle for Germany's existence you decided to leave your homeland and come to England?"

"Now you sound like Dr. Goebbels," Weber said, and Carlo caught a trace of that smile again. "Yes, I can give you a reason," the physicist added dejectedly, "but then you will think me mad like the others."

"Not at all." Carlo shook his head. He thought the professor excessively logical, and in a grudging way rather respected him—though he would never dream of admitting such a thing to the professor. Perhaps for Carlo, and certainly for the professor, that was a pity.

"I'll tell you, then," Hugo Weber said, "and now you really will think I'm crazy. The angel Rahab told me to do it. At first it was only a dream, you understand." The physicist seemed anxious to justify his vision. "The angel Rahab appeared to me in a dream and commanded me to go to England. It claimed that it had so commanded Hess." Weber smiled sadly. "And if he obeyed, who was I to refuse? But refuse I did—like Jonah. So you can say this of me, Herr Peat, that I am a man who refused an angel's command. To cut a long story short, the vision began to appear in my working hours and, as a consequence, my research suffered. But I am nothing if not methodical, and if I could not investigate the atom then I would investigate this angel. My investigations, and I will pass over their more distressing aspects, taught me that this particular angel was destroyed by God for refusing to separate the upper from the lower waters at the Creation, and was destroyed yet again for trying to hinder the Hebrews' escape from the Pharaoh's host in the crossing of the Red Sea. To me this double destruction of an evidently indestructible entity came to symbolize the fissile capture of neutrons by the atomic nucleus, each capture leading to a further fission, and so on and so on, the whole chain reaction leading up to the final cataclysm. But nothing is really destroyed, Herr Peat. It is only the energy bound up in and binding matter that is being released, matter *becoming* energy. Nothing is really destroyed, just as the angel was not really destroyed. That was the kernel of my vision—*Kernphysik*, you know, is the German word for nuclear physics—and thus I sought to reason with myself and my by now constant familiar, the angel Rahab. But angels, as I found out, are not amenable to reason. Do you know what the name of this angel means, Herr Peat—this Rahab? It means violence."

"Yes," Carlo said. "In the Babylonian Talmud, Rahab is one of the names given to the Angel of Death."

It was Christmas Eve, 1944.

Outside Weber's door the sentry snapped to attention as Carlo left. Collinson, waiting with the key to lock the door, said: "I think I should tell you that I was listening."

"I would have been surprised if you weren't," Carlo said.

"What's your opinion? What do you make of him?"

"If I were you I'd take the strong clothing off him and give him a decent suit of clothes and writing materials."

"Then it is not a psychosis, after all?" Collinson seemed relieved.

"You're the doctor," Carlo said.

4: KATHERINA WEBER

She was at a house in Clifton Road in suburban York. Roman, Saxon, Dane, Norman—these the town had known, to be conquered, finally, by the suburbanite descendants of the chocolate manufacturer. Carlo was oppressed by jaded thoughts.

Katherina sat quietly watchful in the living room by a Chippendale cabinet full of willow plate. Carlo appraised her as he would a horse, for he had yet to be persuaded that women, apart from eugenic purposes, were members of the same species. Katherina had her father's high complexion, and she was, thought Carlo, too thin, perhaps even undernourished. She wore her hair in braids around her head. It was a deep auburn, and with her coloring and her brilliant, lucent, pale blue eyes made for an odd combination. Her cheekbones were gaunt and angular, and her teeth too big. At least they were her own, Carlo thought cold-bloodedly. She wore no makeup, and it would not have mattered if she had.

Her appearance made him wonder all the more about Stengel, and Stengel's interest in her. He came straight to the point, and was totally unprepared for her reaction. She laughed.

This is the story that Katherina Weber told Carlo Peat on Christmas Day, 1944.

"Did it not occur to you that my father might have something to hide? *He* was Stengel's hobby, and this is how it came about. Last summer, it was after July twentieth, after the assassination attempt against Hitler, my father began to develop this obsession with angels. He tried to disguise it at first in a number of ways, all equally peculiar, pretending an interest in Jewish mysticism, in the Cabala and the

37

Zohar. These interests became something of a joke around the Virus House. Stengel, who was then quite often in Berlin-Dahlem on business connected with foreign visits and visas, heard of my father's obsession and mentioned quite casually to him that he happened to know the whereabouts of Rabbi Moses de Razin, the French angelologist and internationally renowned authority on the Cabala. De Razin was at Sachsenhausen, only a few kilometers north of Berlin, and Stengel could easily arrange a meeting at the concentration camp, if my father was willing.

"Of course, he was. The circumstances of this meeting, which took place in September, were detailed to me by my father, who was then in some distress, on the evening of the same day. Shortly afterward he had what I suppose you would call a nervous breakdown, and tried to commit suicide."

"How?" Carlo asked.

"By cutting his wrists. The rabbi, he said, was brought to him in a special hut, obviously designed to impress the international Red Cross with the humanitarian nature of the camps. For example, there was a vase of cut flowers on the table. According to my father, no one else was present at the meeting between Moses de Razin and himself, which lasted for a quarter of an hour, though he had the feeling that their conversation was being monitored throughout. My father has evidently told you about the angel Rahab. De Razin identified this angel as the prince of the primordial sea, an angel of insolence and pride. He mentioned also that in at least one tradition Rahab, Leviathan, Behemoth, and the Angel of Death are regarded as interchangeable.

"At the end of fifteen minutes Stengel returned and the interview was over. Much against my father's wishes, Stengel insisted that they should tour the camp together. After half an hour, in which time, my father told me, he saw terrible things, they came to *Bad und Disinfektion*—the showers.

"My father, and you must believe this, did not realize that the showers were in fact gas chambers. He was asked, forced would be a better way of putting it, to look through a glass spy hole. Inside the gas chamber he saw a group of human beings awaiting death, and among them recognized Rabbi Moses de Razin. Later, so the point of this demonstration was not lost on him, he was forced to view the bodies as they were brought out of the gas chamber, and was at this time able to make a positive identification of de Razin's body."

Sitting in a comfortable armchair and contemplating Fräulein Weber and the Chippendale cabinet, Carlo listened to this story and reserved judgment. Fräulein Weber had not finished speaking, and Carlo was as polite to women as he was careful of horses.

"I know you will ask me this question"—Katherina Weber looked at him through those terrible, pale blue eyes—"so I might as well give you the answer. You would like to know how Rudolf Stengel found out about my father's obsession. I told him."

"That is very frank of you," Carlo allowed. It was not, of course, a statement he could verify. "There is one other question that I must trouble you with," he said. "Does the name Haigerloch mean anything to you?"

"Of course. It will be the site for Germany's first functioning atomic pile, and the plutonium from the pile will be used in making an atomic bomb."

"Then there is definitely such a project, is there? To make an atom bomb?"

"After what I have told you," said Katherina Weber, "how can you possibly doubt the answer to that question?"

"And your mother, Fräulein Weber," Carlo countered, "where is she?"

"In hospital in Stuttgart." Katherina showed no surprise. "She needs special care. She is—how do you say it?"

"A vegetable." Carlo said it. She was very good, he thought.

He took the ghost train back to London, traveling with a whisky salesman who said his name was Norris. Carlo believed him.

Studying Norris—pencil-mustached, thin, balding, hip-flasked and talkative, as who wouldn't be on this of all nights—Carlo reflected on what a perfect disguise the truth was.

"A drink, old boy?"

Carlo accepted the proferred flask. It was good whisky, mellow and smooth.

"The twelve-year-old stuff," Norris said. "What line are you in, old boy?"

"I'm a classicist," Carlo said, wondering how true that was. His first love had been the Chinese. *Ex oriente lux*. Sun-tse, in his *Treatise on the Art of War*, written in the fifth century before Christ, had listed five kinds of spies: the native spies, the spies within, the spies that return from the other side, the spies of life, and the spies of death. Carlo wondered what sort of spies the Webers were. He tried not to think of them and their angelic familiar. It was a good story, unverifiable, the kind he might have concocted himself, which made him wonder whether it had been intended especially for his ears, paranoia being merely an occupational neurosis of spies.

Carlo thought of his Uncle Alex (his mother's brother), a navy friend of Mansfield Cumming's, the legendary founder of the service—"C." It was Alex who had recruited Carlo, who felt that he owed it to his dead father. *Pro patria mori*. Yes, and how many more? Carlo thought of the dead schoolmen who had debated how many angels might dance on the head of a pin. He had judged Hugo Weber as vain and ambitious, a not-so-angelic traducer, a man perplexed, certainly, yet one incapable of a scientific lie. Which meant that Weber was very possibly right, and Heisenberg very possibly wrong, about the neutron flux.

A scientific lie? Wasn't that, in a certain sense, the truth? A contradiction in terms, at any rate. The best kind of spies, Carlo reflected, were scientific liars. How could you detect the inner spy, how snare the innocent traitor?

Clickety-clack, the tracks sang out. *Snicker-snack*.

"What does a classicist do?" the whisky salesman asked. A good question, Carlo thought.

"Translate things," Carlo said. "Teach, read a bit of history." Obsolete truths. After the war, perhaps, there would be a research post for him at his old college.

The whisky salesman seemed disappointed. "This Ardennes thing can't last," he said. "It'll all be over in a month. You'll see."

"Possibly," Carlo agreed.

Knowledge of the future was what Sun-tse had called the divine secret, the most priceless possession of the lord and master who must control his spies' work in person. Who controlled the Webers? Carlo wondered. Was it the mysterious source Bandersnatch, or was he in turn controlled by the lord and master? And the future—who controlled that?

"His last throw," the whisky salesman said. "He always was a gambler."

5: JOHNNY SCARR

Early in the new year of 1945 Johnny Scarr saw the man with the mustache and rotten teeth. He saw him in the gilt mirror in the bar of the Push Inn in the Yorkshire market town of Beverley where Scarr was celebrating with a couple of Polish DPs his release from a Swedish internment camp.

Johnny was telling the Poles about his war in the desert, how, toward the end of 1940, he had captured an entire Italian armored brigade near a place called Sidi Barrani: "There were four of us, see? All we had were a few rubber tanks, inflatable, you know, like, like"—Johnny blew out his cheeks—"like water wings. A few rubber tanks, a number of strategically placed firecrackers, and one Bren gun carrier."

The Poles laughed when he laughed, drank when he drank, and Johnny wondered if they understood a single damned word. Sidi Barrani—that was before friend Yuill stepped on the land mine. New Year's Day, Christ, 1941; Yuill dead four years. The hell with that.

Johnny ordered three more pints and looked up.

In the mirror the man with the rotten teeth was smiling at him. He was one of the watchers from the Friends, and his name was Sweet.

Scarr turned round. "Piss off," he said. "This is a private conversation."

"I say—" Johnny's seedy familiar began. He had truly appalling teeth, like bits of rotting coral.

"Stow it, friend," Scarr said. "I'm telling you, leave me alone, leave me well alone."

Johnny Scarr decided to make himself scarce. He muttered something to the Poles, suddenly threw his pint of beer in the face of the man called Sweet, punched him once in the stomach, then plunged into the cold, clear light of the market square. It might have been a streetscape by Gainsborough, cobblestones, gaslights, Georgian façades dominated by the single rose window of the minster staring down like an eye.

Glancing over his shoulder, Johnny Scarr saw the man called Sweet scurrying after him through the narrow pedestrian arch of the town gate.

"Hey, you there!" Johnny Scarr heard the cry, and was abruptly familiar with the mosses colonizing the cracks between the paving stones.

Scarr was on his knees, looking almost penitential. He gazed up at the watcher with the funny teeth and at the baby-faced man. Too late he realized there was a third. He heard the crunch as his assailant swung the life preserver down on the back of his head, then his ribs felt the boot go in. You're out of shape, you are, he told himself. There was nothing he could do. . . .

The shifting war in the desert sands had interposed a fine screen of irreality between Johnny Scarr and the world outside. In the land of mirages, capturing the Italians had almost been a mirage itself, the kind of thing that happened from the outside, like a movie. The death of his friend Yuill had happened that way, too. "Got to take a piss," Yuill had said, and had wandered off into the desert with an imaginary hound he kept, a hound called Frog. Johnny Scarr remembered how the horizon had jumped when Yuill stood on the land mine. He remembered the purplish brown jets of the explosion followed by a dull, flat detonation that sounded like a harmless thing, the cordage of black smoke coiling above the desert until it was no more than a smudge against the blue Mediterranean sky; and he remembered running and shouting and waving his arms. And screaming, Johnny remembered that, though at first he'd thought it was Yuill who was doing the screaming. But he wasn't. Yuill was dead by the time Johnny Scarr got to him, his legs torn off by a razor-sharp chunk of still-smoking shrapnel, his mouth open in a great airless gawp, as

44

though he wished to protest but could not somehow find the words, Yuill, standing freakishly on what was left of his thighs, truncated like a circus dwarf, a tattered and torn clown daubed with red, the sandpit in which the slapstick blast had thus deposited him devouring his blood like a giant sponge, like blotting paper, Johnny Scarr thought.

Before the war he'd worked in Germany, buying and selling space for the Hamburg-Amerika Line. Johnny's father ran a shipping and forwarding business in Hull, and had many connections across the sea. The boy "did well," the ultimate parental accolade. Johnny did well because he was lucky; everyone agreed on that; Johnny was lucky at whatever he turned his hand to, fortune's child in war and peace.

The Nazis simplified life for Johnny Scarr, who had watched the U-boat pens being laid down in the canal port of Kiel and who saw the *Bismarck* slide down Blohm and Voss's slipway on St. Valentine's day, 1939, a ceremony attended by *der Führer* himself and the swaggering Nazi top brass in their gaudy uniforms, the festive crowd cheering lustily to see Bismarck's granddaughter, Dorothea von Loewenfeld, christen the steel warship with the name of the Iron Chancellor. Battleships in port, girls in bars, Johnny went around like a camera, recording everything, forgetting nothing. It seemed only natural that when the army had done with Johnny Scarr, the Friends should ask him to spy for king and country; and in September 1941, Johnny Scarr, who didn't know any better, had agreed.

"You'll be using the name Heller," the baby-faced man had told him. They met in the fog-infiltrated second-class waiting room at Euston. "Johann Heller, 'Johnny' to your friends, a small-time cargo mover from Altona on the Elbe. Your contact works for a very reputable Gerhoffstrasse trading firm, Rheinhold and Company. His name is Hans Schmidt. We think he may be a double agent, but you can leave us to worry about that. We'll fly you to Landskrona, and from there you'll catch the Oresund ferry to Copenhagen. There's a Hamburg boat due in on the twenty-fifth. Your reservation is already made, of course." The baby-faced man had handed over a bundle of papers, which Johnny accepted like a benediction.

"Good luck." And so saying, embraced by tentacles of the kraken fog, Carlo Peat had plunged into the blackout gloom.

Johnny's contact was supposed to show up on the steps of the Rhein-hold Building, a copy of *Das Reich* under one arm, a rolled umbrella in the other. The appointed hour arrived, but not Herr Schmidt. Eyeing the gray stone building on the other side of Gerhoffstrasse, Johnny Scarr felt that it—and the two trench-coated figures standing on the steps—were waiting for him. The two men, looking as gray as the stonework, were still there twenty minutes later when Johnny Scarr, peering out from behind a copy of the *Völkische Beobachter*, rattled by in a tram. Of Herr Schmidt there was still no sign.

Johnny began to wonder whether Herr Schmidt's existence was anything other than notional. How else could things have gone so very wrong? Both alternatives were equally unpleasant. Either Schmidt was the bait for a trap, or the contact had been arrested and tortured. Both ways, that was the fate awaiting Johnny Scarr, should he attempt to pursue the *Treff.* Johnny believed in his luck; he even blamed himself for it, thinking that was why friend Yuill instead of him had stepped on the land mine; but then, in the graying light of that Hamburg afternoon, Johnny began to wonder if Lady Luck was playing him false.

He got off the tram at the Alster. Johnny knew what he had to do. He had a list of girls in his address book, the kind of thing that Johnny Heller from Altona might have. But these were Johnny Scarr's girls. He would have to start calling them up, one by one; but he needed some Dutch courage first.

Johnny blew a packet of forged Reichsmarks on a slap-up meal in the Vier Jahreszeiten hotel, washed down with beers along the Ree-perbahn. It was after ten when he ran into an old flame in the Valhalla Club.

"Ach, Johnny Scarr!" she'd exclaimed, still burning.

Johnny sat down at her table, fast. He wondered if her name was in his book with the others, then realized, dismally, that he couldn't remember it anyway. Eva? Elsa? The most important thing in the world to him now, and he couldn't remember it.

"Listen," he pleaded, "I have to get to a ship, any ship." He kept his voice down for fear of being overheard. "Any *neutral* ship, but, well, you know how things are."

"Ach, Johnny Scarr!"

She knew.

The girl told him there was a Swedish ore carrier in port. "The *Ostersund* out of Bergshamra. I know some of the crew," she added modestly. "If that's any help."

"It's a start," said Johnny Scarr, for whom anything was a help.

Together they went on a dock-land pub crawl, looking for the crew. They found some of them in the middle of a melancholy sing-along in the Metropole Bodega. The girl explained Johnny's predicament. "But you do not look like a Swedish sailor," one of the crew protested, and volunteered to return to the ship for some clothes and papers. Johnny spent a nervous forty minutes waiting for this mission to be accomplished. At one o'clock that morning, he was just another drunken Swedish sailor kissing his girl goodnight.

He was to spend the next three years trying to remember her name.

"You did very well in getting out of Hamburg," the baby-faced man was saying to Johnny in the back of the Black Maria; "believe me, it wasn't our fault you spent three years in internment." Actually, things couldn't have turned out better, Carlo Peat reflected. This way Johnny Scarr was alive, just when they needed him most. Lucky Johnny Scarr. "So you do see, don't you, that if you won't cooperate with us, we simply have no choice but to turn you over to the secular arm?"

The baby-faced man had just finished telling Johnny Scarr that he was a murderer, something to do with a pub fight. "I didn't kill anyone," Johnny protested. His head ached as if his brain were gyrating inside his skull, which it was. Johnny closed his eyes and watched the eidetic replay of the fracas in the pub, old coral teeth, sudsy with beer, folding over; then scampering nimbly after Johnny through the arch. Johnny watched the replay again and again.

"Not me," he said. "Not me."

"Frankly, your attitude surprises me." The baby-faced man did not look surprised. "We have the coroner's report, the death certificate, and the body. No shortage of those, you know, Johnny. Plenty of eyewitnesses too. The court would probably take a lenient view because of your war record, but that would only mean a mental hospital, or, worse, a prison for the criminally insane. I mean, imagine how it would look on your psychiatric report. 'Cannot remember actions. Total amnesia.' Very bleak. Oh, I expect it would be Broadmoor for you. So let's be sensible, Scarr, do."

"I don't suppose I have any choice, do I?"

"None whatsoever," the baby-faced man replied.

"Where are you taking me?"

"South of the river, to a place called Winthorpe, near the Lincolnshire coast."

"Why?" asked Johnny Scarr.

"I was beginning to wonder when you'd ask," Carlo Peat murmured. "We need Johnny Heller again," he said, adding a bit shamefacedly this time: "I knew you would see reason, Johnny; I knew you would."

6: WORST CASE

*"No deception link should ever be used for any
intelligence purpose other than deception."*

—David Mure, *Practise to Deceive.*

Memo to: H.C.P.
From: H.A.R.P.
January 10, 1945

<u>ULTRA SECRET</u>

Source BANDERSNATCH indicates following developments in
German scientific war effort. Shuffle in GOERING's War Research
Pool (Wehrforschungsrat) as a result of criticism by Reichsmin-
ister of War Production SPEER: Prof. Walter GERLACH appointed
Chief Coordinator Nuclear Research, with "DE" clearance
(highest priority); Von WEIZSÄCKER evacuated from Strasbourg
last November, before US ALSOS team raided his lab, to HECH-
INGEN, joining Walter Bagge; Werner Heisenberg, and others;
Research Station "D" of the Kaiser-Wilhelm Gesellschaft now at
BISINGEN, near HECHINGEN, where work has started on ten-
million-volt cyclotron; DÄLLENBACH, Director of Forschungsstelle
"D," reported in Switzerland last month (December '44). Source
indicates installation of Otto HAHN's branch of *KWI für Chemie*
at TAILFINGEN, near HECHINGEN, and of the Institute's Measuring
Methods Section at HAIGERLOCH; also near HECHINGEN. Source

reports Adolf HITLER, at Führer Conference dated 3 January '45, appointed SS Standartenführer Rudolf STENGEL as head of security to A-bomb project code named PROJEKT ALBERICH, stating that the war is lost unless Germany can produce the bomb in two months. Source further states that STENGEL has personally assured the Führer that this target date will be met.

"Let us hope to God not," Carlo said, voicing everyone's thoughts.

The council of war was held in his room at Baker Street, an attic hideaway distinguished only by a bust of Julius Caesar, to which was appended the motto: "I love treason but hate the traitor," a college scarf tied around the truncated plaster neck. Freezing rain lashed the attic windowpane, which rattled.

David Sweet was present with Philby and a man who said his name was Brown, "from Tube Alloys, don't you know." The tubular man doodled algebraically in a notebook. He wore a houndstooth jacket with leather patches at the elbows, and had an abstracted air that went with a curiously militant presence. The tubular man was reputed to have the prime minister's ear.

Someone knocked at the door.

"That'll be Lucas from the Air Ministry," Carlo said.

He opened the door to reveal a long-faced man who looked as though he had been up all night pressing his group captain's uniform.

"Lucas," the long-faced man said, nodding. Clutching his briefcase, he sat down in Sweet's slipstream, inhaling a heady blend of wintergreen and halitosis. The group captain's nose, like his trouser creases, was sharp. He frowned at Sweet, who grinned back at him, a ghastly sight.

Lucas fidgeted; Carlo said, helpfully: "I understand you have some pictures for us, Group Captain."

"Oh yes. Ra-ther." Lucas, galvanized into a nervy response, unhasped his battered and scarred briefcase, delving within for a set of aerial reconnaissance photographs which he began doling out, Carlo thought, like a visiting great-aunt her snapshots of Brighton beach.

Lucas began his commentary: "In the first set of photos the road you can see is the Hechingen-Rottweil road, the railway line crossing it is the Stuttgart-Zurich line, and the river is the upper course of the Neckar. Hechingen, a small textiles-manufacturing town about twenty-five miles south-southwest of Stuttgart, is situated between the watersheds of the Neckar and the Donau rivers. It has so far been completely untouched by our strategic bombing campaign—a relatively easy target, I would say, but for political reasons . . ."

"Political reasons?" the tubular man echoed.

"The Swiss border is only forty miles away at its nearest point."

"You don't mean to tell me, do you, that forty miles is an acceptable bombing error with you people?"

"No." Lucas overlooked the insult. "But there could be trouble with downed or damaged aircraft. I should say they did the same thing with the Zeppelin yards in the First War, thinking we'd never dare bomb them so close to the frontier. Well, we attacked those targets then and we can attack these targets now; it's just that—so far at any rate—there has been no good reason to justify a raid on these towns and villages. I might add, by the way, that another good reason for locating in the general area south of Stuttgart, east of the Black Forest, is that the enemy has plenty of hydroelectric power from the Falls of the Rhine."

Lucas looked from one man to the other; he was quite calm and patient now, though there was a certain prissiness to his manner. The tubular man, silenced, renewed his doodling, leaving Carlo to wonder at his apparent animosity to Lucas.

"All right," the Air Ministry man continued. "Mount Zollern lies immediately to the south of Hechingen, this craggy outcrop here"—Lucas pointed to a white pimple-like excrescence on one of the photos—"with Hohenzollern Castle on top of it—a good aiming point, gentlemen . . ." Carlo smiled at this clipped reference to the historic home of Germany's kaisers. "Haigerloch lies some five miles to the southwest along this side road off the main Hechingen-Rottweil road," said Lucas, "and it is not an easy target, gentlemen, not by any means an easy target."

The group captain began handing out another set of photographs.

"If you look at the first one closely," he went on, "you can just see the entrance to the wine cellar mentioned by your source Bandersnatch, and the Webers, as the site for the installation of the Berlin pile—the so-called Speleological Research Unit. The arrow here points to the cave mouth at the foot of the river bluff; the edifice next to it is the Swan Inn. On top of the cliff, you can see the church, the château, and the prison."

"Château?" Philby queried.

"*Schloss*, I suppose. Really more of a manor house. Dates back to the fifteenth century, with the church and the inn."

The tubular man sighed.

"But look at these now." Lucas sensed his impatience. "This is the first shot blown up. You can see they're running power lines from the back of the inn into the cave, digging trenches (for buried cables, I'd say), and generally mucking about. This photo was taken last December, just before Christmas. In this much more recent one, you can see they've brought in some flak. There are also some armored units of an SS Panzergrenadier division dug in around the village. And that's not all. Look at this. We've circled the really interesting stuff, just to make it plain."

"What are they?" asked Carlo. He made out some vague-looking blotches against the snow; and something else, too, something that looked like birds' feet.

"This," Lucas indicated one of the blotches, "is an armored personnel carrier; these are portable Freya radar antennae with their trailers," the group captain's finger moved on, "and this—this, gentlemen, is a Volkswagen jeep."

"What's so bloody remarkable about that?" the tubular man asked.

"We know their totem," Philby said. "The latest decrypt came in from B-b-bandersnatch yesterday. He says a Luftwaffe outfit has moved into the area. Their markings are a *W* over an *8*, a kind of f-f-fraction. Unusual, really, for the Germans, almost a pun: the *8* gives you *Achtel*, for one-eighth; plus the initial *W* equals Wachtel, Flakgruppe Wachtel—a Luftwaffe unit named after its CO. We first noticed them at Peenemünde, then at Creil near Paris, but it's quite a while since we saw them last. Flakgruppe Wachtel is a f-f-flying bomb outfit."

"That clinches it then," said Lucas. "These other marks you probably noticed are V-1 launching skis. 'Sludge pumps.'" He turned to the tubular man, and Carlo was astonished to see the group captain smiling happily. "That's what you people thought they were when we photographed them at Peenemünde. Sludge pumps. This would be a good site for sludge pumps, too. You can see that the river bluff is ringed with them. The new building under construction here is probably a *Stofflager* for fuel storage, and this long, low structure over here will probably house the missiles. Yes, I'd say that clinches it. Definitely." Lucas began collecting his photos. "It wouldn't do to let them get mixed up," he said. Everyone was looking at the tubular man.

"They couldn't put a nuclear warhead in one of those things, if that's what you're all thinking," he said. "I reckon they're for a last-ditch stand against the Americans, or anyone foolish enough to attack the place. It's one way of explaining the Ardennes offensive, by the way; perhaps the only way. He was protecting his establishment here by attacking farther north."

Lucas nodded. "Yes, I'll second that. All of it."

The tubular man shot him a snide who-asked-you look. Malice suddenly inspired him. "I must say," he declared, "that if the Germans were to produce the bomb in a couple of months, it would be a magnificent achievement—considering the state of things over there. Aren't we supposed to have bombed them into the Stone Age?"

Things were getting out of hand, Carlo thought. Lucas wasn't that sort of flier anyway. The group captain flew Mosquitoes, and if anyone could drop a bomb—an ordinary, conventional, high-explosive bomb—in the Haigerloch cave mouth, Lucas could.

But the group captain had already thought of that. "It's not simply a question of bombing," he said patiently. "They've already installed blast doors in that cave, and there must be a hundred and fifty feet of solid rock above the cellar. I'd say the place was virtually impregnable from the air. And there's another consideration, too. If you want to go in, it would have to be through the front door. But you'd want to come out again, of course, and the best we could do for you might be the worst—to cause a landslide, I mean."

Carlo looked at the tubular man. "Two months. Can they do it?"

The tubular man shrugged. He hated being put on the spot, Carlo thought. Just like a backroom boy.

"I can tell you what I know," the tubular man said; "and if these reports are accurate, I can tell you what our chances are."

"All right," Carlo agreed.

"Well, we know that back in June 1942 Heisenberg told Field-Marshal Milch that a piece of uranium the size of a pineapple would be enough to destroy a city, a large city. The theory is simple enough," the tubular man said. "Assuming a sustained chain reaction, then it's enough that, on average, just over one neutron per fission event is captured by another U^{235} nucleus to create an explosion of quite unimaginable force: let's say something in the order of twenty-five thousand million kilowatt hours, if all the energy in that pineapple-sized piece of uranium were released; or, to put it another way, an explosion equivalent to twenty thousand tons of TNT from one kilogram of uranium. No one knows yet what the actual critical size of the bomb would be, but, taking what must be absolutely the worst case from our point of view, a one-ton atomic warhead in a V-2 rocket could give an explosive potential equivalent to twenty million tons of TNT." The tubular man stared at Lucas. "That's an awful lot of thousand-bomber raids," he said, lending Carlo a shuddering insight into the true source of his animosity toward the group captain. Thousand-bomber raids were *inefficient*. All that time, effort, and extraneous *energy*, and they still couldn't achieve what the tubular man was proposing—vaporize entire cities in milliseconds.

The tubular man worshipped efficiency.

"Actually"—he sounded quite regretful, Carlo thought—"there are several theoretical reasons why the explosion would not be quite so large. For one thing, no conversion of matter into energy is ever one-hundred percent efficient. There is always some entropy in the system, but I don't want to bore you with that now. To tell you the truth, no one really knows what the total effects of such a weapon would be. If the target were a city, a large city like London, you could reckon on complete devastation over an area of some ten to twenty miles out from the point of impact. I couldn't even give you an estimate on the fire-storm and blast damage. Incalculable, really. Many people might die from suffocation, others from the concussive effects of the blast. Some would be burned to death; many, in a city like this, would drown. Hospitals, if any were left standing, would not be able to cope. And I am speaking only of physical casualties, you understand; not to mention the long and short term effects of radiation on biological materials, plants and animals, crops and so forth.

"Vegetables," Sweet objected; "you're talking about vegetables. What about people, for Christ's sake?"

"We believe it may make them quite ill," the tubular man responded. "Depending on the type and duration of dosage, it may even be fatal, though not immediately so."

"Not immediately so?" Sweet parroted.

"We lack empirical data, of course, but it seems that a person in a position to receive a lethal dose of radiation would, in all probability, die of other injuries first."

"That's reassuring, that is," declared Sweet.

"We already know that the missile is unstoppable." The tubular man ignored him. "However, there are tactical circumstances in our favor. Their only launching sites at present are on the other side of the Scheldt River, and in two months they may not even have those. Of course, that's not to say they might not hit on some other delivery system, some sort of stand-off bomb, an air-launched V-1, even a suicide mission. We would have some sort of defense against these." The tubular man began an aggressive series of quadratic doodles. "If they do have the bomb and if they really want to use a V-2, I'd say their greatest difficulty would be getting the two together. I think we should be on the lookout for something else, something quite primitive and therefore unexpected."

"Such as?" Carlo prompted.

"Oh, good lord . . . a floating mine, a radio-controlled aircraft, a balloon perhaps, with the bomb in the gondola. You name it." The tubular man suddenly looked up from his doodling. "You know,

we've only been talking about uranium so far. Suppose they're working on something else? Just a few grams of plutonium in one of those
'conventional' warheads, and you'd have yourself a pretty poisonous
weapon. I'd expect to find cases of unexplained sickness around the
points of impact—some sort of epidemic, you know. It's something
I've often thought of myself," the tubular man concluded cheerfully,
"radioactive contamination."

"That still doesn't answer my question," Carlo observed. "Is two
months a feasible estimate, in your opinion?"

"I can't read the future any more than you can," the tubular man
responded testily. "I agree with Hitler on this: if they don't have the
bomb by the middle of March, they have lost the war."

"And if they do?" Carlo pressed him.

"Then they've beaten us to it," said the man from Tube Alloys.
"And if they deliver the goods, they've won the war."

"Ah, but deliver them *where*—isn't that the question?"

Carlo was startled by Philby's voice. Harold had lit his pipe, and the
atmosphere had become quite fumid in Carlo's little attic room. Now
Philby laid his pipe aside, and speaking in a voice such as the poet
W. H. Auden used, a voice at once hesitant and tentative yet full of
grave ironies, and looking like the young Trevor Howard looked, his
jaw jutting forth in a characteristic pose, he began to develop the
thesis that the Friends would soon be hearing from their source again.

"I know the enemy," this former apostle of the Anglo-German
Fellowship remarked. "He'll want to strike a bargain soon. You mark
my words. He'll be in touch with us again before the week is out."

A screaming came across the sky, the sonic double boom of a V-2's
passage and arrival. Carlo leaped to the rain-lashed windowpane,
which had rattled again in the wintry blast. Across the wet gray slate
rooftops of the winnowed city, the smoke hung over the horizon like a
genie uncorked.

"South London again," Carlo said.

7: THE SHAPING OF THE SWORD

An oasis of sorts, RAF Winthorpe lay abandoned in a tawny expanse of fenlands bordered to the east by the gray North Sea, and to the west by the Lincolnshire Wolds, a low line of distant hills almost inseparable from the clouds.

A satellite base, disused now that the strategic air war against the enemy's cities was winding down, Winthorpe bore witness to the fallibility of men and their machines; the fire-blackened hulks of Liberators, Lancasters, Halifaxes, and B-26s lay abandoned in the salt grasses that encroached on the cracked and blistered tarmac. The windswept haunt of the curlew and the skylark, Winthorpe presented a melancholy aspect, like that of some saurian graveyard of long ago, a place where these gaunt black birds had come to die. For these returning wounded, their bases farther inland, the sky and the distant hills had proved all too separable.

It was the beginning of February, a light sprinkling of snow on the tarmac. To Carlo Peat the tire tracks across the snow had the look of some indecipherable god's script. He had driven up from London with David Sweet, and they had pulled over on a low rise overlooking Winthorpe. As he rolled down the car window, Carlo heard the crackle of automatic weapons' fire from the base. A line of khaki-clad figures broke from one of the Nissen huts, scattered across the tarmac, and disappeared into the grasses. Carlo studied the footprints in the snow as he would some demotic scrawl on an ancient palimpsest. These evidences of intelligent purpose caused him to shiver. Anyone else studying the ground from his vantage point would have spied six maniacs charging around down there, armed with Sten guns, grenades, and a mortar, for Carlo now heard the crump-crump of a Stokes trench mortar and watched the daubs of white smoke, drifting, it seemed to him in a suddenly childish access of imagery, drifting across the base like Red Indian smoke signals. War was noisy. Carlo sighed, and told David Sweet to drive down.

"Slowly, David. I want to see if there's anyone else about."

Carlo, who enjoyed code names for their own sake, had dubbed Scarr's people Force Vorpal, after the blade that slew the Jabberwock in Lewis Carroll's nonsense poem. Vorpal numbered six members: Scarr and a nuclear physicist from the Cavendish Laboratories, Richard Prentice; two survivors from Scarr's Long Range Desert Group, a demolitions expert, Roger Innis, and a weapons specialist, Ian Roberts; a sergeant W/T operator from the Second Commando Regiment, Frank "Bony" Wilkes; and Charlie Page, the team's parachute instructor from the Royal Parachute Regiment.

By the beginning of February, Force Vorpal, all of whom were fluent German speakers, had mastered the SOE refresher courses in sabotage, small arms and automatic weapons, plastic explosives, unarmed combat, astral navigation and W/T operations. Each team member was intimately familiar ("and I mean 'intimately,'" their cartography instructor had told them, "your map is your mistress") with a several-hundred-square-mile segment of Württemberg bordering the Black Forest, from Stuttgart in the north to Schaffhausen across the Swiss frontier in the south. They knew its watersheds and waterfalls, its rivers and river crossings, roads, railways, towns and villages, castles and farmhouses; in particular they knew the two-mile stretch of road from Hechingen Airbase to the Hohenzollern Castle, and the five miles of side road from the castle to the village of Haigerloch. The village they knew as their own minds, perhaps better; from three-dimensional models they knew the *Schloss* on top of the river bluff, the fifteenth-century church and jail adjoining, the Swan Inn and its outbuildings at the base of the cliff, the wine cellar in the cave, the new barracks, flak emplacements, guardhouses, barbed-wire entanglements and electric fences, the V-1 launching sites ringing in the village, the *Stofflager* for the buzz-bomb catapult fuels stored in separate compartments, *Z-Stoff* or sodium permanganate, and

T-Stoff or hydrogen peroxide—fuels that could not be mixed without explosive consequences; they knew the antimagnetic *R-Haus* that housed the missiles, and they knew the details of the Argus ramjet tube that powered them; in fact, Force Vorpal knew more than enough about the V-1 missile, the doodlebug. They also knew about the heavy-water tanks buried outside the cave mouth at the entrance to the wine cellar of the Swan Inn. Only one team member, the nuclear physicist, Dick Prentice, knew why the Germans had heavy water at Haigerloch, but he wasn't saying, not yet.

Scarr's people were often cold, hungry, and tired, but they were always sober and mostly happy. Among themselves they wondered about their training and the construction underway night and day in the base's old main hangar. Prentice knew about that, too, but kept himself to himself, a man apart from the others, knowing much, saying little.

"They want us to take out a V-1 base, you see," declared Bony Wilkes, who knew about that sort of thing. "Why else all this stuff about buzz bombs? I bet they want us to pinch one, to see how it works."

The last week in January changed his mind forever, when the German lady introduced Vorpal to the mock-up in the old main hangar.

The Dustbin, they called it.

"Katherina Weber's been working with them on a mock-up of the Berlin B VIII pile," Carlo told David Sweet on the way down to the base. "We're to have a demonstration after lunch."

"I don't trust that woman," Sweet said dourly.

"It's not a question of trust, David. Anyway, I'm giving her plenty of rope. You might say I'm just uncoiling it. She hasn't jumped yet, you know."

"Neither has Vorpal," Sweet reminded him.

Carlo changed the subject. "Did you know the Americans have an operative in this area?"

Sweet shook his head. He pulled up at the guardhouse and, wheezing, produced a pass from an inside pocket.

Carlo waited until the sentry disappeared with the pass before shoving a photograph at Sweet. "Take this," he said. "Seek him out, watch him, David."

There was at times a portentousness about Carlo that irritated Sweet.

"It's not a very good photo," he complained.

"It's not a very good war," Carlo said as the sentry returned with the pass, saluted, and waved them through the raised barrier.

"Herr Peat, how nice to see you again." Katherina Weber wore gray overalls and her hair in braids. She stood next to Johnny Scarr, who was armed with a clipboard and stopwatch, and Charlie Page, squat, muscular, and apelike, a Sten gun slung from one shoulder.

The Dustbin loomed behind the little group under the glare of the hangar lights, a concrete box seven-feet high, ten wide, with a smooth, metallic liner big enough to hold a couple of men.

Carlo nodded at Katherina. "A colleague," he excused Sweet's grinning presence. "All right, Fräulein; let's begin," he said, turning to watch the show.

Two white-suited figures, wearing heavy protective clothing, face masks and filters, lumbered from the shadows and began scaling the side of the pile. One of them, Prentice, carried a specially designed lead-lined case, wire cutters, and tongs; the other, the demolitions man Innis, two pounds of mock plastic in an oilskin packet with a detonator and fuse.

At the top of the Dustbin, Innis reached out to press a button that activated the electric motor of an overhead portal crane. Looking monstrous, zombielike in his radiation suit, the big Scotsman peered up as the crane hook swung down out of the lights' baleful, blinding glare to his eye level. Innis grappled with the hook, and, kneeling awkwardly, guided it into the Dustbin lid's retaining ring. Standing up, he jabbed a gloved finger at the return button and stepped back as the pulley lines tautened, the block and tackle taking the strain.

Katherina said: "The pile's outer wall is actually an aluminum boiler from the Berlin firm of Bamag-Meguin. It measures two hundred and ten point eight centimeters in diameter by two hundred and sixteen in height, and is lined with ten tons of graphite slabs that have been shaped to fit it. The graphite serves as a reflector, and the lid of the reactor vessel is similarly lined. The vessel itself, which is made of a light magnesium alloy, fits inside the graphite reflector and measures one hundred and twenty-four centimeters in diameter by the same in height. The vessel will hold approximately one and a half tons of deuterium oxide—heavy water to you, Herr Peat."

Carlo watched as the lid came away. Dangling underneath it, looking like nothing more than a giant Christmas bauble, hundreds of shimmering cubes turned and twinkled in the lights. "The same amount of uranium, about one and a half tons, will be found in the actual pile," Katherina said. "For technical reasons, we have found that the cubes are the best configuration."

"Tube Alloys would like one or two for testing." Carlo turned to Sweet, then watched as Prentice snipped at one of the cubes, first securing it with his tongs as a dentist a tooth, before dropping it into his lead-lined case. The cube was quite small, no more than two inches square, and Prentice moved on to snip another, repeating the performance with his tongs.

Sweet asked if Vorpal couldn't do the assay with a Geiger counter.

Carlo shrugged: "Tube Alloys are afraid the claim might be salted," he said.

The demolitions man, meanwhile, had dropped out of sight into the pile liner where he was laying his charge of mock plastic. He popped up again a few minutes later and gave the thumbs-up sign. Both men started to make their way down from the pile.

"Six minutes thirty seconds." Johnny Scarr looked up from his stopwatch. "Maybe we could shave another minute off. A lot depends on that damned portal crane working the way it's supposed to."

Charlie Page laughed. "That has to be the least of our worries," he said.

Carlo Peat laughed too. Privately, he agreed with Charlie, but he said nothing. Instead, he watched Katherina go over and strike up an animated conversation with Dick Prentice at the base of the pile. Carlo drew Charlie Page aside and beckoned Johnny Scarr over to join them.

"You know, I've been thinking about that," he said. "I've been thinking of a way to crack the Speleological Unit. Gentlemen, how would you like to join the Luftwaffe?"

8: BANDERSNATCH

Memo to: H.C.P.
From: H.A.R.P.
February 7, 1945

ULTRA SECRET

Source BANDERSNATCH reports shipments of radioactive isotope U^{235} and heavy water (for pile moderator) from BERLIN to SPELEO-LOGICAL RESEARCH UNIT, HAIGERLOCH; also delivery of aluminum boiler (216cm x 210cm) believed to be reactor vessel or *Uran-brenner* (Uranium burner) from the firm of BAMAG-MEGUIN. (Separate ULTRAS confirm this.) Source urgently requests meeting to establish bona fides beyond dispute. Suggests LUGANO, Switzerland, if acceptable, on Saturday 17 of this month, 9:30 A.M. local time, to hand over the plans of two (2) proposed nuclear devices, GROSS ALBERICH and KINDCHEN ALBERICH, FAT and BABY ALBERTS. Contact and fallback procedures to follow. How about sending Balthazar?

The road from Bellinzona drops steeply from the valley of the Ticino, twisting and turning through the villages of Giubasco and Taverne until it finds Lugano almost as if by surprise, contoured against the foothills of the Lepontine Alps with a view like that on a Swiss-cheese label.

The man the Friends called Balthazar radiated bonhomie in bulk.

His dramatic presence he owed to his board-treading days at the old Variety Theatre as the Amazing Doctor Waldemar, mesmerist, clairvoyant, and master of prestidigitation. The use to which he put his talents was not listed on the bill. Miles Cavendish, aka The Amazing Doctor Waldemar, had been a society dip, until Carlo had rescued him from prosecution. Now he could pick more than people's pockets, and it was legal. The Friends called him Balthazar after the wine bottle that holds thirteen quarts U.S., a tribute.

Balthazar had caught the overnight milkrun to Bern, picked up the embassy Citroën, and had spent the predawn hours racing across Switzerland only to wait at the Gotthard, still closed at this time of year, for the car train to take him under the Alps. The train, an exemplar of capitalism, worked on the supply-and-demand principle. When enough people had gathered at the Göschenen end of the tunnel, the train was telegraphed from Airolo, and vice versa. Scrutinizing his fellow passengers at the little Alpine station—a commercial traveler from Fribourg, a skiing instructor from Oberalpstock, and a languid Italian count who claimed, improbably, to have been the model for Thomas Mann's Settembrini in *The Magic Mountain*, Balthazar wondered who among them was a spy, and whether any thought the same of him.

The train, when it arrived, rattled with neatness, and as it plunged into the tunnel the count was heard to remark, in the moment before the lights went on, that he had often traveled on such a train in his days at the sanatorium. He was going to Lugano, he said, to take the waters.

Balthazar, who had seen quite enough hairpin bends for one morning, drove the last few miles from Bellinzona delicately. He was beginning to feel the effects of last night's supper at Claridges—forced grouse washed down by a rather sweaty Calvados which had not traveled well, a profound disqualification for a man who thinks from his stomach.

He parked the Citroën in the cobblestone forecourt of the ornate Victorian *stazione* at 9:20 A.M. A couple of minutes later he turned left out of the yard and walked north up the hill he had just driven down. At 9:25 he crossed the road and began conspicuously admiring the view. Below to his right the placid blue lake reflected a placid blue sky; above to his left Lugano's hotels and apartments, the Alpine huts of the fabulously well-off, looked sedately down from their mountainous backdrop. In this town the embassy Citroën was conspicuous next to the procession of Rolls Royces chauffeuring along as if in some vast funereal cortege. The town was a terminal rest home for inmates with unnumbered bank accounts, a sausage-maker's paradise dripping with scenic views. Balthazar shivered, his mortality aroused at the passage of a berouged crone in a wilted boa, death the senile flapper smiling at him from behind the mask.

"Pleasant, is it not?"

The bearer of this sentiment was a thin man with a thin mustache, the kind favored by Panzer commanders and intelligence officers alike. The thin man wore a dark hat, dark glasses, dark clothes. His right hand wore a shiny dark glove. Balthazar decided that the hand was artificial. In his left hand the thin man carried a briefcase apparently bulging with documents. Balthazar put his age at around sixty-five.

"Is this your first visit?" the thin man inquired, and Balthazar said that, yes, it was, but not, he hoped, his last—a double lie.

The thin man was wreathed entirely in insincere smiles. "Dorf," he said, clumsily changing hands with the briefcase and extending his left hand, which Balthazar shook. "Colonel-General."

"Carstairs," Balthazar grinned. Carlo had once said of him that he had so many names he could put Somerset House out of business.

"Pleased to make your acquaintance, Mr. Carstairs." The German invested this name with a sinister inflection. Balthazar, wishing to hell that the thin man would take his glasses off, was amazed when he did exactly that, revealing a pair of glacial blue eyes, Prussian eyes turned down at the corners, eyes that blinked too much, though whether from sudden admission of the light or nervous strain, Balthazar could not say. The gesture convinced him that Dorf really was Dorf's name, and that he was probably an amateur.

This last assumption he modified a moment later under the blinking regard of those blue eyes when Dorf said: "You will not find my name on the latest Active List. I have just been recalled from retire-

ment to head an army group in the south. My troops are Württembergers, loyal to the memory of Field-Marshal Rommel and the
conspirators of July twentieth." Dorf paused. "Now that I have been
honest with you," he said, "I think you should be honest with me.
Your name is not Carstairs."

"Does it matter what my name is, Herr Dorf?" Balthazar hid his
surprise at the mention of Rommel's name in connection with the
anti-Hitler plot. The connection made sense, however. Rommel, like
many of the conspirators, was from the state of Württemberg.

"To me personally, no," Dorf replied; "but to my associates, very
definitely yes."

"Associates?"

"The agent you know as Bandersnatch is, of course, a fiction.
Evidently you have not realized this. Frankly I'm surprised, and not a
little disappointed. Nevertheless, I am empowered to tell you that I
represent an organization known as Degussa. . . ."

"Degussa?"

"That is correct. The German Gold and Silver Refining Company,
Deutsche Gold und Silber Scheideanstalt. Degussa is the parent company of the Auer Gesellschaft, a well-known German chemical concern. Perhaps you have heard of them?"

Balthazar said that indeed he had.

"Very well," Dorf continued. "Degussa refined the uranium for
Reich Research Council's atomic pile in Berlin. I regret that I cannot
go into details." Dorf raised the briefcase that he held in his shiny
black-gloved hand. "They are all in here. But my associates do insist
on your proper name for purposes of verification. When they know
who you are, they will know with whom they are dealing. This is far
too serious a business to play at spies. Furthermore, Degussa has
international connections. Believe me, we are not to be trifled with."

"I believe you." Balthazar tried not to look at the briefcase dangling
from Dorf's artificial hand like bait on a hook. He could scarcely
credit that Dorf would hand it over, not without some major conces-
sion, and Balthazar was not empowered to enter any negotiations. Of
course, that was not to say he couldn't lie a little, and so he began by
telling the truth:

"My name is Miles Cavendish. I'm an officer in the British Secret Intelligence Service, section six of MI6. My trade names are Carstairs, Carruthers, and, occasionally, Venables. My friends call me Balthazar. I don't know why."

The German blinked.

"Unfortunately, I'm not carrying a pass book," Balthazar added.

The German blinked again.

"Now that I've established my credentials," Balthazar went on, "supposing you clarify a few points for me?"

Dorf gave a thin smile. He nodded.

"My chief is very worried about the heavy water," Balthazar said. "Where does it come from?"

"It's old stock. We acquired some in 1940 from Joliot's lab in Paris," Dorf was smiling bleakly, "on the understanding that it be used for peaceful purposes only. We were the masters then, and Joliot could hardly refuse, but his German colleagues felt they had to salve his conscience with this assurance which was, of course, a lie."

"And the uranium?"

"The ore is from Joachimstahl, the Schmiedeberg lode in the Erzgebirge. We also imported some from Union Minière of Katanga. Several tons were refined at Degussa's number-two factory in Frankfurt. When that was partly destroyed by the bombing, we moved some of the equipment to the Chemische Fabrik Grünau, where we started production last December. Degussa's principal works at Oranienburg has been in operation throughout the war, with the Joachimstahl ore as its source of supply. Most of the *Spezialmetall* from there went to Heisenberg, first at Leipzig, then at Berlin, and now to Haigerloch. The last ton and a half will be shipped on the twenty-third, next Friday. Naturally I cannot guarantee its arrival." Dorf gave his characteristic smile. "But I can assure you that every effort will be made to ensure that it does arrive safely. Without this fuel the *Uranbrenner* cannot possibly make the plutonium for the bomb. But you must be wondering why I am telling you all this and what advantage our proposal has for Degussa?"

Balthazar, who was not aware that there had yet been a proposal, said: "Something of the sort, yes."

"Degussa believes that under the present regime there is a good chance that our research effort will be abused."

"No; really?" said Balthazar.

"The assembly and delivery plans for a German atomic bomb are already in place. All that is lacking is the plutonium. Let me tell you something, Herr Cavendish, something that very few human beings on this planet are aware of." Dorf's eyelids worked like semaphore shutters. "Some years ago the Reich Research Council conducted experiments with cylindrical charges of TNT and deuterium. Heavy paraffin was used as the deuterium carrier with silver foil underneath to record the radiation traces. The idea was to implode the TNT, so creating a pressure of many millions of atmospheres at a temperature equivalent to that of the sun's. This, it was believed, would cause a fusion reaction essentially the same as the one that powers the stars—in a word, Herr Cavendish, a hydrogen bomb. These experiments failed, and were later repeated using deuterium-filled silver spheres surrounded by a TNT charge. Again the experiments failed, but only because the scale was too small. A conventional explosive was hardly enough to begin the hydrogen-burning sequence. Only an atomic bomb could trigger the fusion reaction, which meant that it would be necessary to build a bomb within a bomb.

"Given Germany's military situation, it was decided temporarily to scale down the quest for a hydrogen bomb and concentrate instead on the search for an atomic bomb. Had the scientists who were involved in these experiments used plutonium instead of deuterium, they would have succeeded in creating an atomic bomb. But at that time they had no plutonium because there was not anywhere in the Reich an atomic reactor that had achieved a self-sustaining chain reaction. Now both these goals are in sight, the chain reaction and the plutonium. You do not seem to realize the danger, London does not seem to realize the danger—perhaps now you can understand why my associates felt that this meeting was necessary. Germany is perhaps a month away from producing an atomic bomb—two months away from using that bomb as the trigger for a deuterium superbomb many hundreds of times more powerful than even an atomic bomb."

Balthazar, eyeing the briefcase in Dorf's gloved hand, was hooked. "You mentioned a deal," he said. "What is it?"

"First things first." Dorf raised his good hand. Balthazar considered pinching the briefcase. It would be an easy thing to do, though it would spoil the whole point of the *Treff*, which was to find out what these people wanted. Anyway, Balthazar didn't like the look of the way Dorf's hand was fixed to the handle of the briefcase. He could just see himself scurrying back to London with the briefcase, the prosthesis still attached like some kind of artificial hand of Orlac. Actually, now that he came to think about it, Dorf *did* sound rather like Peter Lorre.

The German was talking about the delivery plans for the superbomb. "By rocket attack from the Hook of Holland, or, should the military situation prevent that, by a suicide-bomber attack. Hitler insists that London be the main target because he claims that British intransigence lost him the war. This ultimate vengeance weapon will reduce London to a pile of radioactive dust." Dorf paused to let that possibility sink in, and very carefully transferred the briefcase to his good hand.

"Now, Herr Cavendish," he continued, "my associates at Degussa sincerely believe that if this terrible new weapon of war is to be used at all, it must be used against the Russians. As a soldier I would have to agree with them. It is the logical choice when the Soviet armies are massing for the assault on the Oder whereas the Anglo-American forces have reached the Rhine only in the south. Degussa, you see, is only too well aware of Operation Eclipse, the Allied plan for the occupation and partition of Germany. We know that this plan calls for the Western powers to halt their advance on the line of the River Elbe while the Russians are allowed to take Berlin. Naturally, Degussa cannot agree with that. Our first condition therefore stipulates that local and ad hoc truces be arranged in the west, freeing German soldiers to continue the battle against the Russians in the east. In order best to give the appearance of spontaneity such truces would be arranged by the commanders in the field. In return, Degussa solemnly undertakes to prevent the use of nuclear weapons against the western Allies. Moreover, we are in a position to guarantee this undertaking. As commander of Army Group Swabia, under the terms of Operation Gunderic, I have the power to occupy the secret research establishments in the south and seal off the whole military district from the outside world."

"Gunderic?" Balthazar queried.

"Yes, a contingency plan, originally, to be enforced if the government in Berlin were to lose control of the political situation. This operation divides the Reich into independent sectors of command, but in view of the present military situation Gunderic has taken on an altogether greater significance. Gunderic will be implemented when the bomb is ready. All our reserves will be thrown into the Hechingen military district to form a *Festung* against the Americans. As commander of Army Group Swabia, of course, I shall control the final dispositions for the delivery of the bomb. So you see, Herr Cavendish, how Gunderic could be to our mutual advantage, but only on condition that the terms of your Operation Eclipse—unconditional surrender and the partition of Germany—are not enforced to the letter in the west."

"I am not in a position to give you such an undertaking," Balthazar said truthfully.

"No, we did not think you would be," Dorf replied. "That is why we are prepared to surrender these documents in an effort to convince your scientific people that the threat is real. And believe me, they will soon see that it is once they get a look at the plans for Gross Alberich, the deuterium superbomb, and Kindchen Alberich, the atomic bomb. But, before I forget, there is one other condition."

"One other condition?"

"Yes. Degussa sincerely regrets that during the course of Germany's heroic struggle it was expedient to use concentration-camp labor. We found that many of our laborers, their resistance lowered by an inadequate diet, their constitutions weakened by contagious diseases, when exposed to radioactive materials actually died."

"Actually died?" And Dorf was supposed to be a good German, Balthazar thought.

"Correct," Dorf acknowledged.

"You're not responsible for that, of course?"

"Certainly not. I find the subject extremely distasteful. As a soldier I happen to be on the board of directors for propaganda reasons only. Many giant corporations like the prestige that a military title lends to their letterhead. It is the same in your country as in mine. I do not wish to press the point, but Degussa sincerely hopes that in any postwar settlement the matter of forced labor could be overlooked."

"I'll pass it on," Balthazar said. "Now let me see if I've got this right," he went on blithely. "We're to call off Monty if you'll spare us from Fat Albert and his baby brother. In return for this we get the plans and you get to fight the Bolshies, but not us, a separate peace, in effect. *Korrekt, Herr Generaloberst?*"

Dorf eyed him levelly, then blinked. "Very good." He nodded. "However, I would like our dealings to be open and aboveboard, as they should be between partners. Therefore I must tell you that we have a V-Mann operating in the Skegness region of the Lincolnshire coast. His code name is Oskar, and until recently he was providing us with rather routine intelligence on the disposition of the Allied air forces in East Anglia. But all that has changed now. I'm afraid Oskar is going to be a bit of an embarrassment."

"Oh?" Balthazar was instantly suspicious, the more so because he knew that Dorf meant to allay his suspicions.

"Please let me explain," Dorf pleaded. "Oskar is—or was—an Abwehr agent. But the Abwehr is no longer under Wehrmacht control. Therefore I regret that I cannot tell you the identity of this agent, merely that he exists and that he has reported the formation of a commando group at a place called Winthorpe."

"So what?"

"He was able to describe a girl who could only have been Katherina Weber."

"Ah, yes." Balthazar was equal to this. "The poor girl is most anxious to know about the state of her mother's health."

"The SS are holding Frau Weber at a private clinic in Stuttgart," Dorf replied. "As for her health, she is—how do you say?—in the pink."

"A hostage?"

71

"Of course. The only reason Stengel let the Webers go was to cast doubt on Germany's nuclear capability. If Katherina is helping your people, then her mother will be in some danger. You should see to it that she is removed from the base forthwith."

"This Oskar," Balthazar began, "who told you about him?"

"Stengel, of course." Dorf gave his thin smile. "Oh, do not worry, Herr Cavendish. Degussa and the Wehrmacht will take care of him." The Generaloberst looked at his watch. "It is getting late," he said, handing over the briefcase to Balthazar: "Bandersnatch expects your answer within three weeks."

"It's not much time," Balthazar grumbled.

"Perhaps all of us have not much time, Herr Cavandish. In three weeks the plutonium will be ready for the bomb. *Auf Wiedersehen*, Herr Cavendish."

Balthazar watched him leave, a thin man with a thin smile, dark hat, dark clothes, dark glasses—and then he raced across to the court-yard of the railway station to make a phone call.

Dorf's briefcase was in the diplomatic bag to London that night.

9: THE GREEN MAN

"There's a new lot moved in up at the base, then."

Charlie Polk, the tailor, was built like a Toby jug. He was small, round, fat, and bald. Hollow, too, Crimshaw, the landlord of The Green Man, was thinking.

"The base?" Crimshaw's gaze narrowed. He was a red-faced, porcine man, and some people said he was his own best customer, Charlie Polk among them.

"Winthorpe." The tailor wiped the foam from his handlebar moustache. He looked expectantly at Crimshaw, his eyes bright, seeking approval. The landlord didn't seem to know what he was talking about. Or care.

"I didn't think that place was used any more," Crimshaw said.

"Well, it is and it isn't," Charlie Polk replied in the vexatious whine of one who knows much and will soon tell all.

"That'd be no good in my trade," grated Sam Morrow from the corner of the snug.

"How's that, Sam?" Crimshaw affected interest. He was trying to work out what Charlie Polk had been doing at Winthorpe, and had difficulty reconciling what he knew of the tailor with the war effort. The two were as far apart, thought Leonard Crimshaw, as cheese and chalk.

"You have to be one thing or the other. Not both, see?" Sam Morrow wheezed sulphurously. He had a face like a gargoyle, and cigarette smoke poured from his nostrils. A wine glass sat before him, holding a reddish amber liquid. Brandy and port, Samuel Morrow was an undertaker.

"I mean it's not used for flying, not any more, except as a satellite base—for emergencies only." Charlie Polk strove to redress the situation. He did not like Samuel Morrow or his business. "But they've got a new lot up there. And I'll tell you something else, too." Charlie put his pint mug down on the bar. "They're running around in German uniforms."

"No kidding," Crimshaw said, without much enthusiasm.

"Gospel truth, Leonard. I'll have another pint, please."

Crimshaw pulled the pint, and watched Charlie Polk drink half of it, his Adam's apple bobbing up and down like a ball-and-poppet valve.

"Commandos in German uniforms leaping around all over the place and letting off a lot of smoke bombs." The little tailor smacked his lips. He was obviously pleased to be the center of attention.

"You've seen them, have you?" asked Crimshaw.

"Not personally, no," answered Charlie Polk, leaving Crimshaw to wonder how the tailor could see things impersonally. "This wing commander—he's a customer of mine—told me about it. You know what I think? It's my theory that they dress our boys up in these Jerry uniforms, then if they get shot down or something, they can pretend they're the other lot's night fighters. Of course"—Charlie Polk contemplated his half-empty mug—"they'd better speak German, otherwise they might be in a bit of a pickle."

"You're not serious?" Crimshaw was intrigued in spite of himself.

"Christ, no," Charlie Polk giggled. Sometimes he thought Crimshaw had a screw loose. The landlord was from Grimsby, not Skegness. That had to be it, or else the drink. "But it's queer, isn't it? What do you think, Sam?"

"Nowt but foolishness," the resident oracle uttered.

"Paddy's not in yet, then?" Charlie Polk took refuge in the obvious. Paddy would be interested in his story. Paddy always was.

Crimshaw looked at the clock. "He's got a minute to go," he said. The horse brasses started rattling again. Funny, but they always picked up the vibrations first. Crimshaw and the other two men listened to the pulse of heavy bombers climbing over the Lincolnshire coast. No one said anything.

"Another pint, please, Leonard." The little tailor rubbed his hands. "Make that two, will you?" Charlie Polk had just seen his friend the Irishman enter the snug. No one knew his real name; everyone just called him Paddy, which suited him well enough.

"Just like bloody clockwork," Crimshaw grumbled. "I wonder who wound him up."

"Lay off it, Len," Charlie protested. "Paddy's all right."

"Evening, Paddy." Crimshaw was smitten with hospitality.

"Good evening." The Irishman was lean and well tanned. He was always polite—too polite for a Paddy, Crimshaw thought.

"Charlie's got a funny story for you tonight," he said, watching for the Irishman's reaction.

"Is that right?" The Irishman smiled.

"Daft bugger, 'e is." Sam Morrow was thinking of what it must be like to be on the receiving end of a thousand-bomber raid. Profitable, in his line of business, but distasteful all the same. These days everything was mass-produced. Samuel Morrow lit another cigarette. He was happy: on his third brandy and port, in heaven without the formalities. "According to him those planes you can hear are being flown by German-speaking pilots in Jerry uniforms. Daft bugger. Next thing you know, they'll be dropping Jerry bombs on us, and I'll tell you," Sam chortled, "bombs speak the same in any language, bombs do."

"True enough," the Irishman said.

"The only good German," Leonard Crimshaw declared unctuously, "is a dead one."

10: THE RABBI MOSES DE RAZIN

Balthazar returned from Switzerland on the morning of Monday, February 19. Carlo spoke with him briefly over the phone from Skegness where Sweet was pursuing a lead on the American OSS operative, a spy in the ointment. Carlo set up field quarters in the local police divisional HQ. He had a scrambler installed and slept in the cells. When he slept.

In London, Carlo had checked out Katherina's story of the Rabbi Moses de Razin, gassed at Sachsenhausen concentration camp. The rabbi, Carlo discovered, was the author of a commentary on the *Yordei Merkavah*—the "descenders of the chariot," an interpretation of the famous Talmudic story in which four renowned rabbis were allowed to enter paradise "for a look." The first went mad, the second became an apostate, the third died; only one of the rabbis, the most learned, was allowed to look and depart in perfect peace. Carlo's sources indicated that Moses de Razin had died in Sachsenhausen "sometime toward the end of July 1944," which would tend to confirm Katherina's story. Yet the presence of Stengel, Hugo Weber, and a French angelologist at Sachsenhausen concentration camp, practically next door to the main Auer chemical works in Oranienburg, had troubled Carlo. It seemed too pat, given Weber's obsession with the Angel of Death, too much of a coincidence.

Carlo had several lengthy sessions with Katherina that week. Try as he might, he could not shake her story about her father and Moses de Razin. Carlo had asked her what kind of work went on in the camp and chemical plant, and she told him.

"Auer's rare-earth department was at Oranienburg; I believe that

77

Degussa acted as the subcontractor. The ore was refined at the camp factory, then shipped to one of Degussa's two plants in Frankfurt. When the bombing put a stop to that, they switched the shipments to the Chemische Fabrik Grünau in Berlin-Grünau. It was much nearer. I remember there was one early process where metallic uranium, which had been refined from ammonium uranate, was mixed with coal dust and pressed into blocks, using tragacanth gum as a binder. Filthy, dangerous work; I believe they used camp labor for that sort of thing."

"Would the rabbi have been involved, do you know, Fräulein?"

"I—I can't honestly say."

Prentice, the nuclear physicist from Cavendish Laboratories, had sat in on several of these sessions, and had asked her technical questions.

"The coal dust—what was that for, Fräulein?"

"For use as a moderator. Other carbonaceous materials were used, too. Paraffin—in one of Heisenberg's experiments—paraffin and uranium oxide. The neutron source would be introduced to the center of the pile and we'd sit around measuring the flux at the edge. It wasn't until the end of 1942, when he started using heavy water as a moderator, that he got any results. But he'd changed the configuration of the pile, because he'd been listening to my father, you see. We were using frozen heavy water then, with ordinary ice as a shield, about one hundred and sixty liters of heavy water and five hundred kilograms of uranium."

"With what results, Fräulein?"

"An increase of one-and-a-half in the neutron flux. Later, using the cubes instead of a layered arrangement, we succeeded in obtaining a tenfold increase."

"But no self-sustaining reaction?"

"I expect the pile will go critical any day now."

"How is it shut down, Fräulein?"

"Cadmium metal," Katherina replied. "Cadmium is a strong absorber of neutrons and we always kept enough ready to drop into the pile through the chimney at the center. The source is introduced in the same way—five hundred milligrams of radioactive beryllium.

78

Once that has been injected into the pile core, we start pumping heavy water into the vessel and plot the reciprocal of neutron intensity against the amount of heavy water pumped in. The heavy water, as you know, acts as a moderator on the fast neutron reactions, allowing the thermal neutrons to build a sustained chain reaction. We have found that once the heavy water becomes irradiated with the by-products of nuclear fission, it can be very corrosive, and we have discovered that using the plastic hydrocarbon strips to hang the uranium in the moderator solves this problem."

Prentice, who had worked in Berlin before the war at Otto Hahn's lab where Lise Meitner had first reported splitting the atom, nodded. What disturbed him was that the Americans had encountered the same problem of pile poisoning, and had solved it in a typically American way by canning the uranium slugs. The German solution seemed as elegant, to say the least, and if they had encountered and overcome identical problems, then their technology had to be equivalent.

"I think you will need my help on the site," said Katherina Weber.

"Yes, Fräulein," Prentice agreed. "I think so, too."

She seemed prepared to talk, and Carlo had let her talk, about the nature of her work and life under the Nazis. "In a way it is a beautiful thing," she had told both men, "to believe in the truth, always to be looking for the right way." Carlo would remember that phrase, which he thought almost Confucian. He had been looking for the right way himself for years.

Katherina told both her inquisitors how her former colleagues had known that Hugo Weber was right, and Heisenberg wrong, about the ratio of captured to free neutrons in fissionable materials, but, because of the system, had deferred to Heisenberg, the top dog and a Nobel laureate besides. "Maybe I can't blame them for that," she had said, "but he was wrong and my father was right, and that was the only thing that mattered to me at the time. When you're involved in a project like that, you want to see it work. That is the main thing. You don't think too much of the long-term consequences except in scientific terms—the blast, radii and degrees of destruction, the density and types of radiation—that sort of thing. Scientists are not cruel people, they don't want to harm anyone. It's just that it's easier to talk about lethality than killing. What I am trying to say is that one kind of truth blots out another. I think I was taught to lie with the truth. I didn't always think so, but that is what I think now. You can lie by telling the truth, or just that part of the truth you think people need to know."

Carlo would remember this too; how could he ever forget? Things were exactly the same in his line.

Prentice had agreed with enthusiasm, but Carlo had been considerably less than enthusiastic. He knew that he had to sort out his feelings toward Katherina. He respected her intelligence; in some ways he pitied her for it, a dangerous indulgence on his part, Carlo knew. But perhaps it really would have been better if she had been stupid as well as everything else—gaunt, toothy, ugly, and stupid, then no one would have paid her the slightest degree of attention.

That she was honest and truthful in most things, Carlo did not for a moment doubt. At the same time, if the account Dorf had given Balthazar in Lugano was to be believed, Katherina had certainly been lying about the state of her mother's health. And so had her father, so indeed had Hugo.

Carlo did not confront the daughter with this, not immediately. By the middle of the week he knew he would have to make the time to see Hugo again. Carlo also had a fairly shrewd idea that he was being "drawn in," that Hugo Weber, his daughter Katherina, the state of Frau Weber's health, Generaloberst Dorf, a spy called Oskar, Projekt Alberich, and a dead French angelologist, the Rabbi Moses de Razin, were linked by a certain indissoluble black thread—SS Standartenführer Rudolf Stengel.

But of the nature of that thread Carlo had no idea.

It rained that week in Skegness, a hard, cold, driving rain that came in off the North Sea in sheets. Carlo spent most of the cold night hours in a DF van with Sweet, listening for Oskar. But Oskar was silent—or dead.

Sweet had first raised that morbid possibility while they crouched over the direction-finding equipment in the back of the van, the rain beating down on the roof as Carlo scanned the wavebands.

"Oh, no, David," he had objected; "I don't think so. Why else would Dorf tell Balthazar about him? I reckon that if you can find the American, then we'll flush out Oskar. How's it going, by the way?"

I left my bloody umbrella in London," Sweet complained bitterly.

"Why not put in for another, David? I'm sure we could spare the expense."

"Operational reasons. A man under an umbrella in these parts would be conspicuous, wouldn't he? After all, this is 'sunny' Skegness, isn't it? Or could I possibly be mistaken, do you think? 'Sunny Skegness,'" Sweet snorted derisively, "you see those posters all over the place." Carlo let him go on. Sweet lit a cigarette and inhaled deeply. "There is a man who says he might recognize that photo if I buy him a brandy and port in The Green Man. I'd hate to disappoint you, though, Carlo. The contact's an undertaker," Sweet declared rapturously. "It'd be too bad for us if he recognized one of his clients, wouldn't it? By the way, where did you get that photo from?"

"Harold gave it to me. It seems this agent is one of their *Alsos*."

"*Alsos* ran. Why don't you just call the Cousins and ask them the favor? It'd save me a soaking."

"Ah well, there's this and there's that. For one thing Harold's afraid they might start developing an interest in speleology. It seems the Cousins don't want to share the candy with their friends any more. We have to think about Baby Albert after all, if he becomes an orphan. I think we could give him a better education than the Cousins, don't you? It would never do if they found out we'd been talking to his present guardians. You know how sensitive they are. Then there's Scarr's people. The Cousins hate baby snatchers; so—all in all—I'm afraid we simply can't pick up the phone and ask them to do what you say. You should cultivate this undertaker, David; buy him a couple of drinks. More, if he needs it."

"Don't you ever get the feeling with those people that they're sizing you up? It's the way they look at you, as if to say 'you're next.' Why don't we just leave town?"

"I've been thinking about that," Carlo said. "I should talk to the Fräulein again."

He spun the dial. Nothing, there was nothing; only static and the rain beating on the van roof.

"Like a bleeding Chinese torture," Sweet said.

"I have a message for you, Fräulein Weber."

"A message, Herr Peat? But who from?"

"From Oskar."

"But I don't know anyone called Oskar."

"No? Nevertheless, he sends you his greetings."

"You are joking, Herr Peat. I see it in your eyes."

"Perhaps I have made a mistake, Fräulein; perhaps the greetings were intended for your mother."

"You know then?" Katherina Weber sat stonily across the table from Carlo Peat. She had a hut to herself at Winthorpe, furnished in Spartan furniture, and she was kept guarded around the clock. Carlo wondered whether she knew, or cared.

"We know that she is alive and well," Carlo said.

"For how long?"

"I beg your pardon, Fräulein?"

She gave a kind of smile: "I meant, for how long have you known this?"

"Since the beginning of the week," he said, surprised that he was answering her questions and looking for a way to reassert himself.

"But you guessed it earlier, did you not?"

"Yes, to be frank, I did," Carlo replied, discomforted by her stony regard and the fact that, undeniably, she had the advantage over him, though he did not know why. He searched that great mare's face with the overlarge teeth, looking for some answer; he found it in her eyes. Contempt. She despised him.

"Your mother may be in some danger, Fräulein," he said. "Perhaps it would be wise to remove you from Winthorpe and from the project."

"Don't you think that is what they want?" She gave him that look again.

"Perhaps," Carlo acknowledged.

"I am very sorry but I have lied to you," she said, though it was not an apology. Then, her Adam's apple working up and down: "I wonder how I can make you understand."

"Try," he said.

It was Sunday before he could get away to York. Nine weeks to the day had passed since he had interrogated Hugo Weber on Christmas Eve, and during that time the professor's condition had improved remarkably. He was pinker and sleeker; no longer wrapped in a straitjacket, he wore a gray serge suit with a white, open-necked shirt that gave him a Byronic look. The scars on his wrists had healed, and he seemed in every way a changed man, even, Carlo thought, a happy one.

"Herr Peat! What a surprise! But, actually, I must confess that I was expecting this visit."

"You were?"

"Indeed. Katherina called, you know. She said she'd told you about my experience with the rabbi. It was terrible, terrible. You can have no idea. The shock of seeing his body so soon after I had been talking to him. And such a loss to scholarship. Can you wonder that I didn't want to talk about it?"

Carlo beamed sympathetically. "That's all behind you now," he said. "I want you to forget all about the rabbi. It's a man called Dorf I want to talk about today—Generaloberst Wilhelm Friederich Dorf. You know him, I believe?"

"*Ach, ja.* Dorf is on the board of Degussa, the gold and silver people. They handled the uranium contracts for the Virus House."

"What's he like? Trustworthy?"

"Yes, I would think so. An old-line German conservative, good family. He was badly wounded in Russia, you know. I would say you could trust him."

"Dorf told us about some experiments conducted with deuterium. Something about imploding spheres."

"Yes, yes. Sachsse and Trinks. They wanted to make a hydrogen bomb. Imagine! I told you that German theoretical physics was ahead of the rest of the world, but here was one case where it was ahead of itself. What is the English expression? Something about putting the horse behind the cart. Well, they were putting the horse behind the cart all right, making a hydrogen bomb before an atom bomb. Impossible!"

"But if someone else were developing the atom bomb?"

"Heisenberg with his lumps of ice and paraffin. Worthless!"

"Then these experiments were of little value?"

"Of *no* value. In order to initiate the reaction, they would have needed a start-up temperature of some four million degrees with an initial pressure of two hundred and fifty million atmospheres, plus an implosion velocity of two thousand five hundred meters per second. Any fool could see that the inner spheres were far too small—about two inches in diameter—to accommodate such parameters. If they had succeeded they would have made pocket hydrogen bombs. As it was they did not even record a residual trace of radioactivity. Does that answer your question, Herr Peat?"

"Oh, yes, I think so. I'm very grateful to you, Professor Weber. By the way, there was one other thing. Your mentioning the rabbi just now reminded me. Rudolf Stengel has quite a sense of humor, hasn't he?"

"I beg your pardon?" The color drained from Weber's face.

"It was Stengel who dreamed up the Angel of Death, wasn't it, Herr Professor?"

"I don't know what you're talking about," Hugo Weber said weakly.

"I think you do. Stengel dreamed up Rahab the Angel of Death—not you, Weber; you wouldn't have had the nerve. It was Stengel who dreamed up this angelic fixation of yours in order to explain how a prominent nuclear scientist and his daughter could slip out of the Reich in the middle of this war. It must have been the rabbi who put it into his head, unintentionally of course. Or maybe it was his own invention completely, in which case when he found out that the Rabbi Moses de Razin was a prisoner at Sachsenhausen it must indeed have seemed like a heaven-sent opportunity. The angel Rahab—that was damned clever. But de Razin? That was just a little too clever, Weber. If only Katherina hadn't been such a good storyteller! Because it was a story, wasn't it, though in a sense you could plead that it really was the angel of death who told you to come to England. It was Stengel, Stengel was behind everything. He threatened to throw you and Katherina into the camp. You'd seen those people in the Oranienburg works often enough, you must have known what conditions were like, you didn't *need* any demonstration. Stengel wanted to use you as his stooge, didn't he? All you had to do was be your usual self and pour scorn on all your colleagues and their research, tell us what fools they were with their pocket hydrogen bombs—and we'd be lulled into a false sense of security. I bet Stengel could hear us saying, 'Ah, that Weber. He's not as crazy as he seems to be. What fools those Nazis are; they let him go for a crazy man. . . .' And you, Weber, using your daughter to tell me that cock-and-bull story about the Rabbi de Razin, that was the cleverest trick of all, because you very nearly got away with it, Herr Doktor Professor Weber, and you would have done too, but for your wife, her mother—the insurance."

Hugo Weber had turned an awful yeasty color. "No, no, please, you must believe me, *please* . . ."

Carlo had seen this happen before. It was almost like a religious conversion. Despair, guilt, anguish, horror, and above all, in a paradoxical sort of way, relief—these were what Hugo Weber was feeling now, and Carlo made it easier for him by effacing his own emotions.

"Go on, Professor Weber," he said, gently. "I'm listening, I believe you."

"I need to, I need to talk," the physicist began; "you've no idea how I need to talk. Can you imagine what it was like for me, a scientist, a man of reason, to live this grotesque lie? Do you wonder that I tried to kill myself? It was the only way to destroy the lie."

"You could have tried telling the truth as soon as you arrived in England," Carlo said.

"My wife, they had my wife."

A human vegetable, Carlo was tempted to say, remembering the appalling glibness with which Hugo Weber had delivered that line nine weeks ago. Instead he said nothing, nothing at all, regretting even the little he had said.

"Of course I lied about her," Weber continued. "There was no cerebral hemorrhage, but she is in Germany. Stengel threatened to send her to the camp, to Sachsenhausen. 'She can work with the uranium ore, making the *Spezialmetall*, where the rabbi worked.' That is what he said, Herr Peat. You were right about Stengel. It was his idea that I should see the angel. It amused him. But you were wrong about Moses de Razin. That was no story; Stengel did show me his body, along with many others. 'This man wrote about a rabbi who saw angels in paradise and came back to tell the tale' is what the Standartenführer said. 'Now it is his turn, but I do not think he will come back from the other side.' You were wrong about the rabbi, Herr Peat; you were very wrong. Until that day my greatest worry was Katherina. Sometimes I thought I did not have her convinced, about the angel of death, I mean. But when I came back from the camp that afternoon, and told her what I had seen, then she believed me."

Carlo could understand that.

"And the story about your wife, Herr Professor?"

"Stengel thought of that, too. Please, you must believe me. Katherina knows nothing of this. I was able to make it look as if we had thought of it together in Switzerland. 'They will ask about mama,' I told her. 'We must think of something to tell them.' I recognized the import of your question, of course; but—" Hugo Weber gave a terrible sigh. "What could I do? What could I do? 'You must go to England,' Stengel said. 'You must go to England to convince them there is no danger. The timetable calls for Germany to explode her first bomb on April the twentieth, the Führer's fifty-sixth birthday. The English must never discover the truth. *We are a month ahead of schedule.*'"

Carlo got up; Hugo Weber's eyes swam with tears. The physicist sobbed convulsively.

"What would you have done? What would you have done?" he cried.

Carlo left him. Outside in the corridor he ran into Collinson. Carlo asked if he could use the phone.

"Yes, of course. And how did you find our patient this time?" the psychiatrist asked.

"Sane, as usual. Would you do something for me?"

"That depends on what it is." Collinson risked a smile.

"Tell your patient he's being moved to London, will you?"

"Is he?"

"Just tell him. And while you're at it, tell him that his precious daughter is being moved there too, would you? I'd be most interested to hear about his reaction," said Carlo Peat.

11: DAVID SWEET

"Bloody hell, I thought you were a Jerry spy, 'ammering on the door like that ten minutes before opening time."

The landlord of The Green Man wore a rubber apron and rubber boots. His face the same liverish hue as his apron, his straw-colored hair in disarray, Leonard Crimshaw looked as though he had just been surprised in the commission of an indelicate act, Sweet thought. He was right.

"I was cleaning out the facilities," Crimshaw announced airily.

"Yes, well . . ." Sweet's nose wrinkled, his own distinctive odor overwhelmed by an invigorating draft of seaweed, stale beer, urine, vinegar, fish and chips, and vomit—and something else, a chemical reek explained, no doubt, by Crimshaw's reference to the facilities.

It still rained that morning in sunny Skegness, and Sweet stood on the flat, worn sandstone step of The Green Man, the rain guttering off the brim of his trilby hat and collecting in the upturned collar of his navy-blue trench coat. Sweet was fed up with looking for the American, and fed up, too, with listening to the crackling of the ether in the back of the DF van. There had been no traffic out of Oskar all week, not a peep, and Sweet didn't have to be told that it was impossible to get a fix on silence, a silence that grew nightly more ominous. For if Oskar was not indeed already dead, he had to be saving up his air time for one final burst—after which, in all probability, he would be signing off.

In the meantime the sky and the horizonless sea had joined together to swallow Oskar up as surely as if he lay at the bottom of the ocean. Carlo Peat, as usual, had his own point of view.

"You'll just have to be patient, David," he'd told Sweet before departing for York. "Field agents are very anal."

Carlo believed the whole thing would break before the new week was very old. When Sweet had asked why, Carlo had told him that Scarr's people were getting out of Winthorpe.

"I'll try to get back on Sunday night," Carlo had said. "Vorpal will have left the base by then and we'll have to think of a way of spreading the news around."

"Sam Morrow," Sweet had said. "He knows everyone around here. Alive or dead."

It was Sam Morrow who'd suggested that Sweet might buy him a drink in The Green Man. Sweet was masquerading as a Prudential agent in search of a beneficiary. "I know 'im, all right," Sam Morrow said; "'e's an Irishman. We call 'im Paddy. I know everyone around 'ere, alive or dead." And so now Sweet stood on the flat sandstone step under the sign of a leguminous demiurge clad in vine leaves, dripped on and dripping, more dead than alive himself.

"If you don't like it you can grow gills," the jovial publican said. "Police, are you?"

"Not exactly." Sweet wondered what had betrayed him. "Would you mind looking at this?"

The image was soft and the print was dog-eared and wet, but Crimshaw recognized Paddy. He was wearing a Fair Isle sweater and was lounging against a boat that had been drawn up on some beach. Paddy, undoubtedly, though in his younger days, grinning all over his pretty Celtic face.

"Seen him before, have you?"

Crimshaw hesitated. Publicans, like clergymen, value the sanctity of the confessional. "It's not a very good likeness," the landlord of The Green Man complained. "But I might 'ave seen 'im before. Once or twice. Irish; yes, it does have the look of 'im about the eyes."

"He's a regular, isn't he?"

"Just like a copper. Why ask if you know?"

Sweet appeared to consider the question. "Listen," he said, "if this Paddy skips, give me a call, will you?"

"What's this all about anyway—IRA? 'Ere, you the Special Branch?"

"You said it." Sweet searched Crimshaw's dropsical features for a sign that he believed this explanation. The landlord seemed happy to have found a reason for Sweet's presence on his doorstep. "Say nothing to Paddy, mind," Sweet elaborated. "I shall be staying in Skegness for quite some time. You can contact me at the local police station."

"To whom shall I speak?" Crimshaw formulated this question with a grammatical flourish that seemed beyond his means. Mine host had a glum look: Sweet reckoned he was calculating Paddy's nightly worth to The Green Man.

"Prendergast," Sweet said, and the brim of his hat suddenly wilted, the rain pouring on to the tip of his nose. "Aren't you supposed to be opening?" he asked hopefully.

"I was getting ready when you knocked. If it's a drink you're looking for, I suppose you'd better come in." Crimshaw spoke as to a leper.

Sweet shuffled after the landlord. He stood miserably in a widening puddle of runoff while Crimshaw glowered at him from behind the bar.

"What'll you have?" the publican demanded.

"A pint of bitter, please."

Crimshaw pulled the pint, which was flat and tepid. Sweet scrutinized it as a fortune teller the glass. It foretold a cloudy future. Crimshaw rang up the pint and held out his hand. "This isn't a bloody charity ward, you know," he grumbled, handing Sweet the change from a ten-shilling note.

As this transaction took place an expression of great wariness crept into the publican's narrow eyes. He looked at Sweet, and was puzzled. A man like that, what was he smiling at? And why? For Sweet was smiling, and it looked horrible.

"You know," Sweet began, affably enough. "I heard a story once about a German fighter pilot who strafed this town during the Blitz. At great personal risk he flew out of his way during a raid on London especially to shoot up the beach at Skegness. Not that there was anybody on it, oh, no. They were all sitting around in the pubs with knotted hankies on their heads, suffering from sunstroke, when this Hun started strafing the beach. Do you know why he did it, his motive

91

for this atrocity, Mr. Crimshaw? He'd spent a holiday here before the war, you see. So I was told—but I didn't think the story was true, until this week, until today. I hope they gave that fighter pilot the bleeding Iron Cross; he certainly deserved it. Thank you for all your help, Mr. Crimshaw. You may go back to cleaning out the facilities now."

Sweet counted his change on the steps of The Green Man. Crimshaw had shortchanged him but it had been worth it, Sweet thought.

At the police station he ran into a man called Raymond Thring, the Detective Chief Inspector for the Parts of Lindsey.

"Been swimming, have you?" the DCI chortled.

"Name me one good man in this town," said Sweet darkly, "and I'll buy you a pint in The Green Man."

"Sam Morrow," the DCI replied unhesitatingly. "If you can't trust an undertaker, who can you trust?"

"Funny you mentioned that," Sweet said. "I'd like Sam to run an errand for us."

"No foul play now." The DCI had stopped at the door of his office. "By the way, Mr. Sweet," he said, "there's a phone call for you."

12: UNDERTAKINGS

Crimshaw observed the horse-drawn hearse coming down the front just before opening time on Monday morning. It was high tide and the waves slopped against the concrete, salt spray dousing Jephthah's flanks and causing the horse to frisk a little. What a swaybacked nag that was, thought Crimshaw, and Morrow thinking himself so high and mighty for not using a motor hearse like everyone else in this day and age. The publican noted the damp black plumes on Jephthah's head, which meant that the undertaker must be going to pick up a body. But whose could it be? Crimshaw hoped, piously, that it wasn't one of his customers. Paddy hadn't been in last night; maybe he had met with an accident. Or had he heard that the cops were looking for him? Crimshaw wondered if he should call the police, then thought better of it. If the bobbies couldn't find their man, why should he help them?

Leonard Crimshaw busied himself with the glasses behind the bar, looked at the clock, and decided that he might as well open up.

His first customer of the day was already standing on the step. It was that cop back again, the one with the mustache and funny teeth. Over his shoulder Leonard Crimshaw caught sight of the hearse rounding the corner to the coast road. Samuel Morrow and Jephthah were heading for the base at Winthorpe.

Crimshaw said: "Hello. I was just thinking of giving you a ring."

Morrow's progress was monitored by Carlo Peat, who had returned the night before, and Raymond Thring, who was sitting behind the wheel of the police Wolseley. The DCI was a large man, and at the moment a gloomy one. He had arrived equipped for the hunt with a shooting stick, binoculars, and an ancient 30-30 Winchester lever-action carbine. Raymond Thring was suitably costumed in a hacking jacket, oxfords, and a pair of heavily welted brown brogues on his size-thirteen feet. Having adopted, at his wife's insistence, this form of the national costume in defiance of the adversary, Raymond Thring felt honor-bound to protest what he regarded as a low subterfuge.

"Sam Morrow's as straight as a die, if you'll pardon the expression, Mr. Peat," he declared, watching the hearse retreat down the coast road. "He buried my old man and he'll probably bury me as well. I hate playing tricks on him like this."

"It can't be helped," Carlo said wearily. "When the day is done, I'm sure Sam will have a tale to tell."

"Having him gallivanting around at his time of life. Do you want me to follow him?"

"No, I don't think that's necessary. All we have to do is sit tight and wait. Quite honestly, I'll be glad of the rest."

And so they waited; for half an hour, for an hour, for an hour and a half, until, after the better part of two hours had passed, an exasperated Thring saw Jephthah pulling the hearse down the coast road with Samuel Morrow aboard, as the DCI would later remark, like Bela Lugosi trying to beat the sunrise.

"He's found out the birds have flown leaving no carrion," said Thring, watching Sam dismount outside The Green Man.

Carlo nodded glumly. "Talk about bolting the stable doors after the horse has gone," he said. "That's almost as bad as putting the horse behind the cart."

Thring stared at him in astonishment.

"Oh, nothing," Carlo said. "He's gone in. Sweet's in there. I hope we haven't hurt Sam's feelings."

"Sam'll do the rounds this morning," Thring said. "It'll be into The Lincoln Imp after The Green Man, then The Marquis of Granby, if I know Sam. He'll be quite exercised, I can tell you."

"So will his horse," Carlo said. "Here's Sweet."

Sweet wheezily unfolded his lanky frame in the back of the car and lit a cigarette. He coughed, filling the Wolseley with a blend of ill humors, the topmost of which was Crimshaw's best bitter.

"You smoke too much," Carlo said.

"No, I damn well don't," Sweet responded with sudden asperity.

"What happened?"

"You were right." Sweet glanced at Thring, who grinned at him in the mirror. "You should have heard him going on about cruelty to dumb animals. He said he got the call at nine-thirty this morning. He said the caller had told him there'd been an accident at Winthorpe and his services were required. 'How many bodies?' Sam had asked. 'I'm only a one-horse undertaker and the animal does like to have a bit of a lie in.'" Sweet was racked by coughing. "'A one-horse undertaker!' It was all I could do to stop from laughing, knowing who the caller was." Sweet gazed at Carlo and coughed again. "When he got up to the base, they were all gone. 'Lock, stock, barrel, and bodies, living or dead,' he said, 'and I know everyone around 'ere—alive or dead. It's just like the *Marie Celeste* up there,' that's what he said, poor old Sam. He must be on his fifth brandy and port by now."

"We'd better get going." The DCI brought a size-thirteen brogue down on the clutch pedal and turned the ignition. "It'll be all over town by this afternoon."

Thring drove with more enthusiasm than skill, his appetite sharpened by the long wait for the one-horse undertaker to return from the now deserted base. The only cloud on Thring's horizon, at the moment, was that this business might not be over by teatime, in which case he would be answerable to his wife, Alice, who was having visitors. Visitors, as a rule, fell into three categories: the vicar, police wives, and charities, only on some grisly occasions in the Lenten season the three categories merged. This was to be such an occasion, and as much as he despised the charity mob gathering at his house, Thring lived in greater fear of his wife's wrath should he fail to take a bow as the representative of law and order, the more so as he knew that she pictured him, gun under arm, striding on cue into the drawing room—the spy-catcher. It was all very fine, but he didn't see how he had a hope in hell of finishing the business by teatime, and Alice so hated unpunctuality.

The DCI drove along the coast road, making a left turn past the main Bomber Command Base at Ingoldmells, then another left a few miles farther on. The road was straight and flat, the land featureless. Thring pulled the car off the road at the crest of the slight rise from which, three weeks ago, Carlo had studied the cryptic signs in the snow. It had stopped raining, the pale sun testing the gray skies over the fen.

"We can watch from here," the DCI announced, and busied himself with setting up his shooting stick. Sweet watched, amused.

"Well?" he asked.

"Scarr's people should be dropping out of the skies over Welsh Wales by now." Carlo looked at his watch. "If Weber's telling the truth we've got about two weeks, David."

Sweet said nothing. He lit another cigarette and chewed on it.

"The girl's father was coached, and well coached by Stengel," Carlo went on. "I suspect that old Hugo still half-believes in the cause. The question is, how much of that has rubbed off on his daughter? I arranged to have him find out that she's been moved to London, by the way. In case his paternal affections fail him, Hugo's going to find out that he's being moved as well."

Sweet inhaled; a rheumy look came into his eyes. It might have been mirth. "Let him sit and stew," he said.

"I will, David. It's the acid test. Here's Thring."

The DCI returned complaining of the cold. "There'll be hell to pay if I'm not home by four," he said. By 3:10 he was showing visible signs of restlessness. Thring had ventured back from his second pee of the afternoon, and was stamping his brogues on the road and slapping his hands together when Carlo said: "Here we go, Mister Thring."

A lone cyclist was approaching the base from the opposite direction. Thring picked up the binoculars and watched the cyclist turn off the road, wobble past the guardhouse, and stop.

"Who is it?" Sweet asked.

"Don't know. He's got his back to me," Thring said. "God, I'm cold." Thring watched the cyclist lay his bicycle down on the gravel path and dart sideways into the nearest building, a Nissen hut. "Damn," Thring said. The cyclist reappeared at the other side of the hut, and Raymond Thring watched him turn around to get his bearings. "Paddy," he said, "and he's going to have a visitor."

Carlo and Sweet watched the car turn into the drive, a Morris.

"Crimshaw's car with Leonard driving," the DCI said. The Morris pulled up at the guardhouse and Crimshaw got out to look at the bicycle.

The DCI said: "Leonard's got a gun, Leonard has." Thring dropped all thoughts of Alice and the cold. Wordlessly, he watched Crimshaw plunge into the nearest hut, emerging at the other side, as Paddy had, to make for the newest and largest of the Nissen huts. Crimshaw disappeared inside: a flock of pigeons scattered; a crow cawed. "Look at that!" Thring cried, still hanging on to the binoculars. Crimshaw had come out of the building and was running. The publican looked over his shoulder once, ran around the back of the first hut, and staggered toward the Morris. Sweet, Carlo, and the DCI watched him back up over Paddy's bicycle, swing the Morris around, and exit through the gates of RAF Winthorpe.

"Don't worry about him," Raymond Thring said. "We know where he's going. Gentlemen," the DCI turned the ignition key, "let us go and see what makes Mr. Crimshaw run."

The Wolseley reached the base in less than a minute, Thring driving like a man bent on self-destruction. "There," the DCI reflected after throwing the car into a sidelong skid past the guardhouse, "this is the building. Have you got a gun, Mr. Sweet?"

Sweet shook his head.

"I have," Carlo said, and produced a Webley .45 service revolver.

"Good. I'll take this and go first. After all, it is my manor." The DCI cradled the carbine as he got out of the car. "You'd better cover me, Mr. Peat, just in case Paddy decides we're unwelcome. He has to be in there somewhere."

Carlo and Sweet watched the DCI stroll leisurely over the black tarmac and kick open the door of the Nissen hut, which swung on its hinges.

"Paddy!" he shouted, and the echo answered him deep from within the cavernous building.

"Mr. Peat!" Thring called. "Come and look at this. You too, Mr. Sweet," and the DCI disappeared from view like Paddy, like Crimshaw.

"Looks like a big pressure cooker to me," he said when Sweet and Peat joined him inside the hut. The huge concrete structure loomed in the glare of the lights slung from the cross beams under the arching roof of the hut. Sweet and the DCI, their footfalls ringing throughout the building, climbed the scaffolding to the top of the pressure cooker, followed by Carlo clutching his service revolver. An aluminum vessel nestled inside the concrete shell, the top of which was about seven feet above the hut floor. An open hatch in the middle invited entrance to the inner vessel, which was no more than four feet deep. Raymond Thring peered through the hatch and made a noncommital grunt to hide his disappointment. The cavity was empty, smooth, innocent. No Paddy. Paddy was not in the Dustbin.

"Where the devil has he got to?" the DCI addressed this question to Carlo, who shrugged and pocketed his revolver. The DCI looked at his watch. "Damn," he said.

Sweet meanwhile was conducting investigations of his own. He circled the top of the concrete shell and stopped halfway around, his attention drawn by some suspicious-looking spots on the concrete. Sweet got down on his knees for a better look. Oil, he decided, when more of the sticky fluid dropped on the back of his neck. Catlike, he dabbed at it experimentally. Another drop fell, and another, this time narrowly missing him. He looked down and saw where they had fallen with the others, deep dark red splotches. And then, with growing apprehension, he looked up.

Through the glare of the lights Sweet made out the soles of a pair of shoes, the toes pointing down at his head, gently circling in space. Slowly, imperfectly at first, he understood that this must be Paddy, suspended somehow from the hook of a portal crane that traversed the ceiling of the hut.

Sweet cringed. His first reaction was that Paddy was going to fall on him. But then, as he realized that the body was more or less a permanent fixture, a shiver of revulsion ran down his spine.

"Good God," David Sweet gasped, and the other two men looked up.

Sweet gradually became aware of other things, too, things he would ordinarily have noticed before, like the electrical-control box on the gantry to his right, toward which with childlike fascination, still on all fours, he extended the sticky finger of temptation.

"Don't touch that button!" Thring cried, at a bound clearing the hatch to land at Sweet's side. "Dabs, Mr. Sweet. Fingerprints. You'll have me all of a lather, you will," the DCI breathed heavily, perspiring. Delicately, as a magician about to perform a trick, he draped his handkerchief over the box, then completed Sweet's action with a stab of his own finger at the down button. "Who knows, Mr. Sweet, but he might just be alive," Raymond Thring allowed, without much conviction.

The body twisted slowly in its earthward transit, turning its face toward the three men on top of the concrete shell so that they could plainly see the tip of the hook sticking out from under Paddy's chin like a gaffing iron. It had gone in through the back of his neck.

"An outside chance, mind," the DCI murmured as the body touched the floor, sagged, and crumpled like a puppet whose strings had been cut.

Raymond Thring was suddenly overcome by forensic interest. He scrambled down the scaffolding, and while Peat and Sweet peered down ghoulishly from above, the DCI felt the body for vital signs before he began the postmortem ritual of emptying Paddy's pockets.

"He's still warm and there's no sign of rigor," the diagnosis floated up. "There don't appear to be any other injuries, though it's a bit hard to tell at the moment. I'd say he's only been dead for five minutes. Crimshaw's the guilty party, but then we know that, don't we? Yes, Len's the one. It's a million-to-one chance, but I reckon they must have struggled up there where you gentlemen are, and Paddy here lost his footing or was pushed—it amounts to the same thing—falling backward on to the hook. Our Len must have hoisted him up—out of sight, out of mind, so to speak—and then panicked. Aye, that's it." Raymond Thring straightened up over the body. "That's what made Leonard run."

Carlo recovered first. "Is there anything we can do?" he enquired.

"You can come down the ladder," said the DCI, "and tell me what this thing is all about."

Carlo displayed surprising nimbleness. "It's a mock-up of a nuclear reactor, chief inspector, with a body—but of course I don't have to tell you that. A foreign body, you know."

"Well, it's no mock-up for Paddy, I can say," Raymond Thring remarked feelingly. "What's the matter, Mr. Sweet; cat get your tongue?"

"Certainly not," Sweet replied stuffily. "I was trying to think where I'd seen something like this before."

"And? Do tell, Mr. Sweet. Comparisons broaden the mind. A policeman's life is such a narrow one."

"The slaughterhouse, after the beast has been skinned."

"Ah." The DCI looked on Sweet with renewed interest. "So it does. Contents of wallet," he enumerated grimly, "one cleaner's ticket—I shall not make the obvious remark—ten pounds in fivers, two in singles, a ten-bob note, a driver's license by the name of Rourke, Patrick," the DCI sniffed, "and half a quid in change. Foreign body, Mr. Peat?"

"His name is O'Driscoll. He's an American citizen, an operative with the OSS."

This time Thring could not forbear. "He's not operative now, if you'll pardon my saying so, Mr. Peat." Raymond Thring looked at his watch, and a great burden was lifted from his mind. It was 3:35. If he acted now, and with dispatch, the case could be wrapped up by four. "Len's pulled his last pint," he remarked, charged with sudden energy. "We really will have to pull him in before teatime now. Funny, isn't it, the way things have of turning out? We'll have to leave the inoperative here by this thingamajig, whatever you call it. I wonder if I can find a phone? There ought to be one in the guard-house. That thing really does look like a pressure cooker, doesn't it, a giant pressure cooker. You know, Sam Morrow isn't going to believe this."

Raymond Thring made his phone call, and drove back to Skegness in maniacal fashion, racing against the clock. He made one comment en route: "You know, he never could keep good ale." In the flat vowels of Raymond Thring this sounded like a terrible condemnation, a sentence of death.

The Green Man was cordoned off by a line of rifle-carrying bobbies.

The DCI held a hurried conference with a uniformed sergeant who told him in stilted officialese that the police had gained access to the pub and that the suspect had secured himself in an upstairs room.

"Is he alive?"

"Oh, yes, sir. He's rigged up some sort of aerial out of the back window."

"All right, sergeant. Well done. Follow me." And so saying Raymond Thring led the way into The Green Man, through the bar, and up the stairs at the back of the pub.

Raymond Thring knocked on the door at the head of the landing.

"Leonard Crimshaw," he began, and was answered by a shot.

"Blast and damn," he said, and put his foot to the door.

Sweet was amazed to see the man move so swiftly. Thring's size-thirteen brogue connected with the lock, shattering the wood. It seemed a commonplace thing to open a door this way, but what had happened to Leonard Crimshaw, that was not commonplace.

Thring burst through the door followed by Sweet and Carlo Peat, who looked around the room in much the same fashion as he had ten weeks ago in Professor Weber's room at the Retreat. Crimshaw was curled on the floor at the foot of a roll-top desk, an overturned chair next to what was left of his head. The radio, no surprise, was inside the desk, and Crimshaw must have been sending to the last for there was a one-time pad on the desk next to the *Afu*'s transmitting key. Carlo walked over to the half-open window. He took a deep breath of the clean sea air. There was a tiny hole drilled through the woodwork of the window frame. An open window would have looked suspicious in the middle of winter. Normally Crimshaw must have threaded the wire through the hole, opened the window, then fixed the line to the aerial before closing the window again. It would have been easy to run the aerial along the kitchen-roof gutter so that it could not be seen from below. This time Crimshaw had been in too much of a hurry.

Carlo closed his eyes. He turned around, owlishly blinking. The curtains billowed; somewhere downstairs in the back of the pub a woman sobbed uncontrollably.

Carlo forced himself to study the one-time pad.

"That barmaid must have had a soft spot for him," he heard Thring say. "It's not even opening time yet, so what's she doing here?" the DCI went on. "We'll have to pull her in. I don't think it's worth my while sticking around for the pathologist. This seems like a pretty open-and-shut business to me. Oh, sergeant, would you call my wife and tell her I might be just a couple of minutes late? There's a good chap." Callous bastard, Carlo thought. But was he really? The DCI smiled at Carlo and shrugged. "Women," he said.

The DCI, making his exit, was already thinking of his next entrance. What would he say to Alice? "Spot of bother up at the base . . ." Something like that. "We got him; he's dead." Thring looked at the body again. Mr. Crimshaw, you got yourself, he thought, and then, because he could think of nothing to say, Raymond Thring lightly tapped the paunch of the baby-faced Peat and clapped the sickly Sweet on the shoulder.

"Fine day," he said, and, looking at his watch, was gone.

Sweet was staring at the corpse on the floor when the blow from the DCI almost did him in. A Luger pistol lay on the carpet next to Leonard Crimshaw's outstretched hand. He had blown away the top of his head like an eggshell and his scrambled brains steamed and dribbled down the floral wallpaper, forming, in Sweet's fevered mind, a vile melange with rugosa roses.

He had to excuse himself. Outside on the landing a young police constable told him, in solemn and hushed tones, that they had discovered a photographic darkroom in the cellar.

Sweet remembered the smell of Leonard cleaning out the facilities. Leonard must have been developing his pin-ups, Sweet thought. He looked out the landing window and saw Sam Morrow's glass-sided hearse draw up in the street below, Jephthah happily feeding from a nosebag while his master shouldered his way through the curious gaggle of spectators with the air of one who at last knows when his services are required.

"This time I 'ope I've come to the right place," the one-horse undertker said at the top of the stairs.

"Ee, Leonard." Sam Morrow drew his breath in when he saw the corpse. "I wouldn't have known thee." The undertaker looked up at Sweet. "It's the truth," he declared. "I wouldn't have recognized 'im, and I know everybody around 'ere, alive or dead."

102

13: REQUIEM FOR OSKAR

Stengel's assistant, Major Karl Kroll, brought Oskar's last message across from the Tirpitzufer on the evening of Monday, February 26. Kroll had been with Stengel for little more than a year, since the SD had "coordinated" the Abwehr in February 1944. He was a small, lithe figure who reminded Stengel of a ferret. A former *Korpsstudent* (hence the saber scar on the right side of his jaw), he was neat and punctilious, shaving twice a day lest the scar, with its tendency to show a livid white against his blue jowls, should make him look more sinister than he really was. Kroll was methodical, astute, and diligent, and his army file held unstinting praise for his powers of observation, which Stengel tested from time to time, using the little major to spy on his army comrades.

The Standartenführer did think that Kroll, for one so mindful of his appearance, should have been more careful of his opponent's blade. He could never have guessed that Kroll's wound was self-inflicted, a stage prop like so much of the methodical major's personality. In this he had something in common with his fellow countryman, Adolf Hitler. Kroll was an Austrian.

He was full of news as he laid Oskar's last message on Stengel's desk. There were signs of a new Allied offensive in Italy, but the Oder front had stabilized with the Russians being held fifty miles east of Berlin. In last night's air raid, the grounds of the Biological Institute in Dahlem and Ribbentrop's fashionable home in Zehlendorf had been hit.

Stengel glanced through the decrypt, a list of names and aliases:

1. Innis, Roger, 30, Captain, technical specialist, Long Range

Desert Group (LRDG) = Ahrens, Konrad, Major, Wehrmacht LXV Korps.

2. Page, Charles, 32, Captain, 2 Battalion, 1 Parachute Regiment = Unger, Otto, Hauptmann, Flakgruppe W8.

3. Roberts, Ian, 27, Lieutenant, Long Range Desert Group (LRDG) = Vogt, Hardmuth, Leutnant, Flakgruppe W8.

4. Prentice, Richard, 31, physicist, Cavendish Laboratories = Berger, Julius, affiliation *Deutsche Gold und Silber Scheideanstalt* (Degussa).

5. Wilkes, Frank, 25, Sergeant W/T operator, 2 Commando Regiment = Ernst, Hans, Oberfeldwebel, Flakgruppe W8.

6. Scarr, John, 32, Captain, Long Range Desert Group (LRDG) = Heller, Johann, Oberstleutnant, Flakgruppe W8.

"Anything else?" Stengel knew that Kroll was watching him.

"This was sent in the clear, Herr Standartenführer." It was just the one word:

Freischütz

"A code name, do you think, Herr Standartenführer?"

"Try the opera, Kroll."

"Von Weber!"

"Exactly. Do you know where he died, Kroll?"

"Where he died? No, Herr Standartenführer."

Stengel's fingers drummed on his desk. Oskar's last signal referred to Carlo Maria von Weber, whose opera *Der Freischütz*, about a rustic Faust who had made a pact with the devil in order to win his loved one in a shooting match, was first performed at Berlin in the year 1821. The composer had been born in Stengel's hometown of Lübeck. Had he been, perhaps, a distant relative of the Webers?

"London," Stengel said; "he died in London."

"But what can it mean, Herr Standartenführer?" Kroll was at a loss.

"It means they have moved one or the other of the Webers, perhaps both, to London."

"Extraordinary!" the little major declared, and it was. Kroll hesitated. He gave a little cough.

"Yes, Herr Major; what is it?"

"The girl, Herr Standartenführer. If the English are moving her, there may be some chance that she has been turned."

"What is there to turn?" Rudolf Stengel inquired. "You know, I shall never be able to listen to that opera again without thinking of it as a requiem for Oskar," the Standartenführer lamented. "Major Kroll, see if you can contact Generaloberst Dorf, commander-in-chief of Army Group Swabia, will you?" Stengel tapped the message. "I am sure he will be most interested in this."

14: JOHNNY SCARR

"You're not in the Camel Corps now, Scarr. This is a parachute, not a dromedary, though it does give you the hump." The speaker was Charlie Page, the flying ape from the Parachute Regiment, and Scarr would remember that line, and the occasion, for the rest of his life.

Scarr was on the final practice jump from an Anson, and the sight of the navigator winding down the undercarriage with the hand crank to lower air speed did not inspire confidence. But Charlie Page did. He was squat and stock, long-armed and short-legged, so well-muscled that he seemed to barrel along with his knuckles close to the ground. His father had been a glass blower from the Black Country and had died of silicosis; Charlie had joined the paratroopers looking for a fast death. He once told Johnny Scarr that his commission was a case of dead-man's harness. All the officers who had been in the regiment when he had joined up had since died. "From booze, clap, and the force of gravity," he told Johnny Scarr. "Sand and the force of gravity are great killers, old boy." Charlie Page had a plummy way of saying "old boy," forming his lips around an imaginary marble. Charlie said he could take the piss out of a stone if he wanted to, and Johnny Scarr believed him.

The evening before the jump some panjandrum from the Air Ministry arrived at Winthorpe to lecture Scarr's people. "Now I have got a surprise for you. We're not coming back to Winthorpe tomorrow or ever. We must forget all about Winthorpe, forget it ever existed."

"Just as I was beginning to get fond of the place," Charlie Page whispered loudly.

"Jolly good," the man from the Air Ministry said. "Now, about tomorrow. Just to complicate things you'll be jumping in German uniforms. Each man will be issued fifteen pounds in five-pound notes—made in Germany, I'm afraid. You will find your way to your new home by whatever means seems most expedient to you. The idea is not to get caught, and you will have forty-eight hours in which to complete the exercise. Your new home is Farm Hall in Huntingdon, near RAF Tempsford. Any questions? Good luck."

Scarr's people were jumping over a granitic outcrop called the Long Mynd. It was in the Welsh border country, held, by some god of operations, to resemble the Black Forest. Things began badly enough. Johnny's line snagged and broke as he came out of the aircraft, and the next thing he knew he was plummeting earthwards with no visible means of support. Johnny hit the harness release so he could clear his main chute. Nothing doing. Far above he saw two, three tiny chutes blossom out, spinning. Johnny Scarr tugged at the ripcord of his emergency chute, hoping with a wish and a prayer that it wouldn't tangle in the streamer's lines. The force of its opening flipped him over on his back so that he hung from his navel, fetus-like. You'll do, he thought, floating.

Scarr's drop ended in a slide down the tailings of a disused quarry with Johnny half-buried in a pile of iron pyrites—fool's gold, worth a million to Johnny Scarr, lucky Johnny Scarr.

Johnny waited for the sky to stop spinning. The night before he had packed an old overcoat; now, as he came down from the mountain, the coat covering his SS uniform, Johnny was whistling Hubert Parry's hymn tune to Blake's "Jerusalem." The thought of how he must have looked made him laugh. Johnny Scarr started singing to the sheep:

> And did those feet in ancient time
> Walk upon England's mountins green?
> And was the holy Lamb of God
> On England's pleasant pastures seen?

It didn't matter that this was Wales or that those feet wore jackboots; Johnny Scarr had a plan.

Johnny walked for ten miles or more until he reached the Church Stretton rift valley with the arterial road from south Wales to the north. He didn't have to wait long before he hitched a lorry to Shrewsbury. It was out of his way, but that was part of the plan.

The lorry was old and greasy and smelled of fish. Johnny hunkered down in the passenger seat, staring at the road ahead. The driver was very concerned about his appearance.

"You look as if you just fell off the side of the mountain," he said.

"I just did," Johnny Scarr said.

"What sort of uniform is that you've got on, then?"

"Uniform?"

"Under your coat."

"Welsh RSPCA." Johnny Scarr affected a Welsh accent. "I'm a field inspector with the Welsh RSPCA."

"Now that is what I call a coincidence," the driver said. "You'll never guess what I'm carrying."

"Fish," Johnny Scarr said.

"Winkles, two tons of winkles to market at Birmingham. I don't expect they feel much, not winkles. What sort of animals do you deal with, then?"

"Pit ponies mostly," said Johnny Scarr, "and sheep. We get a lot of those."

The driver dropped him off in Shrewsbury town center, outside the castle. Johnny Scarr watched the truck stop at a set of lights before the railway viaduct. A passenger train, pulling out of the station above the town, seemed to be scaling an almost insuperable gradient, puffs of white smoke daubing the blue sky. A sudden blast from the train whistle made Johnny Scarr shiver. When he looked again, the truck was gone.

There wasn't much of the castle left, a wall, part of a tower, a few eroded ramparts in gingerbread-red sandstone. Johnny found a bench and sat down. The war was a million miles away, he told himself, watching a group of kids who were staring at something in the flowerbeds by the border. There were no flowers at this time of year, and Johnny Scarr wondered what they were looking at. Without being asked, one of the kids told him.

"It's a war of ants," he said. Johnny Scarr had a way with kids, who felt he was on their side. "Red ants against black ants, and the red ants is winning."

Sure enough, Johnny Scarr made out the skirmishing lines and columns of reinforcements. A war in miniature was being fought in the soil, fought much as a human war, for all its panoply of generalship a thing of hazard, bluff, and sudden death.

One of the kids spotted Scarr's uniform beneath his coat. "He's a German!" the kid yelled. "A German sojer!" The kid turned beet red from the neck up and began bouncing up and down on the castle walk, screaming. The others ignored him, intent on redressing the balance among the ants.

"No, no, sonny." Scarr leant over to reassure the child, who could only have been about three or four years old. He was dressed in a terry-cloth blue jump-suit, and his features were torn with apoplectic rage and terror.

"German sojer!" he screamed. "German sojer!"

The others, now, began to take an interest in this adult who was the cause of so much commotion. Scarr stood up, clutching his coat collar.

"No, no," he said, "it's a game, that's all, just a game. Look, I'll surrender. See? I give up." And raising his hands high, he placed them on top of his head like the Italian prisoners he had seen in North Africa. "See? I give up," Johnny Scarr said, and hoped that no one was watching. "I'm your prisoner now. You've captured me."

"C'mon, Jimmy." One of the older children stepped forward to take Scarr's jump-suited denouncer by the hand. "He ain't a German, not a proper German."

"Why not?" asked Johnny Scarr.

"Cos you ain't, that's all," the kid replied. "C'mon, Jimmy. The ants is fighting to the death." And the children turned away, jumpsuit turning around once to rub his eyes and peer at Scarr, who grinned and winked at him. The kid smiled back knowingly.

Johnny Scarr heard a clock strike eleven. He strode out of the castle grounds and turned right, hurrying past an august building that bore a blue light and the legend POLICE above the entrance. Scarr hurried on until he reached the market hall below the railway station. Inside, he rummaged around the second-hand clothes stalls, finding a tattered tweed jacket and an old pair of dress shoes.

"And I'd like that bib and tucker," he said to the stall-keeper, a dumpy blonde who was glad to get rid of the junk, "the dress shirt and the bow tie there. How much are they?"

"Half a crown. Two bob to you. The jacket'll cost you thirty bob with those shoes. You can have the lot for that. Going to a fancy-dress ball, are you, ducks?"

"I've just come from one," Johnny Scarr said.

Johnny handed over one of the forged fivers. It was accepted without a question, probably because it was made out of old clothes anyway, Johnny Scarr thought. He clicked his heels in exuberance, and marched over to the Gents where he spent a penny of his recently acquired change. In the closet he tore the rank badges and insignia from his tunic and dropped them into the bowl. Johnny Scarr girded himself in the bib shirt, fixed up the bow tie, and, bare-armed, slipped on the tweed jacket. The shoes pinched his toes, but Johnny didn't plan on much more walking. He wrapped the jackboots in his tunic and tucked the parcel under his arm. Outside, he paused to look at himself in the mirror. You are the cat's whiskers, he thought, and left to mingle with the lunchtime crowd.

Johnny Scarr went to see a girl who sold pewter things from an Elizabethan half-timbered building in the old part of town. The girl was blonde with freckles. She wore an orange knitted sweater and a gray skirt, and her name was Sandra. She was incorrigibly honest and single.

Johnny Scarr loitered tactically, waiting for the last of the morning's customers to leave and for the girl to hang up the CLOSED FOR LUNCH sign, which she was doing when Johnny Scarr tapped at the door.

"Oh, Johnny Scarr!" she gasped.

Johnny Scarr wasted no time. He was inside the door and talking before she could take her hand away from her mouth. "Look, Sandra, I'm in a bit of a fix. I've got to get to this place in Huntingdon. It's rather obscure, I'm afraid, and, well, the fact is this fellow's after me and means to kill me. I shouldn't be telling you this, really, but I didn't know where else to go."

The girl's eyes were wide open. "What about the police?" she asked.

"They wouldn't believe me," Johnny Scarr replied truthfully.

"And you've got to get to—where? Huntingdon?"

Johnny Scarr nodded. "Yes, a place called Farm Hall."

"My uncle in Church Stretton—he's got an old Bentley he never uses."

"Do you think you could get him here?" asked Johnny Scarr, lucky Johnny Scarr.

15: JOAN-ELEANOR

Stengel met Dorf at Harry Rosse's in suburban Wilmersdorf on the evening of Tuesday, February 27. The Nestorstrasse bar was unusual in that it was frequented by Nazi Party officials and Wehrmacht officers alike, as well as the few foreign businessmen, mostly Scandinavians, still left in the Reich. It was one of those rare places in Berlin where these various elements met to exchange views on the military and political situations, a good place, Stengel knew, to take the pulse of the city. Now the mood of the bar was subdued, the blackout curtains, drawn since twilight, inflicting their own kind of twilight on the patrons, most of whom awaited the first air raid of the night with a sullen anxiety that amounted to a conditioned response.

Alcohol, as Stengel remarked to Colonel-General Dorf, helped to mask the symptoms.

"And how was Switzerland?" He sat across from Dorf in a corner booth. The Standartenführer was not drinking; an ulcerative condition forbade it, he explained. Dorf looked at the glass of schnapps on the table before him and wondered exactly what symptoms he was supposed to be hiding.

"Switzerland was *prima*," he said.

"The girl has been moved to London." Stengel folded his arms and he, too, contemplated the colonel-general's drink. "The British must have found out about Oskar."

"Too bad," Dorf commiserated. He held his glass level in his left hand, the right clumped on the table in a shiny black fist. *"Prosit,"* he said incongruously.

Stengel said: "I'm not so sure—about Oskar. In some ways this might encourage the British."

113

"Possibly," Dorf conceded.

For the first time Stengel became aware of the other's mood. "What's the matter with you?" he asked.

Dorf sipped the schnapps, his peculiar turned-down eyes coldly regarding Stengel. "On my way here," he said, "a group of civilians jeered at my staff car. 'Bloodsuckers,' that is what they were crying."

"Foreign workers." Stengel shrugged. "Agents provocateurs."

"If you choose to believe that"—Dorf finished his drink and called for another—"that is your responsibility."

"There has been an interesting development," Stengel said.

"Oh?"

"Joan-Eleanor."

"Who?"

"Not who—it." Stengel smiled. When the waitress returned with Dorf's drink, the Standartenführer ordered a glass of goat's milk. Harry Rosse kept a supply on hand especially for Stengel. It was illegal, and where he got it from was the devil's own business, but goat's milk was the only thing for the Standartenführer's ulcers. This evening it also gave him an excuse for an unwonted display of humanity.

Stengel studied the waitress, who served the goat's milk in double-quick time. She was an emaciated creature, not much better-looking than the living skeletons he had seen at Oranienburg. Stengel asked how old she was. Eighteen, she said.

"Tell Herr Harry to feed you goat's milk," he said, turning again to Dorf, who was mystified by the display of feeling and also a little unsettled by it. "Joan-Eleanor is a new radio set used by the Americans," Stengel continued. "It operates from the ground to a control aircraft flying at ten thousand meters. Last week the Gestapo picked up an OSS agent who had been dropped in the Stuttgart area. He was asking questions about Haigerloch and the military district to the south. The stupidity of these people! This one lit his cigarettes with American matches. Can you imagine such a thing? Anyway, during his interrogation he let it be known that he had heard about the Winthorpe commando. Apparently, the OSS had a field operative there. It was quite accidental, but the kind of confirmation we like to have. We're playing him back now. Incidentally, Joan-Eleanor tells us that the big push will come on March the twenty-fourth in the north, so your people will have to be ready by then."

Dorf nodded. "Everything is ready for Gunderic," he said. "Degussa are preparing another load of *Spezialmetall,* and my troops are on standby. I will let you know the moment I hear from the British whether or not they have agreed to our terms. Once Gunderic is in force, you can take it that the bomb is as good as on its way."

"But in which direction, Herr Colonel-General?"

"That of course depends on our enemies," Dorf said as the sirens started up, carrying far into the Prussian night like a wolf's baneful howl.

ULTRA DECRYPT

+ + + SOURCE BANDERSNATCH BERLIN FEB 27 1945 0650 ZULU + + +
SOURCE REPORTS PROBABLE LAST SHIPMENT SILESIAN CRUDE U
ARRIVED AUER GESELLSCHAFT ORANIENBURG & CONFIRMS DELIVERY
OF REFINED U^{235} PLUS HEAVY WATER HAIGERLOCH STOP + + +
MESSAGE ENDS + + +

+ + + GENERALOBERST DORF, C-IN-C ARMY GROUP SWABIA, HECHIN-
GEN HQ, TO STANDARTENFÜHRER RUDOLF STENGEL, SECURITY
DIRECTOR PROJEKT ALBERICH, BERLIN FEB 28 1945 1100 ZULU + + + THIS
SENT IN CLEAR + + +DIE MASCHINE GEHT + + + THE MACHINE IS
WORKING + + + MESSAGE ENDS + + +

March slunk in under fog.

Before returning to his Baker Street attic, Carlo dropped in to the
teleprinter room at Broadway on the off-chance that a message might
have come in overnight from the source. Hitherto, the Bandersnatch
decrypts had been handled directly by Harold, either as digests or
memoranda, and Carlo was curious to see one of the originals for
himself.

Lined with intestinal tubes transporting bits of paper from one
floor to the next, the teleprinter room reminded Carlo of the central
cash at a large department store, its denizens displaying all the symptoms of universal busyness. There had to be some law which required
that a communications channel be used in proportion to its capacity,
the sheer bulk of traffic overwhelming the quality of information
sent. But Carlo could have no doubt about the two signals that
Thomas, the Scouse teletype operator, thrust into his hands.

"This one, Thomas, why was it sent in the clear?"

"Search me, Mr. Peat." Thomas was loud and amusing. He wore a yellow shirt and a green tie and grinned at Carlo like the Cheshire cat. "Somebody must 'ave got excited or 'ad an 'angover. 'Ow should I know, really? It's the same difference any'ow. We're reading all their signals."

That, in itself, was enough to convince Carlo that the signal was genuine. In which case it meant that Germany was one step away from the atom bomb.

Carlo went to see Harold. Coming out of the lift cage, he ran into Balthazar, who was carrying a bundle of papers.

"Oh, hello," Balthazar said. "I was just thinking about you. The PUS wants to see you and Sweet. Something about Americans on hooks." Balthazar was his usual jolly self. "By the way, did you hear what happened to Johnny Scarr?"

"No. What?"

"Johnny turned up at Farm Hall in a Bentley."

"A Bentley?"

"That's not all. Charlie Page was driving. Seems that Johnny had picked him up hitching on the A49. Charlie was still dressed in his bloody Luftwaffe uniform. 'You do the driving, my man,' Johnny told him. "With you in that getup, people'll think I'm the cream cheese.'" Balthazar thought this was uproariously funny.

Carlo asked him what he was doing.

"Me? I'm off the project now. Balthazar's blown."

"What happened to the stuff you brought back from Switzerland?"

"The boffins got that. Must rush. 'The cream cheese!'" And, laughing, he stepped into the lift and was gone to his own paper war.

Carlo found Philby writing a memorandum to the PUS. He had already read the signals himself.

"There's one hell of a f-f-flap on," Harold said, lighting his pipe, which spat and sizzled. He looked at it in dismay, banged the bowl on the edge of the ashtray, and began going through his desk for a pipe cleaner. He found one, twisted the bowl from the stem, and inserted the cleaner into the mouthpiece. "The PUS wants to see you and Sweet," he said, drawing the cleaner through and wincing at the nicotinous gunk. "Oh, look at that," he said; "poisonous stuff, isn't it?"

"Those sandwiches tasted foggy," Sweet complained. Fresh from a Lyons Corner House lunch, the two men sneaked into the King Charles Street side entrance of the Foreign Office like Montagues at the feast of the Capulets.

Wentworth, the Permanent Under Secretary, inhabited a nook at the end of a third-floor corridor by the back stairs of the FO—"my *escalier*," according to the PUS. He was a lean man with a Roman-esque face, a civil servant whose job was to mediate between the Friends and the War Cabinet. The PUS suffered from chilly elbows and the intermittent ringing of bells; he spent his days listening for footsteps; occasionally, and always to his great annoyance, this vigil was interrupted by the third-floor fire alarms, despite the fact that there had never yet been a fire in his vicinity.

He was composing an address on the subject when he heard the footfalls of Sweet and Peat in the corridor outside. "En-ter!" Pen in hand, he sprang to his feet and tore open the door, startling his visitors. "One moment, gentlemen—Mackintosh!" Wentworth con-jured his secretary from a cranny—spinsterish, tweedy, balding, female.

"Dictation, Mackintosh. 'Is it not possible'"—the PUS directed his aquiline gaze to the cyclone of cherubs encompassing the ceiling light fixture—"'is it not possible,' I say, 'to cry wolf once too often with these diurnal tintinnabulations? Such all-too-frequent alarums, if persisted in, will have, I fear, cinerary results.'"

The secretary looked at her master, puzzled.

"No, wait, Mackintosh—stay!" The PUS turned to the two Friends. "Well, gentlemen, been dealing with the enemy, I hear? Oh, that's all right, but what's this about the Americans? You can't afford to jeo-pardize the Atlantic alliance by leaving their chaps hanging about on hooks, you know."

Carlo said: "I protest. We did take him down, Under Secretary."

"Oh. Is it in your report? Good. Well then, enough said. Now, Peat, this bomb. Are they spoofing us, do you think?"

"Well, that's the question."

"No harm in taking a dekko, sort of thing. Is that the idea?" Carlo said that it was.

"The whenth?"

"New moon is on the thirteenth, Under Secretary."

"There is some question in your mind about this Dorf, is there?"

Carlo said: "Obviously he's playing a double game. Stengel sent us Weber ostensibly to make it look as though nothing much was happening on the nuclear front. Weber says we can trust Dorf, but Dorf has to be playing a double game with Stengel, who inspired Weber with terror in the first place. I rather fear that Stengel may be a sort of *eminence noir* behind the whole thing."

"To what end?"

"I wish I knew."

"You must have some idea, Peat."

"Well, it could be genuine. Dorf's HQ signaled Stengel yesterday that the pile is working. If true, then they're close to making the bomb."

"Now listen to me, the pair of you. We are cooperating with the Cousins in this project. However, their lordships do feel it is allowable to deal with Degussa because that is private enterprise. In other words, Degussa is not the German government. But you, whether you're aware of it or not, represent His Majesty's government. Now the view has been expressed, only half in jest I may say, that you, were you Imperial Chemicals, could make Degussa a businesslike offer for what is essentially a piece of scientific intelligence. Well, you're not, you can't, and that's that. I quite take the point, by the way, that after the war it won't do to have outfits like Degussa dictating to the nations of Free Europe, but, at the same time, Auer Chemicals—and all that they represent—are going to be around for quite some time. Their lordships have to think of the big picture. They have to consider which side of the Atlantic their nuclear bread is buttered on, so to speak."

"I quite understand," Carlo said.

"I'm not sure that you do. Degussa's uranium-mining operation at Joachimstahl is in the line of the Russian advance. The Erzgebirge field will go to a resurrected Czech state as part of the peace settlement. It's no secret that there are those in the cabinet who would like to prevent that. They regard Dorf's offer as, well, negotiable, while there are those who think that any commerce with the enemy is tantamount to treating with the devil himself." Wentworth's eyes shot ceilingward again. "We are like a ship that must tack before contrary winds," he declared.

"And which way are we tacking at the moment?" Carlo inquired.

"Becalmed, I'm afraid," the PUS replied.

"Under Secretary, you are aware, are you not, that on the seventeenth of last month Dorf gave us three weeks to reply to his terms? There are eight days left. At the same time Hugo Weber maintains that the Germans are ahead of schedule by a month, which means that we have until the twentieth of this month before they explode a nuclear device. Unless we give Dorf the answer he wants, there's a very good chance that the target for that device will be London. It would be an act of criminal folly to do nothing."

"My dear Peat," the PUS leaned forward slightly and rested his elbows on his desk. He winced. How the cold got into his elbows! "Let me give you the official view," the PUS continued, picking his words carefully. "The official view is that Hugo Weber is a visionary lunatic who will say anything that comes into his poor addled head. To base your plan of campaign on the say-so of this wretched bedlamite would certainly be an act of folly, though not necessarily criminal. However, to engage in a separate peace with Colonel-General Dorf, an enemy soldier, could certainly be construed as a criminal act, one, moreover, contrary to the policy of His Majesty's government, which categorirdally forbids you to give the said Colonel-General Dorf any undertakings as to the future conduct of military operations. And, Peat—?"

"Yes, Under Secretary?"

"This is from me. Tell Dorf what you damn well please. His Majesty's government, in its anxiety to see the big picture, sometimes overlooks the details. Scarr's people are details, you understand. Details can be changed or forgotten about; details are deniable. Good luck, Peat. All right, gentlemen, that will be all. Now Mackintosh; about these incendiary alarums . . ."

Carlo spent the rest of the week putting together a complete picture of Army Group Swabia's units in the field, their strength, composition, whereabouts, and signals. It was the kind of ferociously dull work he enjoyed, the bookkeeping of war, devoid of any human complications. Carlo was looking for a unit under Dorf's overall command but separate from it logistically, with its own signals, staff, supplies, equipment, and support personnel—the unit that would deliver the bomb.

Carlo was also on the lookout for any signs that Dorf was preparing to implement Operation Gunderic, the exercise designed to seal off the Hechingen military area from the rest of the Reich and its enemies.

He did not find what he was looking for—at first. A logistical unit certainly would not advertise its presence, except, maybe, for deception purposes. If Dorf's signals people had changed the primary key settings on their Enigma machines, then it might be a while—two or three days—before Cryptographic Services at Bletchley Park could decode the traffic. But no such reenciphered traffic was being picked up, which either meant the unit had yet to be formed or was under a total communications blackout. From previous experience Carlo knew that if the unit did exist it would eventually be picked up, probably from one of Dorf's signals. But this would take time, an element not in great supply, and a slow, reasoning fear began to take hold of Carlo Peat.

Sunday, came a cheery phone call from the PUS. In their wisdom, and with the benefit of scientific advice, their lordships had ruled out the possibility of a rocket attack.

"They don't see how a warhead could be transported down the Rhine, given the military situation. Too risky by far."

Carlo wondered aloud whether this was a case of wishful thinking.

"Oh, I don't doubt it for a moment," Wentworth replied merrily. "Though if they're going to use a rocket, wishful thinking's as good a defense as any. Name a better one."

Carlo was unable.

On Monday, the fifth, Cryptographic Services called to say they had something. They had picked up a reference in a signal not from Dorf but from Stengel, a reference to Kindchen Alberich *und sein Ring.* The ring, in this case, as the Friends knew from the documents that Dorf had turned over to Balthazar in Lugano, was an implosive, high-tensile steel lens designed to focus the shock waves from a multiple-point spherical detonator around a plutonium core.

Carlo was summoned before Philby, who said: "According to Tube Alloys this means that what they've got is as good as anything we've got—if not b-b-better."

Carlo had asked why the traffic was coming from Stengel.

"I don't know," Harold answered. "He must be taking over. Obviously he doesn't trust Dorf, and no w-w-wonder. What the hell are we going to do, Carlo? We can't very well signal Dorf we plan on visiting him at home in the cave. He might not like that."

"Then temporize. Tell him we agree to his terms but need time to get cabinet approval. If Dorf thinks he's got an agreement, it might be just the thing to knock Stengel out of the picture."

"The signal's already drafted," Philby said. "But I have to get Wentworth's approval first. You know how things are."

Carlo had gone back to his signals.

There had been a flurry of traffic from Stengel's Berlin HQ over the weekend, and Cryptographic Services was running slightly behind. Carlo did not have a complete set of decodes until Monday afternoon. The first signals were of a technical nature and dealt with shock wave "interaction lines" from the implosive ring. Carlo turned this traffic over to Tube Alloys.

The key signal had been sent on Sunday night; Carlo had the decrypt on his desk by late Monday afternoon:

+ + + STANDARTENFÜHRER STENGEL, SECURITY DIRECTOR PROJEKT ALBERICH, BERLIN HQ, TO GENERALFELDMARSCHALL KEITEL, FÜHRER HQ BERLIN, 4 MARCH 2200 ZULU + + + CRITICAL ASSEMBLY OF KINDCHEN ALBERICH COMPLETE STOP AWAITING FINAL RESULT OF RING TEST WHICH I EXPECT NO LATER THAN FRIDAY STOP HEIL HITLER STENGEL + + +MESSAGE ENDS + + +

Tuesday, Cryptographic Services caused a minor panic by picking up another reference to Kindchen Alberich. The signal, which again was not one of Dorf's, had been sent by the *Heereswaffenamt*, the Army War Office, Berlin, to a Sturmbannführer Waldmann, chief of security at Hechingen Airfield, and had been selected for Carlo's attention by a sharp-eyed cryptographer at Bletchley Park. The Army Ordnance Division wanted to know the dead weight of Kindchen Alberich, which, so the signal ran, was ready for ordnance testing.

Carlo had found what he was looking for. All he wanted now was confirmation, and that would not be long in coming.

"A mock-up, you know," the tubular man said in Philby's office on the afternoon of Wednesday, the seventh. "It has to be. I mean, they'd never dare drop the bomb without testing it first."

"Wouldn't they?" asked Carlo Peat.

The tubular man picked abstractedly at the stitches on an elbow patch. "That depends on what you mean by test," he replied, forgetting that he was the one who had first spoken of testing. "The scientific stuff is first-rate, though. I'd say you were justified in going. No doubt about it."

"I think you should prepare a final briefing for Scarr's people, Carlo," said Philby.

"Yes, Harold; I think so, too."

This was followed by another flurry of Enigma signals on the eighth and ninth: from Führer HQ to Dorf asking when Gunderic would be in effect, from Dorf to Führer HQ answering ("as soon as feasible"), from Stengel to Führer HQ reporting that the ring test was positive, and from Stengel to Dorf requesting the latter's presence in Berlin ("immediate").

Carlo had his confirmation on Friday. It was a signal from one Luftwaffe unit at Stuttgart Flugplatz to another at Hechingen, commanded by Oberst Viktor von Wenden, asking whether his squadron was ready to receive Kindchen Alberich. Cryptographic Services had no record of the reply, which could have been an ordinary phone call or hand-delivered message. The signal also revealed that Gunderic would be implemented on March 14—Woden's Day, as Carlo noted, in the month of Mars.

The signs were auspicious. Over the weekend they became terrifying.

17: HARRY ROSSE'S

Stengel met Dorf again at Harry Rosse's on Saturday, March tenth. This time he brought along his assistant, Major Kroll, and Dorf was accompanied by his adjutant, Captain Lang, who made a point of cutting Kroll at the first opportunity. It was a mystery to him why a Wehrmacht officer, especially one with Kroll's background, should act as a spy and a lackey to the SS and he saw no reason to hide his contempt. The methodical major was not offended at such treatment, which he had grown to expect. He listened and he watched, for that was his function, his eyes as smooth as pebbles, and as hard. A repulsive specimen, thought Lang, distressed to see the old man fallen in with such snakes.

Stengel began by announcing he had just come from the Führer. In a manner at once direct and insinuating, he asked if Dorf had heard from the English yet.

The Colonel-General blinked. His left hand was wrapped around his customary glass of schnapps; his eyes were red-rimmed, and he needed a shave. Lang had driven him up overnight along Reichsstrasse 96 against the prevailing flow of loot-laden Mercedes and Wanderers bearing hard-faced Party officials away from Festung Berlin as the once-in-a-thousand-year-Reich migration of the Golden Pheasants got under way.

Dorf shook his head warily, preserving the memory of the exodus through the dawn mists. He had half-expected to see Stengel's cadaverous face heading toward him in one of the cars. If Stengel was still in Berlin, things couldn't be so bad on the Oder front.

"Nothing, as yet, Herr Standartenführer."

125

"So, Herr Generaloberst. The ultimatum expires today." Stengel felt he could relax. He sipped at his goat's milk, his eyes wandering, looking for the waitress, who came across immediately. Stengel slipped his arm around her waist. "Harry has been fattening you up," he said. "That's good, *ja?* Maybe we should all have another drink and grow fat together."

"He's fattening her up for the Russians," Kroll said when the girl had gone. "Harry's no fool. How else do you think he's stayed in business this long? He's fattening all his girls up for the Russians."

Dorf and Lang stared down their noses at him as if he had just crawled out of a sewer. "I was only joking, gentlemen." Kroll smiled uneasily. "You must allow me my little joke. Where in the world would we be without a sense of humor."

"Perhaps on the eastern front, Herr Major," Lang said. "You should try it some time."

Kroll took the insult calmly. He raised his stein to drain the dregs, his stony eyes peering at Lang over the rim. "Your good health, Herr Hauptmann," he said, draining his glass.

"So, the Americans have their bridgehead at last," Stengel remarked, pleasantly enough, as if he were talking about the weather.

"The Führer has had the demolitions officer shot." Kroll dropped his ersatz attempt at good humor. "Imagine! Allowing them to capture an entire railway bridge intact. What could he have been thinking of?"

"Perhaps he should have allowed them to capture only half the bridge intact," Lang observed acidly. "Then the rest of them would have dropped into the river to be eaten alive by the Rhine Maidens."

"The Führer has dispatched an armored force to the area." Stengel gave him a long, cold look. "There will be reinforcements from the strategic reserve. The Americans will be held, you'll see."

"The strategic reserve! What strategic reserve?" exclaimed the anguished Dorf. "Most of my divisions exist in name only, and it is the same for every other army group. As for this armored force—four armored personnel carriers! Do you call that an armored force? Four armored personnel carriers to throw the Americans back across the Rhine!"

Lang tried to hush him up, but he would not be quieted.

"And you, Kroll," Dorf turned to the little major, "when the Americans decide to break out of their bridgehead, tell me, what will your Führer do then? Oppose them with more phantom divisions?"

"He's your Führer as well," Kroll responded sulkily, "and so long as he lives he is our Commander-in-Chief, Herr Generaloberst."

"I do not need to be reminded of my duty," Dorf bridled. "As a soldier I have always obeyed orders, even when I found them objectionable or, more often, simply foolish. Obedience has been a principle with me from the start, but it is not the only one I know."

The girl had returned with the drinks, and Dorf gulped at his. It had a steadying effect on his nerves, and he fell into a brooding silence.

Hurriedly, Stengel said: "At least you may rest assured that Haigerloch is well defended, though you must be on your guard against this English commando. What dispositions have been made for Kindchen Alberich?"

"If I might answer that question, Herr Standartenführer," Lang intervened, hiding his dislike of Stengel behind a mask of formality. "The Luftwaffe has a four-engined bomber at Hechingen, ready to receive the bomb when the fuses are calibrated."

"The aircraft will be shot down," Stengel objected.

"The Luftwaffe does not think so, Herr Standartenführer. The aircraft is a Short Stirling bomber, which was downed after a raid on Milan some years ago. The Luftwaffe obtained the aircraft, more or less intact, from the Italian authorities, and has been using it for training purposes ever since. In addition, the Luftwaffe has obtained an 'Iffy'—Identification Friend or Foe—from the wreck of a Lancaster *Terrorbomber*. As soon as the Stirling is within radar range, it will switch on this device and be seen as harmless by the enemy's radar defense. Even if fighters are sent up to investigate, they will see only an obsolescent bomber on a training flight. If the target is London, the Luftwaffe even has a flight plan, a slightly garbled flight plan, Herr Standartenführer, that will further confuse the enemy's air defense. There is no doubt that this intrusion into protected air space will be overlooked, or, if detected, put down to inexperienced personnel—precisely the sort of thing, in fact, that you would expect from trainees. I need hardly add, of course, that the Luftwaffe has dedicated one of its most experienced and senior pilots for this mission, Oberst Viktor von Wenden."

"You say if the target is to be London, Herr Hauptmann. Can there be any doubt? It is the Führer's express intention."

"Nevertheless, Herr Standartenführer, the Luftwaffe—and in this the Wehrmacht concurs—would like to preserve a degree of flexibility in the matter."

"Listen to that, Kroll," Stengel scoffed. "Since when have you people believed in flexibility?"

Dorf's gloved right hand suddenly crashed down on the table. "Degussa agrees," he declared, emboldened by the liquor. "We are agreed that Alberich would better be used in the defense of the Reich against Soviet forces. If this new and terrible weapon is used against the West, we shall be hunted down wherever we go. The world will have no hiding place for us, the first nuclear war criminals. If, on the other hand, we join forces with the West, extending them the hand of scientific collaboration, then the excesses of this present war will soon be overlooked. Degussa has a valuable contribution to make in the continuing struggle against Bolshevism. The company must be allowed to survive. Use this bomb against the West, and you guarantee not only Degussa's annihilation but Germany's also. Stengel, I dread what is to come if this present policy is followed through to its logical conclusion."

"Aren't you forgetting one thing, Herr Generaloberst?" Stengel inquired acidly. "The English have not responded to your terms. And the Americans—as you have been at great pains to point out—are already across the Rhine. Need I remind you, gentlemen, that the whole object of Gunderic is to force a separate peace from the Anglo-Saxons? Even a limited truce would further our aim of splitting the unholy alliance of capitalist and communist against Germany. But let there be no mistake: the English must first be made to realize the deadline of our purpose, and if this means destroying their capital—then so be it."

"Herr Standartenführer"—Lang pressed the army's case for one last time—"what better demonstration could we have than to wipe out the Soviet forces in the Kustrin bridgehead?"

"You do not realize, Herr Hauptmann, what an obtuse race the Anglo-Saxons are. They would rejoice at the Russians' misfortune. And think, Herr Hauptmann, how many atomic bombs do we have? What use is one bomb, even an atomic bomb, against millions of men on a front hundreds of kilometers long? Lang, if we are to make more bombs, we must first secure Silesia. In order to do that, we must free our forces from the conflict in the west. If we succeed in doing that, then we can use these troops to assure a continued supply of uranium ore from our Silesian fields. Hence, priority must be given to securing a truce along the Rhine.

"Generaloberst Dorf, I charge you with this task in the name of the Führer, Adolf Hitler. You must make one final attempt to awaken the Anglo-Saxons to the peril they are in. Should you fail then the Führer has determined London must be destroyed. The English capital must be wiped off the face of the earth, for it will be the English who have cheated us of the final victory. But, Generaloberst Dorf, should you succeed, then Kindchen Alberich will be freed for use against the barbaric hordes who are even now mustering for their assault on the Reich capital. And now, gentlemen, let us drink this toast to the ultimate victory of German arms: to Gunderic, who repelled an earlier invader from the east, to Alberich, who fashioned the ring of the gods—*Sieg Heil*!"

18: IN THE WAR ROOM

ULTRA DECRYPT

+ + + SOURCES BANDERSNATCH BERLIN MAR 10 1945 2330 ZULU + + +
IMPERATIVE ACCEPT TERMS OF FEB 17 STOP KINDCHEN ALBERICH
READY STOP TARGET LONDON STOP REPEAT IMPERATIVE ACCEPT
TERMS STOP + + + MESSAGE ENDS + + +

Carlo Peat was in the teleprinter room with Philby when the message came through.

"I'd like to show this to Hugo Weber," he said.

"Unfortunately, you can't," Philby said.

"Why not? Ah, because he's still in York, you mean."

"Because he's dead, I mean."

"What?"

"Didn't you know? He hanged himself yesterday. You must have been too busy with your signals. Collinson called. He said Hugo was very worried about his daughter. Said he was constantly asking after her, how many miles was she from the center of town. Collinson told him he could join her soon—this weekend. Hugo hanged himself yesterday afternoon, in the hospital washroom, with some torn-up lengths of sheet. I thought you'd have heard."

Carlo shook his head. "Somebody should tell Katherina," he said.

"Somebody already has. I sent Sweet. Can't imagine a more sympathetic chap."

"Where is she now?" Carlo asked.

"I included her on the roster for the briefing at Farm Hall," Philby said.

"You did *what?*"

"Thring called. He said he'd shaken down Crimshaw's barmaid. Seems she was friendly with one of the biographers at Winthorpe, don't know whose. Thring said she got Vorpal's cover down pat, and gave the gen to Crimshaw. She told him you were moving the Fräulein too. All right, C-c-carlo. So it means we can't go in through the front door. Katherina Weber says she knows another way into the Speleological Research Unit—through the church crypt. She also worked on the fuses for Baby Albert. Katherina is going with Scarr's people."

"Oh, good God, Harold!"

"Now just a minute, Carlo. I can see a way of turning things around. We do everything as planned; we send the signal announcing the arrival of Oberstleutnant Heller and party at Haigerloch. If Vorpal is blown, that'll be just what Stengel is looking for. So what'll he do? Triple the guard, stage an alert? But Johnny isn't going to come through the front door, Carlo. Don't you see? When Johnny doesn't show the way he's supposed to, their guard'll be down. Then we take them from the back, Carlo, chop-chop. Scarr's people will break *out* of the cave and be at Hechingen before you can say s-s-snicker-snack."

"So you say. This way into the cave through the crypt. Isn't it guarded?"

"Katherina says they bricked it up last summer then forgot about it."

"And to what do you attribute this amnesia?" Carlo inquired acidly.

"She says very few people knew about the tunnel—the priest and a few of the scientists, that's all. It wasn't the kind of thing they would get too excited about."

"Stengel would know about the tunnel, and Stengel is holding the Fräulein's mother hostage," said Carlo.

"Maybe, but the Fräulein says what is one life against so many millions. I must say that I agree with her, Carlo."

"Why is she so keen to go? Haven't you asked yourself that question? She's an enemy national, after all. This is going to make Scarr's people very nervous, Harold."

132

"My dear Carlo, some of our best scientists are enemy nationals. Look at Fermi."

"Yes, but he's an Italian. And you still haven't answered my question about Stengel. What if she's playing some kind of double game with him?"

"A frontier policeman?"

"He's more than that, and you know it," said Carlo.

"Perhaps," said Harold.

"I can't let her go," protested Carlo.

"What choice do you have? If Kindchen Alberich is ready to fly, the Fräulein has to be there to defuse it. Anyway, you can save it all for the PM, Carlo. He wants to see us in a couple of hours. At Storey's Gate."

Carlo checked the time. It was just a few minutes past midnight.

Wentworth wasn't going to get deniability. It wasn't his fault, or anyone's he could think of—yet; alas, but it was plain to see that the disaster ahead was bound to become common knowledge, in which case a sacrificial victim would have to be found.

"This, then, must represent the gravest danger." The PM's words intruded upon Wentworth's consciousness. "What area could the bomb Fat Albert devastate?"

"Hypothetically?"

"*Thetically*, Mr. Brown. Thetically."

But whom? Thus preoccupied, the PUS was a seemingly passive spectator to the exchange between the PM and the tubular man. In the artificial light of the War Room at Churchill's wartime headquarters in Storey's Gate, just off Parliament Square, Wentworth's Romanesque features gave no hint of despair. That face had an oriental cast that might have belonged to a thin Buddha, and as its gaze lit on the tubular man, who was formulating the answer to Winston's question, it was illuminated by a smile.

Churchill was sitting hunched in a swivel chair, a Mercator map of the world on the wall behind him, the tubular man at the end of the cabinet table. Opposite him, at the other end of the long table, Carlo Peat, aware, like the PUS, that he was witnessing a critical exchange, sat with his head cocked to one side. He looked at that moment like a very clever baby, wise beyond his years.

The tubular man was thinking. Enrico Fermi, the Italian physicist working at the University of Chicago, had calculated that 6000 million times more energy was released by nuclear fission than was needed to cause it. However, Fat Albert was a fusion bomb, and Fermi had also said that the splitting of the atom merely foreshadowed "the largest conversion of mass into energy that has yet been achieved by terrestrial means." Fermi had in mind the reactions that take place in the stars, the conversion of atomic hydrogen into helium by thermonuclear fusion, a process more than four times as efficient as nuclear fission.

Where had the Germans got this stuff from? Brown had gone over the documents that Balthazar had brought back from Switzerland. They were the equal of anything in the Manhattan Project.

The tubular man spoke: "According to Einstein's equation $E = mc^2$, a cubic meter of deuterium would give an explosive yield equivalent to ten million tons of TNT. So to answer your question, Prime Minister, I would say about a thousand square miles."

"Do I understand you correctly, Mr. Brown"—the famous jaw jutted forth pugnaciously—"that this one bomb, if operational, would lay waste to an area of a thousand square miles?"

The tubular man nodded. "At least."

"And the smaller bomb, the detonator? How much?"

"Depending on the height of the air blast, I would say something between ten and fifteen square miles only."

"Only? But this would be some two thousand times more powerful than our Grand Slam. Am I correct, Mr. Brown?"

"Yes, sir. I was speaking for comparative purposes only." Brown winced. That word again.

"Then the baby is father to the beast," the great phrasemaker declared. "How long have we known of this menace—Wentworth?"

The PUS composed himself. "The first I heard of it was when we received the Degussa papers from Switzerland. Three weeks ago, Prime Minister. Naturally, I passed them on to Tube Alloys at once."

"Mr. Brown?"

The tubular man swallowed. "We got wind of this some time in 1943, Prime Minister. Actually, I remember it being put about that the Nazis were looking for a way to ignite the atmosphere. We thought it a bit too *outré* even for them." Brown gave a nervous guffaw. "After all, it's their atmosphere, too."

"A matter of no consequence, Mr. Brown. Does the devil fear hellfire?"

"That is beyond the realm of science, Prime Minister."

"Do you bandy words with me, sir? You are like the Bishop of Cloyne, who said that for a thing to exist it must be seen to exist. In your case, what you cannot imagine cannot exist. So much for your science, sir. Tunnel vision, the science of the molehill and the morass! You." Churchill singled out the baby-faced Peat. "You have a team ready to drop into Germany—is that not so?"

Carlo said that it was.

"Pray tell me, when?"

"Tuesday night, sir."

"Then let us be thankful that somebody was prepared. You will root out this evil, Mr. Peat. You will destroy the means of production and you will destroy the matériel itself. The only condition I insist on for this operation is that I must see the plan of campaign myself."

"Our people will be wearing enemy uniforms, sir."

"Against the Geneva Convention, but the enemy offers us precedents. Belgium, 1914. And we ourselves have been known to hoist false colors from time to time."

"It may mean blowing Ultra to send signals to the enemy, sir." Carlo exchanged a quick glance with Harold, who sat next to the PUS.

"What is a mathematician's bauble to the fate of this city, Mr. Peat? I say do it."

"Yes, sir."

"And, Mr. Peat: let there be no thought of failure."

135

19: FINAL BRIEFING, FARM HALL

"The drop is set for midnight Zulu, one A.M. local time, one mile south of the Hohenzollern Castle on the Hechingen-Rottweil road," Carlo began the briefing at Farm Hall, the eighteenth-century country house that the Friends used as a staging post for SOE agents flying out from nearby RAF Tempsford. "The met people are forecasting a clear night for southwestern Germany, with occasional light winds. No precipitation is expected but the climate book does warn of sudden snow squalls at this time of year. The weather should be okay." Carlo glanced at Johnny Scarr, who was sitting next to Katherina Weber. She had sacrificed her braids for the mission and wore *feldgrau* fatigues. Johnny Scarr, jump suit, chute, and gear on the floor in front of him, looked resplendent in the sky-blue uniform and eagle tabs of a Luftwaffe Lieutenant-Colonel. "I wouldn't count on any Fräulein whose uncle has a Bentley to get you out of trouble tonight, Johnny," Carlo said.

Bony Wilkes giggled. He had an unfortunate laugh, like a hiccuping mynah bird, and he stared fixedly at the cigarette he was smoking as though it had somehow caused this outburst. The cigarette came from a red and black tin that he balanced on his knees. The tin was one of Bony's prize possessions; emblazoned with swastikas and the legend *Köln dankt euch*, it had caused trouble between Wilkes and Charlie Page, who was annoyed that a man could be so attached to an inanimate object.

"Where'd you get that from, Bony? Did the Führer give it to you?"

"Wouldn't you like to know? And my name is Ernst, Oberfeldwebel Hans Ernst."

"Jesus, Bony. If your old mum could hear you now. What did they do to you? Take out your brains and fill up the hole with knockwurst?"

Johnny Scarr studied Bony Wilkes, who was holding the cigarette between one bony thumb and forefinger, gazing at it as if it had just spoken to him. It was a German cigarette and it burned like a fuse. "He ain't a German, not a proper German": Johnny Scarr remembered what the street urchin had said at Shrewsbury Castle. The same was true of Bony Wilkes, Johnny thought. He looked German enough in a long-toothed sort of way, yet for all his German cigarettes and that precious tin, his Oberfeldwebel's uniform and Flakgruppe Wachtel insignia, there was something decidedly un-Hunnish about Bony. It was his laugh, Johnny concluded; no German would bray like that unless he was being done to death, not that it damn well mattered much.

Bony's biographer at Winthorpe had been troubled by that laugh and had told his troubles to Crimshaw's barmaid. That laugh could kill us all, Johnny thought; maybe it has already, he thought, looking at the Fräulein. She was trying to look like a man, he decided. The operational difficulty of jumping in a skirt was not something that had occurred to him.

"All identities are notional," Carlo continued. "Captain Innis is Major Ahrens of the Wehrmacht's Sixty-fifth Corps. Major Ahrens is attached to the office coordinating V-2 missile research with Projekt Alberich. The rocket, as you know, is an Army project, and there is some rivalry between the Wehrmacht and the Luftwaffe on that score. Accompanying Major Ahrens is Charlie Page as Hauptmann Unger, his Luftwaffe liaison officer with the commander of Flakgruppe Wachtel. Ahrens is to report in person to General Heinemann, his former commanding officer at Peenemünde, now in Berlin, who rightly suspects Wachtel of cooking the books on the number of V-1 hits in the offensives against London and Brussels.

"Major Ahrens will be accompanied by his secretary, Fräulein Ritter, alias Fräulein Weber, and Prentice will be along as Herr Berger from Degussa to check out the latest consignment of *Spezialmetall*. I trust you will find that everything is *prima*, Herr Berger.

"Also accompanying Major Ahrens are three other Luftwaffe officers, Leutnant Vogt and Oberfeldwebel Ernst, played by Lieutenant Roberts and Sergeant Wilkes respectively—signals people whom Ahrens has filched for work on the rocket—and Johnny Heller, of course. Johnny is playing a Luftwaffe Lieutenant-Colonel who has the goods on Wachtel. A very ambitious officer, Oberstleutnant Heller. By the way, Johnny, the data you're carrying are almost genuine, so take good care of them.

"Now—as you know—there has been some difficulty with Bony's biographer, who suddenly developed a loose tongue. If Crimshaw did get through, identifying you people, then it's certainly fair to say that you're expected and that your cover is blown." There was a general stir of restlessness among Carlo's audience.

"By the same token," he went on, "the enemy will be expecting you to show up, suspecting nothing, at the main gates of the Speleological Research Unit with all the paraphernalia of passes, identity papers, and so on. The fake signal has already been sent (early this morning), announcing that a Major Ahrens and secretary, with a party of Luftwaffe officers, one of them a Lieutenant-Colonel, and a civilian from Degussa, are expected to arrive at Haigerloch sometime around the breakfast hour tomorrow morning, Wednesday, March fourteenth. By the way, we were cheeky enough to send the signal 'from' Stengel's Berlin HQ, on the Standartenführer's authority. Your exact time of arrival, given the state of military operations in Germany, could not be specified, of course." Carlo looked at the upturned faces before him. "No doubt the enemy will be cooking up some breakfast for you." He joked to relieve the tension. "Well, gentlemen, you're going to be a bit too early for breakfast and you're not going in through the front door."

Carlo took up a pointer and turned to a map of the drop zone. "After the drop, you will use Mount Zollern as your assembly point. You will stow your heavy weapons and equipment in the castle, which was used as an army depot in the First War and has been left empty ever since. Then you will make your way across country to Haigerloch, a distance of some four miles as the crow flies." There was a groan as he said this. "It is actually a mile shorter than the side

139

road," Carlo added; "and Fräulein Weber will show you the way. Fräulein?"

"Thank you, Herr Peat." Katherina stood up and took her place next to the lectern. "It is actually a pleasant stroll from the castle to the village," she said. "We often used to walk that way last summer. There is a path that brings you out by the church, above the village. It would not take an hour."

"We've allowed two hours operational time," Carlo interjected, "which brings you to two A.M. local time. I'm sorry, Fräulein, do go on."

"With pleasure, Herr Peat." Katherina's hand went self-consciously to her newly cropped hair. "Last summer I found out about a secret passageway connecting the wine cellar of the Swan Inn with the crypt of the church. I think it is what you call a priest's hole. The minister there, a Father Gisevius, says it was hollowed out of the rock during the religious wars of the sixteenth century, sometime after the Peasant's War, he thinks. A spiral staircase takes you down some twenty meters or so from the crypt to a tunnel, which slopes down to the rear of the cave, which is about a hundred meters away. There is enough room for a large man to negotiate this tunnel on hands and knees. Professor Gerlach explored the tunnel before the war, and if he could do it anyone could. I myself have been down there and experienced no difficulty, of course. When the Virus House pile was moved to Haigerloch, the entrance to the cave was bricked up, but it is nothing that a small charge could not demolish. The entrance to the stairway in the crypt is through a tomb. Very few people know of this," Katherina added.

"How many people?" asked Johnny Scarr.

The question interested Carlo, too. He watched Katherina, monitoring her reaction.

"Myself—Professor Gerlach, of course," the Fräulein colored. "Perhaps some other colleagues."

"But not Stengel." Johnny Scarr sounded skeptical. "Your head of security and he wouldn't know about this? I find that hard to believe, Fräulein."

"No, really. He wouldn't go within a mile of any church. Then the tunnel opens into a kind of vestibule at the rear of the wine cellar where the radiation suits are normally kept. It's quite a small opening, nothing you would notice unless you were looking for it."

Which, of course, Stengel would have been, Johnny Scarr thought. He looked at Carlo, who shrugged. Both men were sure the Fräulein was lying. For operational reasons, both preferred to leave the implication of treachery unspoken. Katherina's motives remained unclear, however—to Johnny Scarr, as to Carlo, who had warned Johnny before the briefing to be wary of the Fräulein. Johnny was prepared for a trap.

"You'd better take it the church is guarded," said Carlo, covering an awkward situation. "Any more questions?"

"This priest—what's he like?" Innis, the explosives man, asked.

"Father Gisevius is a good man. At two o'clock in the morning he will be asleep in bed," Katherina replied. "And the church is not guarded."

Charlie Page winked at Johnny Scarr. "Sounds like she knows what she's talking about," he whispered loudly.

That was the trouble, Johnny thought; the Fräulein always sounded as though she knew what she was talking about.

"Jock is a big man," Roberts said, referring to the explosives man. "Three hundred feet of tunnel, that's a long way."

"There will be no difficulties," Katherina assured him.

Carlo coughed and looked at his watch. The transport for Tempsford would be waiting. "There's one other thing," he said quietly, and had everyone's attention. "The enemy is much further ahead of schedule than we thought. We've been monitoring a Luftwaffe unit at Hechingen, and it seems they've already done some ballistic testing of the bomb. Apparently Dorf is going to implement Operation Gunderic tomorrow, which means that all roads out of the Hechingen military district will be closed. At this stage we simply don't know—and Dorf is not going to be fool enough to tell us—what his logistical preparations are for Baby Albert—I mean for the housing, transport, arming, and delivery of the bomb. But we do have one quite positive assurance from Colonel-General Dorf," said Carlo Peat, "and that is that London will be the target."

141

He took Johnny Scarr aside as the briefing room cleared. "I think she's got something cooked up with her boyfriend," he said. "The trouble is, no one seems to see it except me."

"I wonder why," said Johnny Scarr.

Carlo smiled. "You've got the mountaineering equipment?"

Johnny Scarr nodded.

Carlo said nothing. Together, they walked down the corridor and out into the courtyard. An army truck was pulled up to the door with its engine turning over, a pile of equipment, all of it Scarr's, by the back wheel. Charlie Page peered out from the back of the truck. He, too, said nothing.

Carlo shook hands with Johnny Scarr. "Good luck," he said, and heaved up a pack into the truck.

It was surprisingly heavy.

20: IN THE FÜHRERBUNKER

Immaculately clad in a white tunic with black breeches tucked into highly polished riding boots, the SS orderly greeted Stengel in the main hall of the Reichskanzlei—Hitler's Chancellory, now little more than a façade fronting ruins.

"Come," the SS man said. "The Führer is waiting." This was Standartenführer Richard Schulze, Hitler's personal adjutant.

Stengel followed him down to the basement, which was flooded. The adjutant balanced his way across duckboards to a door that opened on the Chancellory Gardens. Hitler's teahouse had taken a direct hit. The fountain, which no longer worked, was filled with broken glass from the greenhouses of the botanical station. In December the snow had covered a multitude of evils. But with the spring came rain and mud. Stengel looked back—once. The buildings on both sides of the Wilhelmstrasse lay in ruins, the Chancellory walls were pock-marked and soot-stained, lumps of concrete, uprooted trees, flooded bomb craters, and dismembered statuary adding to the dismal and mangled scene that could have been created by a Kandinsky or a Klee.

Schulze was silent as they descended the winding concrete stairs to the bunker. In the brilliantly lit corridor another SS officer searched Stengel's briefcase and checked in his Walther pistol. Schulze looked on with polite disinterest.

Stengel was surprised to see the corpulent form of Reichsmarschall Göring huddled in a solitary heap on a divan in the foyer. Sweat-stains soaked the Reichsmarschall's pale-blue uniform under the armpits. His eyes were shut and he was breathing deeply. As Schulze and Stengel walked by, however, he spoke:

"It is ready, *ja*, Kindchen Alberich?"

Stengel nodded and the Reichsmarschall slapped his corpulent thighs. He rose, puffing with the exertion, and followed them into the conference room where they were welcomed by Reichsleiter Martin Bormann, who reminded Stengel of an overfed rodent—a white rat or a hamster perhaps. He was rubbing his hands as though they were cold, though it was hot in the bunker forty feet underground, hot and humid.

Schulze disappeared into an anteroom. It was crowded in the conference room, and Stengel observed several things: the faded Persian carpet on the floor, curled under at the edges; the gloomy landscapes by Schinkel; the narrow oak table and the chairs, some plushly upholstered, others plain—the bunker had all the ambience of a furniture mover's warehouse.

The Luftwaffe's Chief of Staff, General Karl Koller, came over to ask if everything was ready at Hechingen. Stengel said that it was. Koller had the Minister of Propaganda in tow. Goebbels limped over.

"This will knock them into the middle of next week," he said, his eyes glittering oddly.

"The Führer is elated, of course," Bormann said, and seemed on the point of adding something when a chorus of *"Heils!"* signaled the Führer's entrance. Hitler, who looked like a walking corpse, gripped Schulze's arm for support. The orderly sat him in the armchair at the head of the table. The Führer wore green tinted spectacles and his head lolled on his chest. His hair was grayer than it had been in December, his eyes more sunken and red-rimmed, his flesh pallid from the artificial light in the bunker, his whole body palsied and trembling. Stengel was appalled to see foodstains on the lapel of the Führer's *feldgrau* tunic. Hitler held his left arm crooked in his right, apparently in an attempt to control or at least conceal the convulsive tremors with which he was from time to time afflicted.

The Führer began to speak. Everybody in the room had heard the speech before; no one seemed to tire of it. A peculiar mixture of fantasy, self-deception, half-truths, and sheer delusion, it was delivered in a croaking monotone, its every word shot through with wishful thinking. Germany's enemies were an unholy alliance of capitalists and communists; such an unnatural coalition would destroy itself, as had the alliance against Frederick the Great; the Anglo-Saxons, if they did not come to their senses, would be solely responsible for the downfall of Western civilization; the General Staff in the First War had been lions compared with today's generals; however, this time there would be no stab in the back; this time there would be no November criminals; this time Germany would not make peace at five minutes to midnight; this time . . .

Bormann, Stengel saw, had opened a notebook, and, with a pencil, was making row upon row of dots. Soon, he had a pageful.

"This time," Hitler electrified his audience, "Germany has the atomic bomb."

A congratulatory hubbub broke out. Hitler jabbed the air for silence.

"Projekt Alberich nears completion," he said. "Unless the Anglo-Saxons accept our terms, Gunderic will be implemented at dawn on Wednesday—two days hence. The aircraft is ready and waiting; the bomb has only to be armed and loaded. Kindchen Alberich—this miracle of German science—ensures victory in the west. The Anglo-Saxons have been notified. They must surrender or I shall annihilate London. Once too often they have made the mistake of doubting my resolve. I will do this thing—a thousand times! For every city they have destroyed I will destroy a thousand of theirs! General Koller"— Hitler turned to the Luftwaffe Chief of Staff—"see to it that Oberst Viktor von Wenden is awarded the diamonds to his Knight's Cross."

"*Jawohl, mein Führer!*"

"And you, Stengel," Hitler turned to the Standartenführer, "you will convey my orders to von Wenden personally."

The Standartenführer nodded, and asked permission to speak.

"Of course, Stengel. What is it?"

"*Mein Führer*, I hereby volunteer to accompany Oberst von Wenden upon this mission. My duty is clear. As head of security to Projekt Alberich, I would like to see it through to the end."

"Then your wish is granted," Hitler rasped. He turned to the softly palpitating, softly sweating form of the Reichsmarschall. A ghastly smile played on Hitler's lips, the spittle dribbling from the corner of his mouth. "You see, Göring," he said, "there is a man. With one bomb he shall achieve what your entire Luftwaffe could not. One bomb! Go, Stengel, and may Providence go with you. But let it be remembered," the Führer shook a finger at the hapless Reichsmarschall, "that it was I, your Führer, who alone possessed the unshakeable will and vision to bring this thing into being while others waxed gross upon the spoils of conquest. Let it be remembered when the name of London has been forgotten, burned from the pages of history! This was Hitler's bomb! No one else's! Mine! And this is only just the beginning, Göring!" the Führer averred modestly, still with that ghastly smile cracking his features. "I haven't even started yet," he said. "Their cities will burn like moths in a summer lantern's flame. Yes, burn, burn, burn, and they will say of me that it was I who brought the sun and the stars to earth."

Stengel managed to creep away unobserved. As he left he noticed that Josef Goebbels, the Minister of Propaganda, seemed to be having great difficulty staying awake and that Martin Bormann, the Reichsrodent, had begun a new page of dots.

21: STENGEL

"Herr Standartenführer! The signal is in! The British commando is coming!" The methodical major tore into Stengel's office at dawn on Tuesday morning.

Stengel rose to receive him. He had been sleeping on a couch underneath a portrait of *der Führer*, and as he glanced at the intercept that Kroll thrust into his hand, Stengel knew that the British signal gave him what he most needed: knowledge of the future, that impossible dream of all spies—the divine secret.

"It means we have them, Kroll," Stengel gloated, amused at the signal's supposed provenance. "It means they are putting their heads on the block. I must fly to Hechingen at once. Kroll, will you call Generaloberst Dorf and inform him of my plans? And, Kroll, you'd better drive me to the airfield, there's a good fellow."

They drove west through the Tiergarten, its once proud shade trees charred stumps, past the ruined embassies and the zoo, past the battle-scarred flak tower, the Giant Würzburg antenna on its roof silhouetted against the first light like a scimitar. On the Charlottenburger Chausée, one lane of the highway was filled with a procession of broken statuary that seemed to be fleeing the city. Only one of these refugees from the Reichstag grounds had survived the *Terrorbomber* raids intact: a blood-red granite and bronze column topped by a winged Nike holding a laurel wreath in one hand and a giant Iron Cross in the other—the Victory Column, its shadow falling aslant the grotesquely disordered cityscape of total war.

Behind the wheel, Kroll was uncharacteristically silent, listening as Stengel outlined the measures he had taken to deal with the enemy.

"I have ordered a company of Waffen SS to surround Haigerloch village. They will be taking up their positions after midnight tonight, and there is already a tank regiment dug in there, not to mention Wachtel's V-1 battery. Dorf's Württembergers will be sealing off the entire Hechingen military district—local troops, they know the area well—and there is a battalion of Jäger covering the mountains to the south. The Swiss frontier will be closed, and I have ordered extra patrols on the lake. I do not see what else I can do."

Kroll, swinging the Mercedes on to the Gatow approach road, agreed that such measures would surely be enough to deal with six of the enemy.

"And the girl, Herr Standartenführer? This Ahrens' secretary mentioned in the signal—surely this must be Fräulein Weber. Can she be working for the enemy, do you think?"

Grimly Stengel remarked that if she were, he would have great pleasure in dealing with the Fräulein personally.

"There's one more thing, Kroll," he added. "Generaloberst Dorf may not be entirely secure in his command. I want you to telephone me tomorrow. Insist on speaking to me personally, you understand. Do not be put off with excuses. If, for any reason, you cannot contact me, alert Sturmbannführer Waldmann at Hechingen Airfield and the commander of the SS troops at Haigerloch, Oberführer Schramm."

Kroll accompanied his master on to the tarmac where the plane, a Junkers 88, was waiting with its engines turning over. Stengel shook hands, an unusual gesture. He gave a kind of shrug as he turned toward the aircraft, and the methodical major was visited by the presentiment that he would never see him again.

"Kroll," Stengel turned around, "call at this time tomorrow morning": he took a couple of steps back toward the major; "call me at Hechingen, Kroll." Stengel came even closer. "I saw the Führer yesterday and I volunteered for the mission, Kroll, so I'll be flying with von Wenden and Kindchen Alberich tomorrow at dawn. I just thought you should know, that's all. *Auf Wiedersehen*, Herr Major!"

Kroll watched him climb the short ladder into the Junkers and saw it hauled up into the belly of the plane as the ground crew dragged away the chocks, and, motors roaring, the Junkers taxied on to the runway. Uncomprehending, oppressed by feelings of doom, the methodical major watched it bounce across the field and climb slowly into the western sky.

The first time Stengel had made this trip had been by road, after the July plot. Himmler had requested that he check out the security at Haigerloch, which was a little too close to Switzerland for the Reichsführer's liking. Stengel had never heard of the place before, though he was not surprised to learn that the Reich's nuclear research effort was being transferred to the south. Then, as now, he had been pleased to leave Berlin.

He had taken time out on that trip to visit some of his old First War battlefields. Staring into the green waters of the Meuse Canal, not far from Verdun, he had been approached by a Frenchman.

"You too, *hein*?"

Stengel had asked him what he meant.

"General Stülpnagel, the military commander of Paris, shot himself here yesterday." The Frenchman had waited for a moment before issuing another communiqué: "For the general, alas, it was not the end."

Stengel indicated a polite interest. He waited while the Frenchman gazed at the waters of the canal and assumed a tragic expression. The Frenchman was racked with sighs. Stengel decided to end the histrionics.

"You mean, then, that he shot himself but survived?"

"*Certainement.* What else? Forgive me, *m'sieur*, but when I came upon you here, I thought that you, too—"

"What happened to von Stülpnagel?" Stengel interrupted the garrulous old peasant.

"They found him floating here in the canal, face up. He had shot out one eye and the other will have to be removed surgically. The general is expected to live. But what for, *hein*? What for?" The Frenchman rolled his eyes and drew a gallows in the gravel with his foot. "And now, *m'sieur*, I shall withdraw. Forgive me for intruding," and the Frenchman indicated the canal with an open gesture of his hand, bequeathing it to all Boche who came this way in search of themselves.

This episode had left Stengel at a loss. Something he did not understand had happened. He had suffered a defeat.

The Standartenführer had felt the need for ritual atonement. He headed east back into Germany, crossing the Rhine at Karlsruhe, and at Pforzheim turned up into the Black Forest. The dark tree-clad line of the ridge, which had been almost an unconscious part of the scenery from the other bank of the Rhine, closed around him, the air filling with the thick sweet scent of pine resin. Stengel got out of the car and wandered about the woods. The midsummer heat made him long for the sea, for something clean, pure, and implacable.

He had returned to the car, where he passed a fitful night dreaming of the Meuse Canal. The Frenchman's mocking face floated in and out of his dreams, sometimes as his enemy and sometimes his friend, inviting him to try the canal, which he now saw was crystal clear, a purifying balm for his soul. A trick, of course. For as he tested those waters they closed over him, foul and green and putrid like the trenches he had seen at Verdun, *les ravines des morts*, those humid swamps of human decomposition overhung with tendrils of poison gas, phosgene drifting wraith-like above the lumps of matter wallowing in the viscous scum below.

Stengel woke in a sweat, his brain filled with fractured images of the artillery park on the left bank of the Meuse. His unit had been unloading a trainload of shells from the narrow-gauge railway when the French artillery started ranging. The troops had ignored the shells bursting above the concrete-lined cutting and had worked calmly and methodically at unloading their own cargo until one of the men gave a cry unlike anything Stengel had heard before or since. He looked up then and saw an uncoupled wagon rolling down the tracks toward his men, the tarpaulin on top of the load wreathed in cherry-pink flames. Stengel saw everything very clearly: the stack of 150-millimeter shells by the tracks, the thick black smoke coiling from the flames above the tarpaulin, the little petrol-engined locomotive racing after the runaway wagon, and something froze in him as he saw the crewmen jump from the locomotive. It, too, was out of control, and careered into the back of the wagon at full throttle, thrusting it and its deadly freight into the buffer at the end of the siding where it erupted in a fearfully intense white flash.

Stengel had watched the concrete walls of the cutting crack and crumble, the earthworks pouring in while the air and ground thundered, plucking at him like the undertow of a mighty ocean. He felt the heat sear his body, yet at no time was he conscious of pain. Bodies and bits of bodies tore past him, the vacuum sucking the air from his lungs until there came a long drawn-out keening that ended in abrupt silence and darkness. The darkness surprised him more than anything else, more than the blast or the flash or the silence. His eyes were open, he was conscious—why then could he not see?

Stengel was destined to replay this scene at intervals throughout the rest of his life. He did so then with what he thought was the dissociated objectivity of a dying man. He saw the wagon rolling down the tracks again, and understood that a hot shrapnel fragment must have touched off the fire on the tarpaulin. The explosion had failed to kill him because it had spent its energies piling up the earth around him. He had been buried alive.

After a while, a length of time he calculated as a whole day, Stengel understood that he was in no immediate danger of dying. The air in his underground prison was not even noticeably stale; it had to be getting in from the outside somehow. The only trouble was, Stengel could not move a muscle. The earth pressed in on him from every side; it trickled into his nostrils and eyes; like a worm he could taste it. Rescue must surely come, he told himself, and once or twice thought he heard the sound of digging. He had tried to cry out then, but could not. He began to itch, his eyes burning like fiery orbs in their sockets, every nerve exposed as if someone were pressing red-hot needles into his flesh. He imagined a million insects nibbling at him, feeding off him, roaches inspecting him with their tiny feelers. Mercifully this torment soon passed, to be succeeded by one more terrible—thirst. The spittle in his mouth turned to acid, his tongue felt as though it had been flayed and stuck to the roof of his mouth, spasms of the vagus nerve emptied the burning juices of his stomach into his throat, and he was forced to swallow them again, afraid to lose this much

151

moisture. He dreamed of cool, clear, limpid pools and when he woke his head reverberated with the dull shoveling of his own blood, each heartbeat measuring the slow bleeding to death of time for him. In his agony he cursed Germany and the war, cursed the insane military policy that had brought him to this pass. The attack should have taken place on both sides of the river at once, any fool could see that. Instead, by concentrating on the east bank, the Germans had offered the French artillery a fine target, and because of this error of the High Command he was imprisoned under perhaps many meters of earth. "Man is a worm!" Nietzsche's Zarathustra had proclaimed. What did he know of it, he who had never been buried alive? Would to God he were a worm! A worm could extricate himself more easily from this dungeon than a man. Was he going to be left here to die of thirst? Had his comrades already given him up for dead? Then at least he had saved the state the expense of a funeral.

It was during this ordeal that the idea of man the mirror had taken hold of Rudolf Stengel's mind. Man was a mirror, nothing more. That this revelation came to Stengel while he was entombed in utter darkness, completely devoid of light, was surely no accident. A mirror could not function without light, but he, Rudolf Stengel, could—a self-reflecting mirror, a mirror with a mind; he knew what he had to do.

When his rescuers dug him up four days later, he was mumbling something in his delirium, something they could not quite catch until they leaned over him:

"I am my own light,' he was saying over and over again. "I am my own light."

At Stengel's insistence the pilot took the Junkers in low over the American bridgehead at Remagen. There was some desultory flak, nothing to trouble this pilot who was more worried by the danger of fighter pursuit.

"Anyone can see that the Americans are going nowhere," Stengel remarked when they had gained some more height. "I wonder why?"

Deadpan, the pilot said: "It must be they're afraid of the Führer's secret weapons."

152

Stengel asked if there was enough fuel to make it to the Swiss frontier and back. The pilot looked at his gauges and nodded unhappily. The longer he was in the air, the greater the chance of being shot out of it.

"I want you to fly down the Neckar, then turn south to the frontier. Can you do that?"

The pilot nodded again, managing to look even more unhappy. A dog's leg, a dog's life, he thought. There was flak from the right bank all the way down the Rhine. Sooner or later he would fall victim to the law of averages. He survived only because the Americans were such lousy gunners. They had more of everything, that was why they were winning the war.

"Everyone needs to practice," he said, and put the plane through a violent series of twists and turns, upsetting Stengel.

At Pforzheim he put the left wing down and banked across the northern slopes of the Schwarzwald.

"Stuttgart is still there," he said, pointing at the smoke on the horizon.

Stuttgart itself had been devastated in the great raid of March 1, 1944, and had been bombed intermittently ever since, but the towns and villages of the Neckar Valley were largely untouched. It was a land of green light and surprising vistas, castled since the early Middle Ages by semi-autonomous barons, each one of whom had his own war to fight against his neighbor. From the air the river looked like a length of gut curling southeast from Stuttgart, then turning southwest to its source in the Black Forest. Taking the Breg road south from Rottweil, it was less than half an hour's drive to the frontier, which jutted north into Germany in a large, almost strangulated salient around the Swiss town of Schaffhausen on the Falls of the Rhine. Stengel assumed the British would take this line of retreat as the shortest. Just to be on the safe side, he had ordered the frontier closed from Basel in the west to Konstanz in the east, an exercise in caution that seemed academic from the air. Stengel didn't think it would come to a retreat.

"Kindchen Alberich is in *Flugzeughalle Eine* with the Stirling. The hangar is cordoned off by Waffen SS with heavy machine guns covering all access points. To gain entry to the base, in addition to one's military identity card, this special *Vorlaüfigergenehmigung* on white paper is needed. Before one can enter the hangar one must have this *Sondergenehmigung* on watermarked paper, and to see the bomb one must have this red *Zusatz*, which is good only until twenty-four hundred hours today." The speaker was a jug-faced man of medium build, Sturmbannführer Waldmann, chief of the SS security detail at Hechingen. He flicked through the various bits of paper like a man checking the numbers on lottery tickets before tucking them back into his tunic pocket, his dull little eyes glinting oddly. Stengel was profoundly depressed.

"Sturmbannführer Waldmann," he began, "as you can see, I am here but I do not have any of these papers." When he saw that this only confused Waldmann, Stengel added: "You are aware, are you not, that an attempt may be made on the base tomorrow morning?"

"*Jawohl,* Herr Standartenführer!"

"I have no doubt, Waldmann, that the enemy will have all the proper documents in his possession."

"Permit me, Herr Standartenführer. Even if the enemy were to gain unauthorized entry to the base, he would not be allowed near the bomb. The color of the *Zusatz,* you see, is changed on a random basis every three days. As I was attempting to say, Herr Standartenführer, the red pass is good only until midnight tonight. Thereafter, for the next three days, one must have a green pass."

Stengel sighed. "What provisions have been made for defense against low-flying aircraft?" he asked.

"The Luftwaffe has several batteries of mobile antiaircraft cannon as well as a full complement of flak guns, Herr Standartenführer."

"Very good. I would like to see the Stirling now, Waldmann—and the bomb, of course."

"Naturally, Herr Standartenführer. First, with your permission," said the doughty Waldmann, pinning a badge on Stengel's lapel.

"A film badge, Herr Standartenführer. In the presence of radiation, the film fogs. A safety measure, you understand, a precaution only."

Machine-gun nozzles poked through the sand-bagged entrance to the hangar. The two men walked together through the defile, Waldmann lagging a respectful pace behind. Stengel was reassured in a way. It would be impossible for the British commando to take the place by main force, but that was never what he had feared anyway.

Inside the hangar, a work crew was putting the finishing touches to a green and brown camouflage job on the Stirling. The underside was painted black, and Stengel made out the RAF roundel on the wing. The original hydraulic turrets had been left in place, .303 caliber machine guns pointing down at the two men who stood for a moment gazing up into the cavernous bomb bay, which, Waldmann explained, had been especially enlarged for this mission.

"It looks all right," said Stengel, in what for him amounted to lavish praise.

"Yes, Herr Standartenführer. But here is our expert now. Standartenführer Stengel, permit me to introduce Herr Oberst Viktor von Wenden."

"Heil Hitler!" The Luftwaffe officer saluted. He was not at all like the pilot who had flown Stengel down from Berlin. Von Wenden came from a different mold. He was young, aristocratic, hard, and ambitious. He was also one of the Luftwaffe's most seasoned bomber pilots. There was something feline about him, something that reminded Stengel of a lynx, a blond lynx. He had no doubt that Oberst von Wenden was imbued with the killer instinct. The Standartenführer approved.

"Oberst von Wenden says that his fitters have done such a good job on the Stirling that it feels just like one of our own machines," continued Waldmann. "Is that not so, Herr Oberst?"

Unsmilingly, von Wenden said that it was.

"Standartenführer Stengel, who will accompany you on this epochal flight, has brought your orders from the Führer personally," the egregious Waldmann went on in his wheedling tones. "That is a great honor, is it not? We all know how highly the Führer thinks of his Luftwaffe."

"For me this mission will be a chance to redeem the service," said Oberst Viktor von Wenden.

"If I might see Kindchen Alberich," Stengel put an end to this banter, "then perhaps I could give the Herr Oberst his orders."

"But of course, of course. This way, gentlemen."

Waldmann led them behind the aircraft, to a small yellow hut in the shadow of the Stirling's huge single fin at the far end of the hangar. The bomb nestled in a cradle inside. Kindchen Alberich, finished in the same obnoxious color as its housing, was about ten feet long, with square box fins welded to its rear end, a livid scar around its waist where additional paint had been sprayed over the clamps and the weld holding the hemispheres together. The assembly reminded Stengel of a large and evil-looking egg.

The Standartenführer noticed the panel forward of the weld. Three holes, each about two inches in diameter, color-coded with the blue, green, and red numerals, I, II, and III, had been tapped in the steel plate, with this warning stenciled underneath:

ACHTUNG!
Z-GERÄT

Von Wenden, observing Stengel's interest, said: "My navigator, who on this flight will also be the bombardier, will arm Kindchen Alberich after take-off. The holes you see are for the fuses—number one for the radar detonator, number two for a pressure-operated back-up fuse, number three for the initiator, a neutron source to bring the plutonium up to criticality."

"And where are these fuses now?" asked Stengel.

"Generaloberst Dorf has them at Haigerloch for recalibration, Herr Standartenführer. It was agreed he would keep them there until the eve of Gunderic."

"What? But that is today. The fuses must be here by midnight at the latest. Oberst von Wenden, your Führer commands you to fly at dawn. The British commando will be held at Haigerloch while Kindchen Alberich is being armed. Our orders explicitly state that we are to attack London tomorrow in broad daylight with Parliament Square as the aiming point. Only if the British accept our terms for a separate peace will this mission be recalled. It is therefore imperative that we secure immediate control of the fuses." Stengel was galvanized into action. "Sturmbannführer, get me a car and escort at once. Call Dorf and tell him I am on my way to Haigerloch. No, wait, Waldmann; do not call Dorf. Call Berlin instead."

"Berlin?"

"Yes, you will speak to my assistant, Major Kroll. Tell him what is happening here. He will know what to do."

During the drive to Haigerloch, Stengel was troubled by the thought that he might have underestimated the enemy. His doubts were soon resolved. Wehrmacht troops—Württembergers—had thrown a road-block across the Haigerloch side road, just south of Mount Zollern.

Stengel recognized the officer who checked his papers. It was Dorf's aide, Hauptmann Lang. "Gunderic is in effect," the young captain told him, adding in a voice that chilled Stengel: "By the way, Herr Standartenführer, where is your assistant, Major Kroll?"

It was not the enemy he had underestimated but his own people.

22: BONY WILKES

In the Dakota over France Bony Wilkes told Johnny Scarr how he had come by the German cigarette tin. "It was because I could speak German, see? I always got landed with these bleeding jobs, interrogating the prisoner." Johnny was half-crouched, half-sitting against a bulkhead, looking at Bony who sat opposite, a Sten gun across his knees. "It was my mother," Bony said, "my mother was a Rhinelander. She married my old man in 1919 after he knocked her up. No secret about that. He was just an ordinary soldier with the Control Commission. No fraternization, that was the rule." Bony frowned. "Though I don't know as you could call what he was doing fraternizing. So he married her and they kicked him out of the army. Just like that." Bony snapped his fingers. He dug the cigarette tin out of his battle-dress pocket and set it on the floor of the aircraft, scrambling around so that he shielded it from the others. "This tin now." Bony gave it a glum look as though it were responsible for the whole fact of his being. "I don't know about this tin. I've never told anyone this story before."

Bony took a cigarette out of the tin and lit it, his face in the light from the match red and raw-looking. Bony shook out the match. "It was after Dieppe," he continued. "We had been dropped north of this radar station near Cape Gris Nez. The main force was supposed to have been dropped right on top of the radar station, and we were to cover them from this Jerry infantry battalion between us and them. Only it didn't work out like that."

"No? How did it turn out, Bony?"

Bony took a deep drag on the cigarette. "Like shit," he said. "We came down in this hayfield. In the middle of the field there was this old bus. Jerry had set up a field kitchen there. We took one prisoner there, and he said he was a cook. 'A cook, eh?' this officer said, he was a lieutenant. 'That's no good. Ask him where the others are.' The cook said his mates had sloped off to town for the day. 'Ask him where the radar is then,' the lieutenant says. The cook hadn't heard of any radar, and I could see that he was telling the truth. Then the lieutenant has an idea. 'Ask him who he's cooking for,' he says. The cook says he's cooking for a bunch of Russians stationed up on the coast. They came down to the bus every night to get their grub. It didn't have to be much, not for Russians, and they were grateful for what they got. The lieutenant had never heard of Russians being in the German army, and neither had I, but we let that pass. 'Ask him how far to the coast,' the lieutenant says. It's thirty kilometers, according to the cook, thirty kilometers and we're damn well supposed to be on it. I could see then that the lieutenant was getting worried. I remember what he said. He said: 'Do you think he's really a cook? I mean, dash it all, this is very awkward. A cook. We can't take a cook back to England.'"

Bony took another deep drag on the cigarette. He shut his eyes, remembering. The cook had offered Bony a cigarette, which Bony had accepted. The cook was about Bony's age and had red hair, which is a sign of bad luck in Germany.

"The lieutenant went away and came back with the captain," Bony continued his story. "Both of them had maps. The captain asked the same questions as the lieutenant and got the same answers, then he asked the prisoner to show him our position on the map. So the prisoner points out this spot, which is not exactly where we're supposed to be, and the captain says to the lieutenant: 'Gather the men together. I must take a short stroll.' That's what he said. Then the lieutenant looks at me and says, 'All right, Wilkes. Get on with the job.' I didn't understand what he meant at first." Bony closed his eyes again.

The prisoner must have known he was down on his luck because he started shaking.

Bony remembered saying to him: "You'll be all right. We'll have to let you go."

The lieutenant spun around in a rage: "For God's sake, Wilkes! Stop torturing the man and get on with the job!"

Bony knew what that meant. This time there was no mistaking the lieutenant's tone.

"I was supposed to shoot the prisoner, you see," Bony explained to Johnny Scarr. "I was supposed to shoot him because this lieutenant couldn't. Well, no more could I."

"What did you do?" asked Johnny Scarr.

"It was stupid, really. I roared at the cook to give me his cigarette tin. I don't know why I did it."

When the captain came back he said: "It looks like he's right. We'd better pull out of here."

"What about the prisoner?" the lieutenant asked.

The captain shrugged and turned his back.

Bony watched the lieutenant unholster his pistol. The cook held out the tin as if in supplication, turning from Wilkes to the lieutenant who hesitated. To shoot a man in cold blood cut against the grain. It was something the lieutenant had never expected to do, something he could not do. He fired one shot—into the ground—motioning with his other hand for the prisoner to run. And then an extraordinary thing happened. The lieutenant gave a little yelp, like a puppy. He fired another shot, this one into the air as his shoulders hunched up and he toppled backward, a red hole open in the middle of his forehead like a third eye.

Bony raised the Sten in his hands and began firing. Three bursts, keeping the muzzle down, tracking as he had been taught. He was like a man with tunnel vision, concentrating on the fleeing cook-prisoner, watching that red head torn back, the tin hurled from upraised arms, tumbling end over end through the air, glinting like a grenade. Bony fired again and again at the muzzle flashes in the hayfield beyond the bus, pausing only to change magazines on the Sten.

The firing stopped abruptly, stopped as abruptly as it had started, and in the immense silence that rose like a pall over the gunsmoke Bony heard the song of a lark ascending. Suddenly he was up and running with his strange disjointed gait, stooping to scoop the cigarette tin where it had rolled from a lifeless hand among the hay, the shiny red tin with its message: "Cologne thanks you," for what Bony had neither the time nor the inclination to think, running into the ditch at the field's edge where he found three Russians in German uniforms, one of them barely alive, the other two dead, sprawled in the ditch surrounded by an incredible amount of food, cheeses, bread, and sausages, the realization slowly growing in Bony that these half-starved wretches must have crept back to the bus to steal the food, which they had been eating when they heard the lieutenant's pistol shot and one of them, panicking, had opened fire, killing the lieutenant.

"They must have thought we were the cook's mates come back from town," Bony said to Johnny Scarr.

"What happened after that?" asked Johnny Scarr.

"We formed up and marched back to the coast. It wasn't until this thing came up that they tried to blame everything on me. They said the cook was some kind of radar expert. Maybe he was. I don't know, I don't know anything any more," said Bony Wilkes. "Do you think I did the wrong thing?"

Johnny Scarr, who wondered what the right thing would have been, shook his head.

"I kept the tin," Bony Wilkes said.

23: SPELEOLOGY

Johnny Scarr jumped at twelve hundred feet. He heard a muted roar like the thunder of surf on a distant shore, followed by the crack of his chute opening and the fading pulse of radial engines. Under the black canopy Johnny stopped thinking of what had happened to him over the Long Mynd and watched the slow cascade of stars: Leo arching across the southern sky, the embattled giant Orion sinking in the west. The air was cold and clear, and Johnny could see the searchlights cutting great swathes through the sky in the direction of Haigerloch. Somewhere down there a motor coughed, disembodied voices floating up as star shells suddenly burst the darkness asunder, their hissing track causing Johnny to flinch in the harness. An umbrella of Very lights spanned the sky over the Hohenzollern Castle, its battlements and turrets glimmering under the ghostly blue light as if it had been conjured out of thin air, a phantom castle at the edge of a phantom forest that Johnny Scarr saw beneath him as a black void, the sweet-smelling pines rushing up toward him, the darkness below fast closing with the darkness above.

Johnny Scarr came down through the great trees that stood like sentinels before the castle. He hit ground, rolled and bounced, his impact cushioned by pine needles, and was jerked upward again as some hidden force tugged at him like a yo-yo on a string. The lines of his chute had snagged in the limbs of a giant pine. Sighing, Johnny Scarr reached for a bayonet.

Three and a half years had passed since he had last been in Germany. Johnny throught of that night in the Metropole Bodega with the crew of the Swedish ore carrier and the girl whose name he could never remember. It didn't matter now; she was probably dead.

Johnny Scarr had been thinking about her, and about the death of his friend Yuill, while Bony Wilkes had told the story of the cigarette tin. Bony's mother was a Rhinelander. Maybe she was from Cologne, which would explain why the tin was such a totem to Bony. *Köln dankt euch*—for the loss of one cook's life, thank you; for the loss of one city, thank you; for the loss of one war, thank you. Maybe Bony's mother wasn't from Cologne at all; maybe the message on the tin held no meaning for him, none at all—like Yuill's famous last words. It seemed a poor sort of testament for a man to leave behind; then, of course, Yuill hadn't known he was about to die. Would he have said anything different if he had? Probably not, Johnny Scarr thought. Got to take a piss was about the score of it. Terry Yuill had liked the desert.

Johnny Scarr hacked at the tangled lines of the chute, silken shreds decorating the trees like pennants. Behind him the castle looked as though Rapunzel ought to be letting her hair down from one of the towers. She should have used a parachute, too, Johnny Scarr thought as his chute billowed and he jumped on it, high-stepping as if in some demonic midnight ritual. Johnny scratched at the earth with the collapsible shovel from his pack; he threw shovelfuls of earth on the chute and heaped it with pine needles, and still it danced diaphanously among the pines like a thing possessed before it gave up the ghost and collapsed at his feet, ready for burial.

Johnny Scarr shouldered his pack. It had several hundred feet of climbing rope inside, crampons, pitons, and an ice pick. Johnny didn't want to use any of this equipment, but something told him he might have to. The Fräulein worried him. She was too confident, almost happy. She had sat with a grim serenity on the flight, looking at Scarr's people as though they were unconscious participants in some experiment. Johnny didn't like the idea of being used as an experimental animal. The trouble was, he couldn't make sense of the experiment and he began to understand how a rat must feel in a maze—inquisitive, cautious, and more than a little afraid.

He heard heavy machine-gun fire, a couple of miles off; then that motor again, revving, and the unmistakable clatter of tank treads sounding like the roosting of many birds in the forest, a mechanical squealing and squawking. What the hell was going on? It had to be some sort of war game, Johnny thought, cursing London.

In the night now he heard an insectile clicking. He was suddenly blinded, caught in the glare of a flashlight beam, a grinning simian face looking out of its nimbus—Charlie Page garlanded with stick grenades, a little metal clicker called a cricket in his hand.

"My, my, but the natives are restless tonight," Charlie said. "Hung up, are we?" He shone the flashlight over the chute rigging.

"Jesus, Charlie. Switch that thing off."

"We have landed in the middle of a war, old son."

"Yeah, I wondered about the fireworks. It must be some sort of exercise."

"Hell," Charlie grimaced, "they must practice hard." Far-off both men heard the *crump-crump* of a flak 88, then a low rumble as the earth shook and the horizon was lit with yellow flashes behind the jagged tree line. "That's a real firefight over on the Haigerloch road," said Charlie. "Come on, while you were swinging in the trees we were stowing the gear. Jock and the boys are over at the castle with the Fräulein." Charlie led the way. "Prentice hurt himself landing," he said.

"Badly?"

"Sprained ankle. It'll be dot and carry one to the cave. But the night is young and we are fresh, Herr Oberstleutnant." More star shells spanned the castle, and there came the sound of the tank engaging some hidden enemy.

"I thought it was for our benefit," Johnny said; "I thought they must have heard the plane."

"You're kidding," said Charlie above the din. "There's a Mark IV squatting on the road just where we have to cross, and they're trying to take it out with the eighty-eights. Don't ask me why, old son, but that lot have had a falling-out among themselves. Things couldn't be better for us, really. Here we are, squire."

They came upon the little group in the lee of the castle. Bony Wilkes was sitting on a boulder apart from the rest. He waved, lit a cigarette from his precious tin, and gathered up his equipment before sauntering over.

"I signaled London," said Bony. "Quite a reception, ain't it?"

"Let's have a look at Prentice's ankle," Johnny said.

Richard Prentice, as Herr Berger from Degussa, wore a double-breasted brown suit under a heavy, fur-collared coat. He pulled out a pair of thick-rimmed glasses, part of his newfound persona, adjusting them carefully. Then he took them off again and handed them to Johnny Scarr.

"Sorry to be such a nuisance," he said. He sat hunched up against the castle wall, one leg stuck out awkwardly in front of him, with his lead-lined portmanteau by his side.

"Here," He followed his glasses with his shoe and sock. "I don't think it's broken, only a sprain."

Johnny knelt down and the physicist winced as Scarr felt his ankle, which was soft and puffy.

"I'll be all right," Prentice said, but Johnny wasn't so sure. Prentice's ankle had swollen to twice its normal size, and he couldn't get his shoe back on properly. "I'll have to leave it unlaced," he said. "I'm sorry to muck things up like this, really I am."

"Okay," Johnny said. "Jock, Roberts, see if you can get him to his feet. I'm gonna take a look at the road. Fräulein?"

"I am here," she said. "And will show you where we must make the crossing."

Johnny Scarr turned around to the others. "You'd better bind that ankle up," he said.

Katherina did it—awkwardly.

"Now I am ready," she said.

The beginning of a pleasant stroll, he thought, taking the Fräulein and a bazooka with him. He didn't know which was the more dangerous.

A quarter of an hour later they lay at the side of the road, having scrambled down from the castle mount. Several times they had stopped to throw themselves to the ground as the shells from the village screamed overhead to land harmlessly in showers of earth, splintered wood, and pine needles. "The track goes uphill from here," Katherina said at the road's edge, but Johnny didn't have to be told that. The 88s were firing over open sights from the high ground in the village, overshooting so that each salvo continued to fall in the woods between the castle and the road.

Johnny understood the situation. Flak guns, the 88s couldn't depress their barrels enough to range the Panzer blocking the road. Johnny looked at the great hulking form of the tank, its turret turning, sniffing, its long 75-mm gun at maximum elevation. The road went uphill to the village, as well as the track, and the Panzer commander, outgunned, dared not advance his tank farther in case he reduced the angle between himself and the flak 88s. A stand-off.

"We have to cross the road here," said Katherina.

Johnny didn't have to be told that either. He was trying to work out who was firing on whom. The 88s had to be Luftwaffe guns under Wehrmacht control, which meant that the tank here was the property of the Waffen SS.

Another salvo whined overhead from the village. Johnny handed the Fräulein an armor-piercing rocket grenade. Kneeling in the ditch, he leveled the bazooka on his shoulder. He was taking aim when the Panzer erupted in a fiery roar, one of its tracks snaking into the air, its turret lifted off the chassis with the force of the explosion. A short round? Johnny wondered, hauling the Fräulein down into the ditch. He felt the warm blast on the back of his neck; blazing gasoline spewed across the road, and the air filled with a fetid carbide stench, the reek of burning batteries mingling with that of burnt flesh. There were five men in the tank and probably something like a hundred shells.

The ammo began exploding; something slithered into the ditch next to Johnny. Charlie Page, his features lit by the flames from the burning hulk, grinning. "Jock and Roberts are coming down with Prentice," he said. "Bony's covering them. Shall we cross the road, captain, sir?"

Johnny nodded. He motioned the girl to get out of the ditch, but her eyes were wild and her nostrils flared, her face a mask of fear—scared shitless, and not at all happy now, Johnny thought. He hoisted the bazooka under one arm and grabbed her roughly by the elbow with the other, propelling her across the road in a kind of half nelson, skirting the lake of burning gasoline and throwing her into the ditch at the other side of the road. A greasy black pall of smoke hung over the hulk of the tank. Katherina gasped and gagged at the stench. Yelling, she tried to get out of the ditch, but Johnny seized her by the scruff of the neck and kept her down as the tank burned an eerie incandescent white, spitting slivers of molten steel, tracer bullets, and shrapnel.

The embers were dying when Bony Wilkes landed in the ditch next to Johnny, who still had his hand on the Fräulein's collar.

"You can let go of me now, Herr Scarr," she said. "I am sorry. I am not used to this."

"Used to it?" Johnny gazed at her incredulously. "Used to it?" he repeated softly, wonderingly. "Well, you'd better get used to it," he said, and then, making amends: "Me neither, I'm not bloody well used to it, not at all used to it," said Johnny Scarr.

Another motor fired up down the hill, a low, almost feral growling, like that of a bear come to look for her cub, followed again by the steel squawking of tank treads. This time the earth quaked.

"Tiger tank," said Charlie Page, "at the bottom of the hill, heading this way. Come along, children, this ain't our scrap."

But whose was it? Johnny Scarr looked at Katherina, who seemed to know even less than he did. She shook her head while Jock and Roberts hauled the physicist out of the ditch and the Tiger barked blindly, once, twice, and was answered by the 88s—whose caliber it matched—sixty tons of Krupp armor beginning its predatory crawl up the hill. Germans were fighting Germans, that much was clear, and it was nothing Johnny could get upset about.

"The way is not so far now," Katherina said, adding: "It will be safer there, *ja*? Where we are going, much safer under the ground."

Watching her at the head of his men, Johnny Scarr thought of the tons of amatol in the V-1 warheads, the potentially explosive mix of fuels in the *Stofflager*, the kerosene dumps for the ramjet-powered missiles, the heavy water, carbon, and uranium in the atomic pile, and Johnny Scarr wondered what it would take to set all that ablaze.

At that moment he couldn't think of a more dangerous place in the world than Haigerloch, under the ground or above it.

"There's no guard on the church," Charlie Page, back from scouting the church, told his comrades crouching among the tombstones in Haigerloch cemetery, "and the crypt is empty. I'll see you down there later. It's not the sort of place I'd be seen dead in."

He went to find Scarr, who was monitoring troop movements in the village below.

"It seems like the girl's on the level anyway," Charlie said.

"Maybe."

"Well, if there was a guard on the church they've pulled it off. What are they fighting about?"

"Damned if I know, Charlie."

The river ran far beneath them, its turbulent course carving the rock that towered over the village like a gnarled fist. Both men looked down on the buildings they already knew so well: the Swan Inn and stables, the Wehrmacht barracks, the *Stofflager* and *R-Haus*, the concrete launching ramps, six of them ringing the base of the river bluff, a couple with missiles loaded on the catapults—both men watching the frantic activity as the Wehrmacht soldiers and Luftwaffe gun crews tried to find some means of bringing the flak 88s to bear on the monster intruder now no more than half a mile below the village.

"They rigged up a searchlight and sent out some sappers a while ago," Johnny said. "No go. One of them's still down there."

"But the Tiger's not firing either," said Charlie.

"No. Maybe he's afraid of hitting the *Stofflager*."

"He must want something, Johnny."

"Or someone. See that? There's an APC at the back of the Swan with its engine running."

Charlie Page said: "We seem to have landed in the middle of someone else's war."

"Let's go back to our own," said Johnny Scarr, drawing back from the cliff edge.

He was thinking about having to climb the cliff—and with Prentice in the shape he was in, that was not going to be easy.

That dank odor of the long dead hung over the crypt of Haigerloch church like a pall. The bones of the Teutonic knights interred therein had long since turned to dust. But not their graven images. Spotlit by Scarr's torch, the naked fist unclenched in prayer, the unhelmeted brow endured on many a sepulcher, often with morbid reminders of human mortality—the worm in the eye socket, the stone skeleton languishing beneath the stone shroud, the lizard, feasting on entrails, glancing up at the living beholder. It was damp and cold and comfortless in the crypt, and it must have seemed at one time like the entrance to purgatory, the beginning of the soul's eternal torment, or, perhaps, rest.

"Here is the place." Katherina rested her hand on the lichen-encrusted lid of a stone catafalque. She was nervous and ill at ease, not at all her usual self, and Johnny Scarr wondered why.

"Bony, cover the door to the crypt," he ordered. "Jock, you'll start down first. Then Roberts, Charlie, Prentice, the Fräulein, and myself with Bony bringing up the rear."

Katherina Weber slid back the lid, stone grating on stone, the narrow, time-worn steps descending inside.

Jock started down the steps. "I'm thinking Mr. Prentice might have a spot of bother," the big Scotsman called up, his flashlight casting long shadows on the smooth walls of the tomb.

"We'll see about that," Johnny's voice sounded in a hollow whisper. "I'm sending Roberts down after you. Okay, Jock? Don't get stuck."

"Aye," Jock's voice rang out full of doom, "you'd have to pull me out by the boots."

Behind him Roberts was muttering something about a place called Tel Algol—the devil's hill.

Roberts was crazy. Controlled, but crazy all the same.

It happened to him at Tel Algol. Roberts had crawled into a German dugout beneath the sand, a concrete room at the end of a tunnel through the rock. Inside, black with putrefaction, four dead men lolled around a table, their tunics, tighter than skin, obscenely stretched over their bloated bodies. The dead men were playing cards. They smiled at Roberts as he walked around the table. "*Willkommen,*" they seemed to say, their grins overexposed behind shrunken black lips. "Come and join the game. But if you don't care to, it's all one to us."

Roberts had looked at the dead men's cards. The four, seven, nine of spades lay on the table, covered by the knave.

The stone lizard in Haigerloch crypt reminded him of that other place beneath the desert sands, how he had prowled catlike around the table, for there was something catlike about Roberts, and something machinelike at the same time—how, in a kind of frenzy, he had gone this way and that around the table like a caged beast patrolling behind the bars of its prison. For in the dugout at Tel Algol the monstrous delusion had grown on Roberts that he would not find his way out—not, at least, until the dead men finished their game.

Jock and the others had found him half an hour later, still prowling around the table. He was babbling something about trumps.

Lizards basked in the tunnel, watching with quick swivel eyes as the sleek brown mammals crawled by.

One of them was screaming. Sunstroke, the others called it, but it wasn't sunstroke at all. It was much worse.

Suddenly, beneath the crypt of Haigerloch church, Roberts had to explain. "Why the hell else would the Arabs have called it Devil's Hill, Jock?"

Jock didn't know, and said so. The only people who did were the Arabs, and they had probably forgotten. Roberts was crazy, no doubt about it.

"Sunstroke, Jock, but how the devil could it have been—*in the shade?*"

Jock told him to shut up. The big Scotsman had found the mouth of the spiral staircase. It was filled with rubble.

"Get back up out of here, damn you," he said to Roberts. "Sixty Christ-fucking feet and filled to the Christ-fucking brim. That double-crossing bitch!"

Johnny Scarr heard him in the crypt. He turned to Katherina.

"The tunnel's blocked," he said.

"I knew nothing of this, believe me," she protested.

"No?" Roberts and Jock emerged from the tomb. "Is that right,

Fräulein? The big Scotsman stepped forward. "What's the matter? Did your boyfriends stand you up?"

"Boyfriends?" She colored.

"Stengel, Dorf. The goose-stepping brigade."

"I don't know what you're talking about."

"Jesus, Johnny." Jock turned to Scarr. "You should take a look down there. Stengel must have used a whole slave-labor corps to fill that shaft and tunnel with rubble. There's no way we could blast our way through that. How could she not have known about it?"

"It was done after I left," Katherina protested. "It must have been."

"The hell with that," said Johnny Scarr. "We'll go over the cliff."

Everyone in the crypt heard the truck climbing up the road from the village.

"Go and see what that is, Bony," said Johnny Scarr.

Bony Wilkes clattered up the stairs. He returned moments later, his face ashen.

"German patrol," he said. "Ten of them, with an officer. They've stopped at the jail."

"Well, that settles it then," said Johnny Scarr, cradling the bazooka that he'd carried from the castle. "We go over the cliff."

24: STENGEL

After Stengel's car was halted at the roadblock, Hauptmann Lang escorted the Standartenführer to Dorf, who was overseeing Operation Gunderic from his command vehicle, the Skorpion, parked at the rear of the Swan Inn.

The Generaloberst was sitting at the radio panel, the table before him heaped with signals, when Stengel demanded the fuses for Kindchen Alberich.

"Later," Dorf waved him aside. "Can't you see I'm busy?"

"Herr Generaloberst, I find your attitude incomprehensible."

"Is that so?" Dorf gave him that peculiar look, those Prussian eyes gazing up at the Standartenführer: "Why?"

Stengel said nothing about Waldmann, who would be calling Kroll in Berlin. Kroll would know what to do.

"You realize, of course, that Oberführer Schramm, commander of the SS panzer units around Haigerloch, will not permit this situation to continue?" said Stengel.

"What situation, Herr Standartenführer? Schramm operates under my command," Dorf replied.

"Is this a military coup?"

"Of course not. Whatever gave you that idea?"

"Then I am free to return to Hechingen?"

"Certainly—without the fuses."

"Impossible! Herr Generaloberst, the Führer has ordered the annihilation of London. I have volunteered for this mission with Oberst von Wenden. We fly at dawn. Would you disobey a Führer order?"

"I have never disobeyed an order in my life," said Dorf. "However, it is still my intention to force a truce from the Anglo-Saxons on the west front. Those are my orders, Stengel, and I intend to obey them to the letter. Therefore, we must await the arrival of this British commando. Then we shall persuade them that London will be destroyed unless our terms are met."

"Persuade them? How?"

"I intend to show them the bomb. Everything is ready, is it not?"

"Of course, but—"

"But what, Herr Standartenführer?"

"You cannot be serious, surely. This is an enemy commando unit you are talking about."

"Come, come, Stengel. We know their plans, when they are arriving, where, and how. What possible harm could they do to us? As for the charge of dealing with the enemy, if that is what you are thinking of . . ." Dorf shuffled through the papers on the table top. "Ach, here we are, Stengel—the signal announcing the imminent arrival of Oberstleutnant Heller, Major Ahrens, and party." Dorf flourished the signal with his good hand, adding, so there could be no doubt of his meaning: "*Your* signal, Herr Standartenführer, your signal."

"That signal is a British forgery, and you know it," Stengel responded.

"Is that so," Dorf mocked. "Listen to him, Lang. An Enigma-enciphered signal. How could that be, Herr Standartenführer? Did you give the enemy our codes? Or perhaps you mean to tell me that the English have been reading our signals throughout the war? Only a man who has volunteered for such a mission as yours could make such a claim as that, Herr Standartenführer. Unless, of course, you have some other motive? Other than serving the Reich and your Führer by annihilating the enemy's capital. Lang"—Dorf reached a decision—"kindly escort the Standartenführer to our prison. Since you will not leave you must stay, Herr Standartenführer. I am sorry I cannot offer you better quarters. Dawn will come, Stengel, never fear," said Generaloberst Dorf, returning to his signals. "Dawn will come."

Lang saluted, turned on his heels, and the cell door clanged shut. It was useless to protest, a waste of energy. Sighing, Stengel stretched out on the cell bunk. Sleep did not come to him at first. He thought of what Kroll had said on the drive to Tempelhof. Katherina working for the British? He could not believe it. Of course, if the British did, that was their business. They would believe anything.

He was awakened at one by what sounded like a plane, then the sound of Schramm's armor moving in around Haigerloch. Kroll must have contacted Führer HQ, and they would have got on to Schramm. The methodical major had his uses.

Stengel wondered if he could have been mistaken about the plane. There was no mistaking the 88s firing from the village, and, half an hour later, the sound of tank ammunition exploding on the Hechingen road.

Stengel gazed bleakly out of the barred window. He had plenty of light—from the moon and the reflected glow of the blazing tank, and from the searchlight that probed the only road into and out of Haigerloch. Another thirty minutes passed before Stengel heard the Tiger tank crawling up toward the village along that road, the Standartenführer watching helplessly from his lofty cell as Wachtel's Luftwaffe crews loaded a couple of missiles on to their ramps. Then, to his relief, Stengel realized that this was a bluff; the V-1s, like the 88s, would overshoot the target.

For a while there was a stand-off. The shooting stopped, started again, then stopped once more as a party set out from the village under a white flag. Dorf had finally come to his senses, Stengel thought, listening as a truck geared up from the village. It was Lang with a patrol, come to parley.

"Generaloberst Dorf presents his compliments," Lang saluted, as he always did, smartly.

"But not the fuses, Lang?"

The Hauptmann ignored this. "Generaloberst Dorf apologises for the inconvenience he has caused you and wishes to see you in his command vehicle again. Germans must not fight Germans. A truce has been arranged. However," Lang hesitated, "the Generaloberst is worried by the possibility of reprisals against himself and his staff. In view of our common interests, it is his earnest hope that this unfortunate misunderstanding can be overlooked."

Stengel smiled bitterly. How like these Wehrmacht swine, to save their own skins while Germany went down to defeat. "I can give no such undertaking, Lang," the Standartenführer said, "until I have informed Oberführer Schramm that I am on my way to Hechingen with the fuses for Kindchen Alberich."

Lang bowed his head.

"Moreover, you can take it from me, Lang, that no such undertaking would be honored until Schramm is personally assured of my safe arrival in Hechingen with the fuses. Furthermore, you can tell Generaloberst Dorf that he must hand over his command to Oberführer Schramm forthwith and allow immediate occupation of the inner security compound by Waffen SS troops. Better than that, Lang; I will tell Dorf myself."

Lang straightened up. "As you wish," he said.

There was a commotion outside in the jailblock corridor. It was the pastor, Father Gisevius. One of Lang's men had found him lurking about the church and had brought him in for questioning. A Swabian, like Dorf himself, Gisevius was horse-faced and wild-eyed. He was also slightly crazed, Stengel thought, and very incensed about something or other.

"Where else should I be but in my church?" he raged. "Where else does a pastor belong?" He glowered at Stengel, whom he had yet to forgive for blocking up the tunnel last summer, though actually the work had been done by army sappers—trailing their mess through the crypt, shoveling in tons of rubble to ruin the work of the ages, a valuable historical relic! He had insisted that they clean up afterwards, the vandals.

"Sit down, pastor." Stengel gave him a gentle shove so that he sat down on the bunk. "How are you?"

"None the better for meeting you," he said.

"A curfew is in effect for civilians," Lang reminded the pastor.

"Curfew?" Gisevius wrung his hands. "What do I, a man of God, have to do with such things? The fighting woke me up. I wanted to be where I belonged, that's all. Then this blockhead turns up." Gisevius gestured at the soldier standing by the cell door. "After the seven comes the eighth, I said to myself."

Stengel sat down next to the pastor. "What was that?" he asked.

"I said after the seven comes the eighth. Him." Gisevius wagged a gnarled finger at the soldier again. "The great beast of the apocalypse."

Stengel stood up again. "Hauptmann Lang," he said with a tremendous sense of foreboding, "summon your men at once. Have them surround the church. And you," he pointed at Gisevius, "you come with me."

25: DER URANBRENNER

They crouched at the edge of the cliff on the far side of the graveyard, their faces blackened with greasepaint. Johnny Scarr hammered the piton into the ground with the rag-muffled ice pick and watched as Prentice expertly wound the rope around himself. The physicist had been a rock climber in his youth.

Johnny Scarr looked up and saw Bony Wilkes threading his way back through the tombstones. Bowed under the weight of his radio, he was returning from the edge of the graveyard, where he had been keeping an eye on the German patrol.

"They're heading for the church," he said. He was out of breath and took great gasps of air in his eagerness to tell Johnny Scarr what he had seen. "They've got the priest and another German with them, an SS colonel. I think it could be Stengel," he said, panting.

"See, I told you it was a set-up," said Jock dourly.

But Johnny wasn't so sure. "They'd have been waiting for us, Jock. Listen, this is what we'll do. We'll suit up here." Johnny began rummaging around in his pack for the lead-shielded suit. "You and me, Jock, that's all—no one else."

"Good, Johnny. It's good to hear you say that," the big Scotsman responded, pleased that the Fräulein was being left out.

"All right? Roberts"—Johnny turned to the weapons specialist—"I want you and Charlie to secure that armored personnel carrier at the back of the inn. You'll take Prentice and the Fräulein with you and hold them there."

"I recognize the vehicle," Katherina spoke up. Evidently she felt the need to redeem herself. "It is Dorf's command vehicle."

179

"So much the better," said Johnny. "We're going to pinch it."

"What about Dorf?" asked Roberts.

"Him as well, if he's at home."

"He might have some staff officers with him," said Roberts.

Johnny Scarr nodded. "Probably. Try not to be too noisy, won't you, Ian?" He began struggling on with the suit, and Jock did likewise, taking the plastic explosive and detonator from his pack and tucking it inside his suit, each man daubing the other with mud as if in some primitive rite of initiation.

"Prentice will go first, followed by Roberts, Charlie Page, Bøny, the Fräulein, then Jock and myself." Johnny glanced at the physicist, who seemed oddly incongruous in his fur-collared coat and thick-rimmed spectacles, the rope coiled over his shoulder. "Think you can lead?"

"It won't be too bad going down," the physicist replied.

"Pain, like fear, is only a state of mind," the Fräulein remarked, making it sound like a manifesto. Prentice apparently agreed, for he gave a weak smile and said that he was feeling much better. A natural bond existed between the two scientists, and Prentice had believed Katherina when she denied all knowledge of the fill in the tunnel. He had always believed her. How could she have lied to him, a fellow scientist?

Johnny Scarr wondered how he looked himself: his face blackened, the bazooka with two rocket grenades in an ammo bag strapped to his waist, a Luftwaffe lieutenant-colonel in a mud-covered radiation suit dropping from the night. Pretty strange, but then he hoped Dorf's people would be too busy to notice.

"We'll set a ten-minute fuse for the plastic," he said. "Jock, don't forget the case for the *Spezialmetall*. We'll have to leave the rest of the gear here. Bony, you can keep a watch on the cave mouth. There's a sentry down there but Charlie will take care of him before helping Roberts secure the APC." The paratrooper ape grinned. "No violence, now, Charlie. Not in public. Remember, you'll have the heavy water to deal with."

"How about if I plant a few charges of my own, Johnny—while you're in the cave?"

"Good idea, Charlie, but not until the Fräulein and Prentice are safely installed in the APC with Roberts looking after them." Johnny looked at the Fräulein. He'd been expecting her to make trouble, but she seemed curiously depressed and withdrawn. She was trouble enough as it was, and he didn't need her in the cave. Johnny thought of the official reason for her inclusion on the mission. The bomb and the problem of its disposal seemed a long way off. Johnny Scarr felt suddenly tired.

He didn't need her in the cave because there was nothing scientific to be done in there. They had rehearsed the operation in the Dustbin many times. Two people were needed in the reactor pit, that was all. And, with the German patrol surrounding the church, it began to look as though Jock was right.

As for Prentice, the chance of his being captured alive was something Johnny did not like to think about. Roberts could look after the physicist and the Fräulein; Johnny had other work to do.

A cry of command echoed across the graveyard from the church.

"We'd better get going," said Johnny. "Mr. Prentice?"

The physicist knelt and looped the rope through the piton. He winced with pain and lowered himself gingerly over the cliff edge. Johnny watched him rappel down, pushing off from the cliff face with his good leg. It looked easy.

"Okay, Ian," Johnny said, looking at his watch. It was 2:50 A.M. They had used all but ten minutes of Carlo Peat's two hours' operating time.

Charlie Page skirted the yard at the base of the Swan Inn, a stuccoed half-frame building, its shutters closed against prying eyes. Behind him the river cliff leaned against the night like a frozen tidal wave, the gorge cleaving Haigerloch in two. Lights playing intermittently across the cliff face illuminated the buttressed chapel at the pinnacle a hundred and fifty feet above the village, plying the night like a Gothic vessel scattering the moon and the stars in her wake. A sentry stood on guard in the cave mouth facing the back of the inn, cables snaking across the yard from the kitchen door, the chugging of a diesel generator audible above the roar of the river in full flood.

181

The lights had made for a tricky descent, and Charlie had been hung up by a searchlight playing on a gorse bush below and to the right of his last rappel. Charlie was afraid that the beam would pick out him or the rope, and he shuddered as he glanced at the cliff again, remembering the slow passage of the seconds until the beam had flicked away.

Charlie waited until he saw Johnny Scarr, the last man down, drop softly to the ground, bringing the rope with him. He watched Johnny stow the rope and join Jock and Bony at the base of the cliff across from the stables. Over his shoulder Charlie glimpsed Roberts, Prentice, and the Fräulein disappearing behind the coffin-shaped outline of Dorf's command vehicle; he tugged at the hem of his jacket and brushed himself down. Then he marched across the yard in the full glare of the lights to where the sentry stood before the great concrete blast doors.

"Son of a Bavarian piss mistress whore! *Achtung!*" he roared. "The major wants to see you in the guardhouse. At the double!"

The sentry assembled himself, saluted, tripped over one of the electrical cables, whimpered, and fled.

Charlie Page waved Jock and Johnny Scarr through the blast doors. They lumbered past him in their radiation suits looking strangely monkish, Jock carrying the lead-lined portmanteau and Johnny the bazooka. It would be a terrible weapon in the wine cellar, thought Charlie. He winked at Bony Wilkes who took the sentry's place in the cave mouth; then he turned to join the others.

Recrossing the yard, Charlie checked out the other vehicles parked there: a Wehrmacht bus, a truck, a Horch Wanderer.

As he approached the flank of the Skorpion, Charlie almost collided with Dorf.

"Lang?" the German inquired.

"Nein. Er kommt, Herr Generaloberst," said Charlie, and hit Dorf in the pit of the stomach, pistol whipping him as he folded.

Charlie hauled him by the jackboots around to the back of the Skorpion. He was rounding the other flank when he saw Roberts laying the driver to rest, Katherina Weber looking on, close to Mr. Prentice and closer to hysteria, Charlie judged. Roberts had cut the driver's throat with a bayonet and was dragging him under the APC.

"No staff officers?" He looked up at Charlie.

"Expected, I believe," said Charlie, and asked Roberts to give him a hand with the old gentleman.

The air filtration system hummed quietly in the wine cellar of the Swan Inn, steel chains hanging down from the portal crane overhead. At the rear of the cave a row of soft white forms clustered along the wall, radiation suits, each with its boots tucked in underneath. Lank and pale, their death's heads masks peering down, the suits looked like flayed victims of the Inquisition. They gave Johnny Scarr quite a start, although he knew from the briefing that they would be there.

Blinking as his eyes grew accustomed to the harsh lights, Johnny Scarr gazed at the suits, then down at the reactor pit. Katherina had not misled them about the layout of the Speleological Research Unit. Everything was just the same as in the main hangar at Winthorpe, except that the pit was sunk in the ground.

Jock's gloved hand brushed against Scarr's canvas sleeve. Someone was working in the reactor pit, a complication Johnny had not expected at three o'clock in the morning.

Oblivious to the two onlookers, the radiation-suited figure crawled on all fours, loosening the locking nuts with a spanner and waving a Geiger counter over the top plate. The counter crackled ominously. Laying the spanner aside, the figure clumsily noted the reading with a pencil attached to a clipboard. Then, still unaware it was being watched, the figure tightened the locking nuts, gathered its belongings together, and squeezed through the hatch to climb out of the reactor body. The figure's canvas paws gripped the ladder supports, its goggle-eyed gaze peering up into the muzzle of the bazooka. The figure halted, astonished; Johnny Scarr motioned for it to continue its climb. The figure obeyed sluggishly. Extricating itself from the pit with a certain top-heavy clumsiness, it threw back its cowl and stared at the visitors in the cave as if they had recently arrived from another planet. Then it spoke, one word—its name: "Katz."

Johnny remembered the name from the roster at Winthorpe. Herr Doktor Katz was a technician who had worked with both the Webers.

"Drop the spanner, Katz, and raise your hands above your head," said Johnny Scarr.

"What is the meaning of this?" demanded Katz. The spanner fell down through the hatch and clanged on the top plate.

"Do as you're told and you'll find out," said Johnny Scarr.

Katz raised his hands slowly. He was bald and wore glasses with steel rims. Behind their lenses his eyes were brown and beady, as if they had been sewn into his head. When he spoke his jaw moved like the lower jaw of a ventriloquist's dummy, two deep lines curving down from his nose like flanges. To Jock, monitoring the brief exchange between Johnny and Katz, the German seemed like a mechanical man made up of glass and canvas and steel, the lights glinting off his glasses and polished cranium.

Pouring his bulk through the hatch, Jock left Johnny to deal with the German scientist and attacked the locking nuts with the spanner, loosening them completely.

"They're free, Johnny." He climbed back to floor level. His voice sounded muffled beneath the canvas hood and he was sweating with his exertions, handicapped, like a prize race horse, by several pounds of lead.

Katz was sweating too. Johnny Scarr motioned him over to the controls of the portal crane while Jock engaged the hook with the retaining ring on the reactor's top plate.

"Hoist her away," said Jock.

Katz shook his head. He made a clicking noise and compressed his oral flanges as if to speak.

"Do as he says." Johnny Scarr raised the bazooka.

Katz blinked and wiped his forehead with a canvas sleeve. "There is considerable activity in the pile," he said. "It is imperative that you remove the radioactive beryllium source and replace it with the cadmium metal."

"No time for that," said Johnny Scarr. He shouldered the bazooka and made as if to fire it at Katz's head. Terrorized, the German jabbed the button and pulled the goggled cowl over his head again.

The portal crane whined, the chains tautening as the reactor top plate slid from its seating, the glistening black film of the carbon reflector visible beneath the gray lead shielding.

"You have no right, no right at all. Stop, please," Katz pleaded as the top plate disengaged with the reflector, seesawing in midair as the hook and chains took the full weight of the shield and pulled it aloft over the pit, cube on silvery gray cube of U^{235} shimmering beneath the top plate like chandelier ornaments. Jock, bathed in baleful blue radiance, snipped at the cubes, dropping them into the heavy lead-lined portmanteau.

"Please, you have no right."

"Every right in the world," said Johnny Scarr as Jock handed over the portmanteau and dropped softly to the floor of the magnesium alloy vessel, ten feet below the level of the cave floor.

He crouched there for a moment, a ton and a half of uranium suspended precariously above him, the lights glimmering. Jock took off his gloves and wiped his hands on the canvas trousers of his radiation suit. Then he opened his suit and reached inside for the plastic, two pounds of it in the oilskin wrapper that he had removed from his pack with the detonator and fuse. The plastic was soft with body heat, like warm putty. Jock stood up in the pit and leaned over the graphite-filled cavity between the heavy-water container and Bamag-Meguin's aluminum boiler, the reactor's outer wall. The cavity between the inner magnesium alloy vessel and the outer aluminum boiler was about seventeen inches across, with a two-inch lip around the top of the boiler leaving lots of room for the plastic.

The army had taught him to be creative about destroying things. Reaching over into the space between the lip and the concrete retaining wall sunk beneath the cave floor, Jock rolled the plastic into a tube and pressed it into place under the lip so that it could not be seen from above—not that this mattered in the slightest, the explosives man thought, wiring the detonator to the plastic and the electrical fuse to the detonator. He looked at his watch. Johnny Scarr had said ten minutes, but it would take a couple of minutes to bolt down the top plate, which, when locked into position, would greatly magnify the blast damage of the explosion.

For a cross-threaded bolt, a slipped wrench, Jock allowed thirty seconds grace. He set the fuse to trigger the detonator in twelve and a half minutes at 3:20:30, then hauled himself out of the reactor core.

The top plate was already descending.

26: HEAVY WATER

Charlie Page saw that Dorf was safely stowed in the Skorpion with Roberts, Prentice, and the Fräulein, before slipping away to the river. As he crossed the yard of the Swan Inn, he took a little black cylinder not much bigger than a cigarette lighter from his pocket, and pressing the lever that would start the acid eating away at the barrier between the volatile chemicals inside, he dropped the cylinder into the gas tank of the nearest vehicle, the Wehrmacht bus.

Charlie waved at Bony Wilkes, still in the cave mouth. Somewhere a dog howled at the moon. A yellow light clicked on in a nearby hut, then went out again. All was quiet from the flak 88s, and Charlie tried to get a fix on their positions. From the yard he made out a camouflage net strung over an emplacement dug into the river bluff, by the road leading up from the village—the road that led to the jail, the *Schloss*, and the church, the only three buildings at the top of the river bluff.

Charlie wondered what had happened to the patrol up there. Searching the graveyard or saying their prayers, Charlie decided. He listened for the sound of a vehicle. There was none. Why would they march down when they had driven up?

The question worried him as he doubled back along the cliff base to find the underground heavy-water tanks where he knew they would be, within view of the cave mouth. If the Germans found Vorpal's abandoned equipment on the cliff top, then the balloon would be going up any minute—the sooner the worse from Charlie's point of view. It would be going up anyway in ten minutes, and he wanted to keep things orchestrated. Which was why the explosive cylinder in the bus gas tank was timed to coincide with Johnny's thing.

187

The storage tanks looked like tumuli, the burial mounds of chief-tains long dead, with cowls and hatches sticking up from their slopes like some kind of fungi. Charlie found a stopcock and opened a valve. A deep intestinal gurgling came from within, the liquid spewing into the river from the pipe looking to Charlie's jaundiced eye exactly like tap water.

He opened every valve he could find. Suddenly, above the roar of the river, the night was shattered by the Tiger's motor.

Charlie retraced his steps to the yard. An alley flanking the inn took him into a street leading to the village square. There, less than a hundred yards away, rested the Tiger, its long-barreled 88 turning silently back along the street toward the inn.

Dorf's command vehicle would be going nowhere tonight as long as the tank remained in the square.

Charlie retreated. On the other side of the yard, across from the stables, a concrete launch ramp loomed like a truncated pyramid, the cruciform missile silhouetted on the catapult rails under its Schmidt-Argus ramjet, which perched on its tail like the barrel of a blowtorch. It didn't seem possible that such a contraption could fly, let alone take off, Charlie thought, computing the angle between the Tiger and the V-1, and it wouldn't fly very far, either, if the shutter valve at the intake end of the Argus tube were closed.

Charlie looked around him. What the heck, he was Hauptmann Unger of Flakgruppe W8 on a service call. He crossed the yard and scaled the ladder to the catapult. Edging along the skids to the missile, he plucked a stick grenade from his battledress, removed the looped firing pin, and kept his finger on the lever. When he drew level with the Argus tube, he reached up and felt for the venetian-blindlike vanes inside. They were closed and would not open until launching, allow-ing the engine to breathe. Charlie jammed the grenade tightly in front of the vanes, making sure that the pin was still depressed, and wedged it against the inside bore of the tube. With any luck the vanes would dislodge the grenade as they opened after launching and the grenade would explode five seconds into the missile's flight.

He checked the time, and the cave mouth. With five minutes left before the bus was set to blow up, Charlie sauntered over to the back door of the Swan Inn.

Charlie kicked open the door. In the kitchen, protected by a wire grille, open at the top, a Siemens generator sat squarely on the red sandstone flags next to a step-up transformer. Charlie unscrewed the air-filter cover and whisked his finger inside. He grinned. It was clean, the filter was clean enough to strain your tea through. Tenderly, almost regretfully, Charlie replaced the cover and unscrewed the fuel cap. The oil tank was nearly full and he had one black cylinder for this, too, a short fuse, one for the pot.

Inside the Skorpion, Roberts slid back the ejector of Dorf's Walther and watched the 9-mm round pop into the breech. He was sitting in the general's swivel chair before the radio table. Dorf was slumped on the floor against the bulkhead. Katherina and the physicist looked on.

"Well, general?" Roberts leaned forward in the chair, holding the pistol in both hands, trigger finger on the guard, his elbows resting on his knees, the snout of the barrel pressed against Dorf's forehead: "The bomb?"

"Really, there is no need for that." Dorf put his hand up wearily. Roberts moved the barrel. "The bomb is at Hechingen Airfield," continued Dorf. "Hitler has ordered the Luftwaffe to attack London. They will be using a four-engined Focke-Wulf Kondor," the general lied smoothly, glancing at Katherina. "To get anywhere near the bomb or the aircraft, one must have a special pass for the base with a colored *Zusatz* for the hangar. The color for today is green, I think. The Kondor is due to fly at dawn. Stengel has volunteered for the mission, but he won't be going anywhere without the fuses."

"And where are they?" asked Katherina.

"Where they have always been, *Fräulein*. Behind the radio panel." Dorf seemed the very abject picture of defeat. "It is useless to resist further," he said. "The SS are occupying the village. Soon they will be here. Soon."

Roberts reached up behind the panel, where he found a steel box taped to the back of the bulkhead.

It was labeled:

ACHTUNG! Z-GERÄT
RADIOAKTIV SPEZIALMETALL

Roberts placed the Walther on the table to open the box. The fuses were inside, three threaded tubes color-coded red, green, and blue.

A boot scraped outside the Skorpion. Roberts looked up and saw a radiation-suited figure climbing through the double doors at the rear of the APC.

"Johnny?" he said. Not Johnny, he realized too late, reaching for the Walther that Katherina Weber snatched up from the table.

Someone else climbed through the doors: Rudolf Stengel, cradling a machine pistol.

"Why, Katherina," he said, "you've cut your hair."

Johnny Scarr was in no hurry to leave the cave after Jock had bolted down the reactor top plate.

"Tell me about the fighting, Katz," he said.

"Hitler has ordered an attack on London at dawn," the technician told him. "Stengel came from Hechingen for the fuses to the bomb, but Dorf, who did not want this attack to take place, would not surrender them. So the SS have come for their man, and for the fuses to Kindchen Alberich."

Johnny Scarr glanced at Jock. "I want to know about the arrangements for arming the bomb."

The technician swallowed. "Normally it would be armed in flight with the neutron source, bringing the spheres close to criticality. The pressure fuse, set to trigger the TNT detonator at one thousand meters altitude, will automatically complete the job, but in the event of failure there is a contact detonator in the nose."

Johnny Scarr looked at his watch. "Katz," he said, "there are two pounds of plastic explosive in the pile, set to explode in approximately nine minutes."

"I am telling the truth!" Katz rolled his eyes, which were bloodshot and tearful. Under stress the Herr Doktor grew quite eloquent. "I beg you," he pleaded, "think of what you are doing here. The uranium in the pile has an explosive power equivalent to one hundred and forty-eight million tons of TNT. Think of what will happen if it explodes, I beg you."

"It'll explode all right," said Jock. "It's just a question of how."

"A nuclear explosion of that magnitude would wipe out the whole of Swabia," the Herr Doktor squirmed.

"We wouldn't have to worry about Hechingen then," said Johnny Scarr. "Katz, is there any other way of detonating that bomb?"

"No, no. That is, yes." Katz's lower jaw worked up and down and he seemed in an agony of indecision. "It could be done electrically, by removing the entire panel and joining two wires together. A simple matter, but it would need specialized knowledge. Even then, without the neutron source—who knows what would happen?" Katz babbled. "Herr Oberstleutnant, Herr Oberstleutnant, I beg you . . ."

"I can't believe they wouldn't have a back-up source, can you, Jock?" asked Johnny Scarr, with studied calmness.

The big Scotsman shook his head.

"There is none! None at all!" Katz screamed. "Only the one in the pile! You must believe me, this is one of those crazy last-minute Führer orders. The only other source is in the pile!"

In the night a klaxon sounded the alarm.

"Let's get out of here, Jock," said Johnny Scarr.

The klaxon was braying, the guard turning out of the guardhouse, when Charlie Page ran into Jock and Johnny Scarr in the cave mouth with Bony Wilkes. He was surprised to see a fourth, Herr Doktor Katz, bobbing up and down with a reciprocating motion as he turned the wheel that wound the great concrete blast doors shut.

"Run for your lives!" Katz cried.

Johnny checked the time. Three minutes left.

The bus blew, early, or it seemed early to Charlie, but that was always the trouble with those chemical fuses. The first wave of soldiers from the guardhouse was engulfed by flames from the blazing gasoline.

"The Tiger's in the square!" Charlie yelled. "I've fixed one of the doodlebugs but I'll need some help."

The air was filled with screams and exploding small-arms ammunition. At the other side of the yard, a detachment of Waffen SS set up a heavy machine gun and opened fire on an enemy they could not see, an enemy who seemed everywhere invisible.

Charlie Page pulled the pin from a stick grenade. Over his shoulder, as he arched his arm, he glimpsed Roberts fleeing the Skorpion with Mr. Prentice. Johnny Scarr saw them too. There was no sign of the Fräulein.

Bullets cracked and whined off the rocks at the cliff base as Charlie hurled the grenade. The blast threw one of the gunners across the breech, his head half blown away; another twitched feebly at the feet of the tripod, a third tottering into the flames, where he spun around, limned by fire, falling.

Johnny Scarr broke to the left with Bony Wilkes, Jock to the right with Charlie Page. Johnny checked his watch again: two minutes. He should have asked Katz how long the blast doors would hold.

Through the flames he saw Dorf's command vehicle backing up. He could see the whiplash aerials curving down from the roof, and the black, white, and red checkered command flag on the front wing. The divisional markings had been masked, the regimental badge a black shield on gray metal, with the word *Skorpion* stenciled underneath in white Gothic script.

The back of the inn blew out, showering the Skorpion's hull with burning timbers. Johnny Scarr watched the heavy armored vehicle slew around, taking what was left of the Swan's kitchen with it. He remembered how, in the desert, they would soak the sand around a scorpion with petrol, light it, and watch the crazed beast sting itself to death in the middle of a ring of fire. Now, the Skorpion was looking for a way out. It swung in a wide arc, nudging the skeleton of the burning bus and dislocating its fiery bones in a shower of incandescent steel. Johnny Scarr heard the gears crash, the powerful Daimler-Benz motor revving, then whining in first gear, as the Skorpion bounced over the burning timbers.

Slit-eyed, lumbering across the yard like some prehistoric reptile, it pulverized the smoldering remains of the Wehrmacht bus in its path.

Only then did Johnny Scarr realize that the lights had gone out in the yard of the Swan Inn.

Bony Wilkes yelled something in his ear about Prentice, and through the clearing smoke Johnny saw Roberts dragging the physicist along the base of the cliff toward them.

He saw something else, too: the Skorpion bearing down on a German officer, who threw up his hands and disappeared beneath the APC's wheels.

On his right hand he had worn a shiny black glove.

"Launch the bluidy thing yourself!" the big Scotsman yelled at Charlie Page, divesting himself of his radiation suit and lead shielding as he blundered past the lanyard that activated the steam-powered catapult. Jock was still carrying the portmanteau when he disappeared from Charlie's view, running at full tilt around the corner of the *Stofflager*, the fuel store behind the ramp on the outside bend of the river.

Charlie tugged experimentally at the lanyard. Nothing happened. "Jesus Christ," he muttered and followed Jock around the corner.

The demolitions man had entered the antimagnetic *R-Haus*, the magazine for the entire battery, which was built at ninety degrees to the *Stofflager*, the two buildings forming a tee. Inside, Jock counted twenty alloy nose caps arrayed on the magazine rack like the Norse helmets. The nose caps contained the V-1's compass and air log, which controlled the distance flown by the missile and would be set, before launching, on target identification. The warhead was located aft of the nose cap, in the midsection of the missile forward of the fuel tank and wing chords.

Wachtel's people had left a fully assembled missile on a trolley inside the double doors of the *R-Haus*. The missile on the trolley was armed. Jock unscrewed the fuse and replaced it with a time-set chemical detonator of the type that Charlie Page had used on the generator in the Swan Inn. Then he left by the back stairs, which brought him out by the side wall of the *Stofflager*, immediately opposite the two adjacent doors separated by a blast wall.

"Jock, Jock, where are you, Jock?" Charlie Page entered through the front doors of the *R-Haus* just as the big Scotsman left by the back stairs.

Every job was a challenge, and the *Stofflager* was no exception. There were no communicating doors between the compartments. Each compartment, however, had its own door, which opened on an antechamber with a valve-and-hose coupling through to the fuel chamber inside. To fuel the catapult, the hoses would have to be connected separately, one to the *T-Stoff*, or hydrogen peroxide coupling, another to the *Z-Stoff* or sodium permanganate coupling, in the respective antechambers of the *Stofflager*. The system was designed to prevent premature mixing of the fuels before launch, and was virtually foolproof.

At Winthorpe, Jock had worked out a simple system of adding the potassium permanganate, the oxidant, to the highly corrosive hydrogen peroxide, a system that would build up an explosive head of steam in the *Stofflager*. He would simply mate the two valves with one hose, then open them separately. Evidently the designers of the *Stofflager* had not foreseen such criminal malice.

Jock had worked this out in the relative peace and seclusion of the English countryside. Now, chaos reigned with confusion in Haigerloch. Firefighting teams had turned out and were running hoses hither and thither, and a violent earthquakelike trembling had set in from the cliff, causing the ground to heave. Jock, like Johnny Scarr, wondered about the blast doors on the cave as he dragged a hose from one antechamber to the next. He worked on the couplings first, making sure they were locked securely before he spun the valves, darting from one door to the next, then charging around the side of the *Stofflager* where he saw steam hissing from the catapult under the missile and Charlie Page, looking a little lost, emerge from the double doors of the *R-Haus*.

The steam suddenly boiled from the catapult. Slowly, as if propelled by an invisible hand, the missile rose from the skids. Jock threw himself to the ground, rolling over and over to escape the all-encompassing steam.

Watched by an open-mouthed Charlie Page, the flying bomb glided silently aloft, and, dipping its nose at the *Brennstoffpunkt*, where the motor should have cut in, it fluttered, wobbled, and stalled, dropping in a ballistic arc over the center of Haigerloch.

The shockwave of the detonation pulsed across the village, a warm wind blowing, bringing in its wake the vinegary reek of vaporized steel as the one-ton amatol warhead blossomed above the turret of the Tiger tank, which was momently illuminated in the orange glow before it disintegrated.

One for Flakgruppe Wachtel, thought Charlie, looking up to see a strange being, wreathed in steam like a refugee from a sauna, running toward him. It was Jock, yelling something about the *R-Haus*.

The *Stofflager* blew first, bowling both men over, a strange, seething explosion unlike any that Jock had witnessed before, the reinforced concrete walls of the *Stofflager* bulging and buckling so that he could see the pale violet flashes reflected from the base of the clouds that boiled within.

Charlie Page picked himself up and made a dash for the yard of the Swan Inn. He saw the Skorpion bearing down on him like a juggernaut threatening to crush him, as it had Dorf, under its bloated wheels. Charlie bared his teeth and danced over the dead Germans around the machine gun. The one draped over the breech he picked up by the scruff of the neck and dropped him with a disdainful, almost fastidious attitude, spinning the machine gun around and opening fire on the Skorpion, which thundered past, bullet after bullet splattering harmlessly along its armored flanks.

He threw himself to one side as the Skorpion careened by, squashing the machine gun and tripod like a stick insect. The last he saw of it, Dorf's command vehicle was heading toward the village square and the wreck of the Tiger tank.

The ground was hot with smoking metal. Charlie looked up and saw Johnny Scarr and Bony Wilkes sprinting away from the cliff mouth. Part of the cliff had detached itself from the bluff. It came away like a fragment of a rotten tooth, and, squirting jets of flame and viscid black smoke, slid toward the river, filling the air with an ominous gurgling.

Charlie Page picked himself up again. On his hands and knees this time, he heard a terrible, forlorn cry—*"Herr Generaloberst! Herr Generaloberst!"*—followed by a single pistol shot.

It was Lang, who had just stumbled across the hideously mangled body of his commanding officer. The adjutant found it hard to believe that Dorf was still breathing, but he was. Lang knelt down and unbuttoned the general's blood-sodden tunic. Dorf's ribs stuck through his chest like bits of broken basketry, his lungs foaming and ballooning underneath. Lang saw other organs too. He unholstered his pistol and dispatched Dorf with a shot to the head, one short, sharp crack reverberating off the cliff and clattering over the rooftops, sounding, to Lang's grief-disordered mind, like the final chord of a vast and cataclysmic symphony.

The Hauptmann had come down from the churchyard to raise the alarm after his patrol had discovered the equipment that the enemy had left at the edge of the cliff. Now, as he knelt over the body of his commanding officer, Lang was utterly unable to understand the nature of the catastrophe, man-made or otherwise, that was overtaking Haigerloch.

A creeping wave extended across the yard of the Swan Inn, the ground undulating toward him like a serpent. Lang was momentarily blinded when the kerosene dump went up, apparently touched off by the *Stofflager*. A searing white sheet leaping up the cliff face, it seemed to turn everything inside out, so that Lang fancied he was looking at a photographic negative.

The Hauptmann watched, paralyzed with shock, as a giant fragment from one of the concrete blast doors fluttered overhead like a leaf, followed by the reactor's top plate, which cartwheeled toward him. He saw it tumble nearby like a child's spinning top, its inertial velocity dwindling. Sundry pieces of lab equipment—vomited forth from the cave—dropped around it. Violet and yellow flames flickered along the cliff face, and a stupendous, deafening drumfire rolled from the *R-Haus. Terrorbomber,* Lang thought, his consciousness ebbing and flowing. He lay on his side, now, contracting into a fetal crouch, his fists clenched. He knew that he should get up and run—but where to?

Everything was silent, as in a movie without a soundtrack. Lang, when he caught his breath, choked on the foul black smoke that blotted out the moon and stars.

He knew that it was carbon from the pile's moderator, carbon burning. Air, he had to get air . . .

He looked up again, and the sky seemed to be falling on the village, a long, slow fall, bringing eternity in its wake.

Lang closed his eyes and put up a hand to parry the blow, but it was useless, a futile gesture in the face of such immensity.

"Mother," he said.

27: STENGEL AND KATHERINA

Through the slits in the armored visor, Katherina saw the English *Affenmensch*, Charlie Page, training the heavy machine gun on the Skorpion. She steered toward him unflinchingly, though it took more strength than she knew to lug the wheel around.

"What was that?" She felt something thunk against the offside hull.

"Nothing, a rock, that's all," Stengel, seated on the other side, said as the Skorpion lurched on. Katherina did not look back and that was all right by him.

Stengel admired the way she handled the vehicle, her composure unshaken by the searing blast from the V-1, though the Standartenführer had a nasty moment when the APC keeled over with a terrible whining from the differential, three of the Skorpion's six wheels spinning on the lip of the smoking crater that marked the Tiger's demise.

Katherina negotiated this crisis, as she had all others, with the same purposeful efficiency that had initially attracted Stengel. Hugo Weber had been telling the truth when he had said to Carlo Peat that Katherina was Stengel's hobby. She represented a unique departure from his normal mode of vicarious manipulation, the remote control of others through intermediaries. At Haigerloch, in the days before the Webers' "defection," he made a deliberate pitch for her. It had not been easy, but they had become lovers—an affair conducted with characteristic, if soulless, efficiency by both parties.

The Webers and Generaloberst Dorf had been on the fringes of the anti-Hitler plot with Gisevius, the priest at Haigerloch and a cousin of one of the conspirators, Hans Bernd Gisevius, vice-consul at the

199

German Legation in Bern. Both the diplomat and the man of God had survived the aftermath of the assassination attempt, and their survival was not accidental.

Clinging to the belief that Hitler's removal would turn the Allies aside from their policy of unconditional surrender, the conspirators had seen their hopes dashed not merely by the failure of the *Attentat* but also by the Allies' refusal to parley. Projekt Alberich had revived their hopes of a separate, negotiated peace on the western front, and Stengel had done everything within his power to nourish this revival.

It was Stengel who had used Gisevius in Bern as a conduit to smuggle documents out of the Reich (the blueprints that Dorf had turned over to Balthazar in Lugano), and it was Stengel who, in his former capacity as head of the Reich's Frontier Service and in his present occupation as Katherina's lover, had arranged the Webers' defection. And he had done this with the full knowledge of the Führer, Adolf Hitler, and the Reichsführer, Heinrich Himmler. This time the Allies must listen, and this time take heed. A separate peace, or annihilation!

Because he was using Katherina, Stengel had assumed, correctly, that she was using him. There had to be a safeguard, and there was. Her mother.

Katherina stopped the Skorpion a couple of kilometers past the village, before the junction with the Hechingen-Rottweil road.

"There's a roadblock ahead," she said.

"Not any more," said Stengel. "There are no roadblocks now."

Katherina asked if he had been surprised to see her. He shook his head. "Not when we found these damned things," he said, struggling out of the radiation suit. "There was something that crazy priest said—'After the seven comes the eighth'—some sort of apocalyptic nonsense. I remembered that tunnel and thought you must have led them to it. If only I could have been there sooner!"

"Gisevius must have seen us," she said.

"He saw you all right. I knew from last summer, when we blocked up the tunnel after the *Attentat*, that there was usually some sort of sense to his ravings. It was Gisevius who first introduced me to the angel Rahab—in connection with the Jews."

"The Jews?"

"Yes, concerning the visitations that the heavenly Führer, the Lord their God, meted out to them in biblical times. This angel was the scourge of the Jews, Katherina. The name occurs in a different context, too—Rahab, the harlot of Jericho, David's grandmother who hid the spies of Joshua in the city. This Rahab was the great-grandmother of all quislings. I was sure that when Gisevius started babbling about the seven that he must have seen you with Scarr's people. As sly as a fox that Gisevius, like his cousin. We surrounded the church, but you'd gone. Then we found the equipment. I put on the radiation suit because I thought I could surprise the raiders in the cave. Then I remembered Lang had said Dorf wanted to see me, and I found you, Katherina." In his cadaverish way Stengel smiled.

"I overheard the conversation with Dorf, by the way," the Standartenführer continued. "He lied about the bomber. It's a Short Stirling not a Kondor, and it's specially equipped to penetrate radar defenses. Dorf didn't mention that. I suppose that when it came down to it he wanted to give us a sporting chance. The English fools will have radioed London by now and they'll be looking for the wrong aircraft."

"I should have known that was why you didn't kill the English-men," said Katherina.

"Well, it wasn't sentiment," Stengel acknowledged with another smile. "I knew they would never come, once they'd flushed out Oskar, unless something changed their minds. It had to be the tunnel. Probably, they would change the time of their arrival, then send the signal announcing their arrival as planned, thinking they were com-ing in the back way. They did everything I would have done, and so did you, Katherina, so did you. Unfortunately, I was unavoidably detained. Otherwise, I couldn't have planned it better myself, even if I'd been in charge over there, doing their planning for them."

"Which you were, Rudolf."

He gave her a quizzical look, and then saw what she meant.

"*Jawohl*, Katherina," he said. "You did very well."

"It was the documents that convinced them. The documents were *prima*, Rudolf."

"It was nothing," said Stengel, modestly. "It's my profession, after all."

"Disinformation maybe, but not nuclear science. The man from Tube Alloys told Prentice it was like looking in a mirror—a magic mirror that foretold the future. He said we were three to four months ahead of them. There was a real change after the meeting with Dorf in Lugano. To begin with, they thought my father was crazy—as you said they would. He tried to kill himself by slashing his wrists, and the English put him in the madhouse when they heard about the angel. But the man called Carlo never believed this story, even when told about the rabbi. This man was very difficult. It was hard to convince him that day follows night and night day. But everything changed once they had the documents from Switzerland. Then they were sure that my father was a plant designed to convince them there was no research effort, no reactor, and no bomb. Then, last Friday, my father hanged himself." Katherina paused.

"What? Hugo? Was there an autopsy?"

"I was not informed of one," said Katherina, surprised. "My father hanged himself with lengths of sheet cut up and made into a rope. The cause of death would have seemed obvious. Carlo Peat, you see, had told my father they were moving me to London."

"Ach! Then he had good cause to kill himself—from their point of view, I mean," said Rudolf Stengel. "He finally met the angel, Katherina. This has set the seal upon the entire operation."

The extent of Stengel's manipulation dawned on her gradually. In a way she found it awesome. This man's whole life, his entire being, consisted of bending others to his will—as often as not while they were unaware of it.

Even disease was something to be manipulated. Hugo Weber had been suffering from an incurable cancer of the blood, which explained Stengel's anxiety about an autopsy.

"The English will have radioed London by now," he said. "It still may not be too late for them to come to their senses. They must know

202

they will have to fight the Russians sooner or later, and they might as well do it with our help as without it. The fuses, Katherina. Von Wenden is a professional. He would not want to fly without them."

She handed them over and, as she did so, kissed him lightly on the cheek. They embraced, a mutually cold and calculating embrace. Both knew they were no longer lovers. Combatants, yes. Enemies in an undeclared war, a war as old as humankind. Perhaps they had known it all along, Katherina reflected, in which case they probably deserved each other. For even as their affair had been loveless, a practical matter, their enmity would likewise be without hatred.

She had no illusions. It was their hypocrisy that made them human, hypocrisy lending each the semblance of human feelings. Love, hatred, these were expensive emotions she could not afford—not, at least, while he continued to hold her mother at the *Institut für Neurochirurgie*, Stuttgart.

Or was this a rationalization too?

She did not hate Stengel; she knew him too well. Yet even Katherina had no idea why he had volunteered for the mission.

To ask would be to invite some zealous profession of fanatical zeal. Nor did she want to ask—yet—after her mother, for to do so would be to remind him of the power he held over her.

She did not understand that this power came from another source, fascination; the hypnotic fascination of hen for hawk, mouse for snake.

But the Standartenführer knew it; as he knew, also, that it is the greatest of illusions to pretend that one is free of illusions.

"Waldmann will be waiting," he said.

The Sturmbannführer was in the control tower at Hechingen, with Oberst Viktor von Wenden and his navigator-bombardier, whom von Wenden introduced as Fliegerhauptmann Schneider. Sallow and dark, contrasting with the blond lynx, he gave a Nazi salute.

Both men wore flying suits.

From the observation deck it was possible to see Hiagerloch burning. Intermittent flashes lit the horizon, followed by detonations that rattled the windows and shook the floors. When he saw Katherina

Weber with Stengel, a spasm of rage contorted Waldmann's florid features, his porcine little eyes opening by several stops.

"You!" he cried, leveling a pudgy finger at her. "You're the one!"

"What are you talking about?" She turned on him, icily.

"Your English friends, Dorf, the security arrangements. Look what has happened! People here without watermarked passes, with no passes at all!"

The Sturmbannführer was scarcely coherent, and Stengel wondered if he was drunk. It was best to ignore him, Stengel thought.

He gave the fuses to von Wenden. "We shall have to run some preflight tests on them," the pilot said.

"Of course," Stengel acknowledged.

Von Wenden glanced at his watch. "We plan on taking off at six-fifteen, in a little less than two hours. The aircraft is presently being armed, and has then to be fueled. Perhaps you would care to see? Then you could suit up and draw a parachute from the stores."

Stengel nodded. "The Fräulein also," he said. "She will be accompanying us."

Katherina started to protest, but he silenced her with a look.

The phone rang. It was Oberführer Schramm with the news that he was pulling out of Haigerloch. The position was no longer tenable.

Stengel asked whether there was any sign of the English parachutists.

"None," the Oberführer replied. "My forces will pull back to a radius of two kilometers around the village. No one will get through, if anyone can get out. The place is an inferno."

Katherina said: "They left their stores at the castle."

It didn't make any difference. The line had gone dead. Stengel said: "Schramm will take care of that. Do not worry. Oberst, Fliegerhauptmann, Fräulein—Kindchen Alberich awaits us."

The hangar doors were open, fore and aft, the Stirling's bulbous nose turret reflecting the lights. Katherina gasped when she saw the bomb. The giant yellow egg with the scarred navel already nestled in its loading trailer. Mechanics, completing the final preflight service, scrambled down from the Stirling's engines and dragged the tubular gantries away from the nacelles.

Katherina watched as the great plane was ingloriously hauled tail-first from the hangar to the brilliantly lit loading pit, Kindchen Alberich following, the loading crew padding behind at a safe distance. She watched as the bomb was slid from trailer to cradle, the cradle offering Kindchen Alberich up on hydraulic arms, the bomb bay accepting this offering, the bomb doors closing. She watched all this on the windswept tarmac, shivering, her heart beating proudly, yet her head could not believe what her heart was feeling, nor could she, Hugo Weber's daughter, believe what she was seeing.

It was an hour before she could tear Stengel away from the assiduously stupid Waldmann. They had drawn their flying gear from the stores and walked back across the tarmac toward the control tower, the bomber, still floodlit, in the background, a fuel truck topping up its wing tanks.

"Rudolf," she said, "why?"

"Only you, my dear, possess the technical knowledge to make the thing work."

He was smiling.

"You're crazy," she said, wondering.

"Katherina, the war is practically over. This is Germany's last chance. I've left instructions that your mother is not to be harmed. She will be taken care of until—until this thing is finished one way or the other. The hospital is probably the safest place for her anyway. Of course, if you do not want to come with me, I could have her released."

She saw him as no longer threatening. In some way she could not understand, she saw that Stengel was offering her her freedom; and she saw, also, that this man, whom she thought she knew so well, she did not know at all.

Perhaps it was death, this freedom; mutual oblivion. Or perhaps it was only another illusion. But whatever her fate, she saw now that she would share it.

"We'll be shot down," she said, and was in his arms again and weeping, for she knew that, whatever his feelings for her, she loved this man.

"Nobody will shoot us down," he said, and meant it. And then with a sigh he saw that, as usual, she had misunderstood him.

28: SCARR'S PEOPLE

Gisevius was tormented by fire and brimstone. The smoke rose from the crypt, driving him out of his church, which was shaken even to the foundations. Verily, the Lord had poured out His wrath on Babylon.

In despair the priest rushed to the edge of the cliff. At the precipice he recoiled, a hot blast catching him in the face. Gisevius thought of Yahweh, God of the Jews, the creator and destroyer of worlds on worlds. Surely he was witnessing His final solution to the problem of the human race.

Gisevius made himself ready for the end. He threw up his hands and was about to jump when an iron grip seized him around the waist and bore him to the ground.

He screamed, until a hand was clamped over his mouth. Gisevius saw the devil grinning down at him, an ape man in Luftwaffe blue, his face smoke blackened, the whites of his eyes staring.

The hand was lifted, the nightmare passed. Gisevius saw that the devil was human, one of the paratroopers he had seen drop from the sky, the first to enter the crypt.

He owed this man more than his life. Charlie Page had rescued Gisevius from the greatest of sins, and the priest did not know how to repay him.

Johnny Scarr had watched Charlie Page swarm over the top of the fractured cliff. In the village the fires spread from rooftop to rooftop, flames and sparks boiling up into the night. Screams and shouts filled the air, and, from far off down the Hechingen road, Johnny heard the

207

squawking clank of caterpillar treads. He went looking for the rest of his men.

Johnny found Prentice cowering at the foot of the cliff with Roberts, who had armed himself with a tommy gun from a dead SS man. They were joined by Jock and Bony Wilkes, lugging his radio across the yard. Johnny told his men that Charlie had found a way up the cliff: "He said he was looking for a place where the waters weren't so heavy."

"Bath, maybe," Jock said.

"Leamington Spa," said Bony, fruitily.

"So there was Stengel and that bitch holding the gun on me." Roberts was explaining what had happened in the APC. "'Give me the fuses,' she said. 'You'd better do as she says,' that bastard said. 'She doesn't like to be crossed.' I had no fucking choice, Johnny. They didn't seem to be interested in me at all. Or Mr. Prentice. Only the fuses. When the alarm went off, I jumped through the side door. Prentice came after me. I didn't see what happened to Dorf."

"The Skorpion ran over him," said Johnny Scarr.

"Shit," Roberts said. "That bitch would have killed us all, you know."

Jock asked what had happened to Katz.

"He jumped in the river," Johnny Scarr said laconically. "You're right, Ian," he turned to Roberts. "She would have killed us all. Jock. You did a good job here." Too good, Johnny thought. "Bony, you'd better raise London. Give 'em the gen on the bird. Tell 'em we'll take it out before dawn." Nobody asked how, and that was fine with Johnny Scarr, because he hadn't the faintest idea himself. Yet.

He looked up at the fissure in the rock, a natural chimney that Charlie had taken to the top. The cliff was overhung with alder bushes that looked like defensive works, machicolations to pour down boiling lead on the enemy below. It was grim, dark, and foreboding, and it was liable to collapse completely at any moment.

Johnny Scarr asked Prentice if he thought he could climb the cliff.

Prentice had no choice, really. Johnny had orders to shoot him if necessary to prevent his falling into enemy hands.

"Use your own discretion," Carlo had said, just like that.

Johnny wondered if the physicist knew. Probably. Johnny couldn't allow himself to agonize over it, though; he was too preoccupied by what might happen if Prentice did make it up the cliff. The physicist would slow them down as he had before, and Johnny couldn't afford to let that happen again.

It was a hell of a situation. He couldn't leave Prentice behind and didn't want him along. He was damned if he did and damned if he didn't; yet he had no choice. None of them did.

It had always been that way.

Bony Wilkes finished transmitting. He lit a cigarette and offered the tin to Jock. The big Scotsman accepted, cupping his hands around Bony's lighter, which was made from an old .303 cartridge. The radio crackled. A stream of Morse bled across the air at signal strength five, followed by some cross talk from the commanders of the panzers surrounding the village.

Bony fiddled with the dial and clamped a set of headphones over his ears. "There's a very weak acknowledgment from London," he said.

"Nothing else?" asked Johnny.

"Not yet . . . wait. The reception's no good. It's that frigging cliff, see? Now I've got them." Bony listened. "They say O . . . U . . . T . . . G . . . R . . . A . . . B . . . E . . ." Bony spelled out the signal: "AND THE MOME RATHS OUTGRABE."

It was the order to break off and head for the Swiss border.

Johnny Scarr said: "Your transmission must have been garbled. Send again."

Bony did as he was told. "This time there's nothing," he reported.

"They can't be reading us right," Johnny said. "We'll try again when we get to the top of the cliff."

Charlie Page landed in a shower of scree. Johnny Scarr asked what had kept him.

"Let me get my breath first." He was breathing hard. "Listen, there's a crazy old gentleman up there who thinks we're angels. A silly old bugger with hands like roots and a nose like an old potato. He says he'll look after Prentice, says he can hide him."

"Where?"

"In the parsonage. And don't ask me for how long. For the bloody duration, for all I care. It won't be long now anyway. Listen, Johnny. It's four miles back to the castle, then half a mile along the road to the airfield. There are frigging troops all over the map and more armor too. If we stay here for much longer we won't have a pot to piss in. If we take him with us"—Charlie Page jerked a thumb at the physicist— "same thing. He's a dead liability, Captain Scarr, Johnny, sir."

"Okay, Charlie." Johnny faced his men. "This time Captain Page will lead the climb," he said.

"Where's the rope, Johnny?" asked Charlie Page.

Johnny had stowed it at the cliff base. He looked around. The cliff had changed shape following the explosion in the cave.

"We'll go without the rope," he said.

"With Mr. Prentice following." The words threaded through the physicist's mind like a looped segment of tape replaying itself over and over again. And Mr. Prentice was following, and making a damn good job of it, too.

"Almost there," Charlie shouted down.

The physicist, looking up, watched as Charlie traversed a ledge to the left. Charlie was a good natural climber, the ape, but why this traverse to the left when it was his left ankle he had damaged, why this sinister twist to the universe tonight? Chance, the physicist supposed, a throw of the cosmic dice, for—Einstein to the contrary—God was the cosmic dicer gaming with his creatures, whole species wagered at a throw, lost.

The physicist thought of the questions he should have asked the Fräulein. How had they separated the plutonium from the spent reactor fuel? How had they prevented radioactive "poisoning" of the pile by fission fragments from the exploded nuclei? What was the cross section of the bomb? Would it reach criticality with fast neutrons alone? Had they used a tamper? If so, what was the material? These were questions the physicist had not asked the Fräulein. She had lied to him, all the time she had lied to him. "Come on, you can do it, you can do it!" the ape was shouting. Prentice saw him wedged in a

210

chimney through the overhang, but he might as well have been galaxies away.

Prentice saw him, the ape of God. He had shifted around in the chimney, wedging himself there with his knees and thighs, and was swinging his right arm down at the physicist. "Come on, come on."

The arm swinging like a pendulum, that great prehensile hand at its end. "Just this ledge now," the ape was saying. "You can do it. Just this ledge now . . ."

The physicist swung his injured foot out across to the ledge, his hand grasping for that other, the hand of rescue dislodging the spectacles which had become such an integral part, along with the pain, of his alien self, Herr Berger from Degussa.

The ape saw them fall, a stray photon from a star reflected in their blank lenses. Herr Berger's spectacles tinkled on the rocks far, far below, the still small sound of their breakage surpassing any explosion the ape had heard that night.

The physicist scarcely heard them. Yes, yes, Mr. Prentice was following. If only he could understand why his foot was taking so long to reach the ledge, an eternity, for it seemed that way to him. There was no sensation and certainly no pain where only moments before every fiber had been awash with vibrant corpuscles of pain. No more. There was only this stasis, this endless descent as if the laws of gravity were in temporary abeyance, the physicist enjoying the brief sensation of free-fall as he came away from the ledge, the cliff face, wrenched away from him, slipping past, accelerating.

In the universe of infinite possibilities, this was one for Richard Prentice—that he asked the right question too late. For another question did occur to him then, only there was no one to answer it, no one except himself, and the time left to him now was of distinctly finite, Newtonian duration. Why, with a ton and a half of U^{235} cubed like dice, U^{235} that would fission spontaneously at the passing caress of a stray neutron—why go to all that trouble of using plutonium in the bomb?

Why? This was the question that Richard Prentice asked as, in gravity's thrall, he hurtled headlong to the rocks far, far below—another cast of the cosmic dicer.

It happened in a glint, faster than the time taken to move the eyes, faster than the hand could react.

"Damn," Charlie Page said.

Gisevius was waiting for him. "Where is the man I was to help?"

"At the bottom of the cliff."

"Then I will go to him."

"He may not know you."

"Dead?"

Charlie looked down at his boots in wordless eloquence. The priest crossed himself, his gnarled hands worrying at the beads of his rosary, his eyes so full of compassion that Charlie was afraid for this man.

Johnny Scarr appeared with the news that Bony had radioed London again—with the same result. No answer.

"Before, they said to break off and head for the border." In front of the priest, he spoke in English. "I don't understand it. Either they didn't understand our signal or they don't think it's us."

"It's those crazy bastards," Charlie said. "They're the ones who don't understand. What are you going to do?"

"Call them again from Hechingen," said Johnny.

"What about him?" Charlie glanced at the priest.

"He stays here," Johnny said.

The priest had been the cause of the row between Johnny Scarr and Innis. "We should shoot him," the Scotsman had maintained. "If we can't take him along, we should shoot him. He knows where we're going, how many of us there are, and he can describe us. We didna ought to leave him here alive."

Scarr shook his head. "He's a civilian."

"How do you know that, sir?"

"Damn it man, he's a priest."

"An enemy priest, sir."

"The hell with that. I'm not in the business of gunning down clergymen," Johnny Scarr had said, thinking of Bony Wilkes's tale of the cook and the cigarette tin. There was something slightly ridiculous in his defense of the priest, Johnny thought. How like the British army: to shoot a cook and save a priest. Another army with a greater experience of cooks and priests, perhaps the French, would have got its priorities in better order.

And now Ian Roberts was wondering who had been in the right. Morally, he had no doubt that Innis was wrong. But militarily? Militarily, Innis had a point.

Roberts voiced some of these thoughts to the Scotsman trudging at his side. "We took nothing from that priest, Jock, except directions," he said.

Savage indignation flared in the stony heart of Roger Innis. As if there weren't enough grief in the world without wanting a share of someone else's. Clergymen were moral Draculas; bloodless, they sucked your blood while at the same time lamenting the base facts of human existence. They could be as sorry and as unhappy about it as they damn well pleased, but that was what kept them in business. Misery gave them their mileage.

"Aye, what did you expect? His blessing?" the big Scotsman said. "I saw them before Alamein, the rented hypocrites. Ask John Scarr if his friend Yuill died full of the consolations of religion." Jock spat. "I tell you, Christianity is a vampire's metaphysics. No one would've been any wiser if we'd have pushed that Gisevius over the cliff, which is where he was going before Charlie Page pulled him back."

"Still, I suppose Johnny was right, though. I mean he was a priest after all, Jock. A man of God."

"A German man, a German God," Innis said, trudging along in dour uncomplicated silence.

"You'd have thought our Panzer friends would have secured the castle, picked it clean," Charlie Page said to Johnny Scarr, who was still carrying the bazooka and the ammo bag.

"I wouldn't doubt it."

"It doesn't seem to worry you."

"Lots of things do. Not that. What's the matter, Charlie? Something on your mind?"

"You could have got that bloody APC," Charlie Page said. "I was waiting for you to fire that bloody bazooka, you know."

"Waste of a round, Charlie."

213

"But they had the fuses, didn't they?"

"You heard what Katz said. Anyway, I didn't believe Dorf. Charlie, I've got two rounds in this ammo bag, and I'm saving them for the plane. Okay?"

"If you say so, Johnny."

"What else is bothering you?"

"I was thinking about Prentice. I was thinking maybe it was all for the best that he had to fall off that bleeding cliff. We might have had to put him out of his misery otherwise."

"Because of his ankle?"

"Because of what he had up here." Charlie Page tapped his head. "That's what I was thinking. I was wondering whether you had orders to shoot him. John probably wouldn't tell me, I said to myself. Then I got to thinking about it some more. If John has orders to shoot the boffin, and something happens to John, who's next in line to do the shooting? Me, that's who, and nobody's told me any such thing. So then I thought maybe he wasn't worth shooting, maybe he didn't know enough, maybe he's just as daft as the rest of us, or was. Maybe he was the wrong boffin for the job. Did you have orders to shoot him?"

"Yes."

"Oh."

"Happy now?"

"No. I'm worried about London. Why don't they reply to our signals?"

"Good God, Charlie, how the hell should I know?" Johnny Scarr remembered once reading in a military training manual that an officer must maintain at all times that he has access to superior levels of command, and is therefore familiar with the "overall situation." Something like that. Laughable, really. Johnny Scarr didn't know what the overall situation was, or even if there still was one. "Maybe the war ended and they forgot to tell us, Charlie," he said.

"Yeah, that would make sense," said Charlie. "What's eating Jock, do you know?"

"It's something he's got about clergymen. He says he was sickened the way Monty flew in all the holy rollers before El Alamein. Jock reckons Monty planned it down to the last dog collar, the last denomination. You know what Monty's planning is like. Jock says he was pissed off by the sight of all those clerical gentlemen ministering to the faithful. He says it turned his stomach."

"That's a lot of holy water under the bridge, Johnny."

"Heavy water, Charles."

The ape grinned. "What happens at Hechingen?" he asked.

"That's the kind of question I like to hear," said Johnny Scarr.

Bony Wilkes stayed out of the way while Jock was urging Johnny Scarr to kill the priest. Bony feared he might be given the job himself, and was glad he'd told Johnny Scarr about the cook. Johnny couldn't very well expect him to kill a priest in cold blood if he hadn't been able to do the same for a cook, though the cook had made things easier for him in the end. But he couldn't expect the priest to do that, and so he had stayed out of the way.

Now he had fallen to the back of the column, and Johnny Scarr had come along to see if he was all right.

"Yes, sir." Bony smartened up.

"It's uphill all the way and it'll be the same coming back," Johnny said.

Bony tucked his thumbs under the straps of his pack. He stumbled.

"Do you want one of us to carry that thing for a while?" asked Johnny. Much use it was, he thought.

"No, sir. I wasn't looking where I was going. I hauled it up and down the cliff. So it can stay with me this much more. It's not far now, is it?"

"Not much further now, no."

Bony liked Johnny Scarr and was glad he hadn't ordered the priest shot. He took this as a good omen. "Sir?"

"What is it, Bony?"

"Oh, nothing," Bony Wilkes said.

"All right, Bony," Johnny Scarr said, but it wasn't all right. He knew what was on Bony's mind, and everyone else's. It wasn't an easy one to ask, still harder to answer.

What if we fail?

Somehow the question became a much more personal one. How am I going to die? And the answer to that question, thought Johnny

215

Scarr, did not matter very much. For if Vorpal failed, the bomb would destroy London and many millions would die. What were five or six lives added to the price of this failure?

Johnny Scarr looked ahead. In the distance he saw the castle. It rose against the fading stars like a gray hand beckoning, yet raised also in warning and admonition.

They had reached the road.

Charlie Page crawled back through the undergrowth and dashed across the road near the burned-out hulk of the Mark IV. "SS," he reported. "A whole company bivouacked around the castle." He'd seen them sprawling against the stone wall where, five and a half hours ago, the Fräulein had bandaged Prentice's ankle. The Germans were breakfasting, which had incensed Charlie, who could smell sausage frying and coffee perking in the pot. "Those bastards, what right do they have to eat?" he said, holding up a canister. "I found this. It's full of flares and a Very pistol."

Johnny Scarr took stock. They had water, picked up at the river, Benzedrine pills, K-rations, wire cutters, their side arms, a machine pistol, one submachine gun, grenades, bayonets, a bazooka, and two rocket grenades. And now Charlie had turned up the flare gun, a useful tool—and potentially deadly.

Johnny wondered if he were grasping at straws.

Charlie rolled over and stretched himself on the grass, yawning. "Why don't we give up and go 'ome?" he said. The ape was nearly beat, he had to be to say something like that.

Ian Roberts said: "This time we don't have any rubber tanks, Johnny."

"True," Johnny acknowledged. He dug both hands into his tunic pockets and pulled out . . . firecrackers.

"Jesus Christ!" the ape exclaimed. "Go 'ome, Johnny! These aren't the bloody Wops."

Johnny Scarr shook his head: "Vorpal is going in, Charlie. The RAF will be making a low-level attack on Hechingen Airfield at dawn. Bony, signal London. And don't wait for a reply this time."

29: VORPAL GOES IN

The enamel desk lamp drooping over Scarr's first signal looked like an alien flower on its stalk. A thermos of black coffee, unopened, stood next to it on the desk. Carlo had decided to wait out the night alone in Balthazar's office so he could be close to the teletype room.

At 3:00 A.M. the telephone jangled. It was Lucas requesting target confirmation for his boys, who would be taking off from an airfield in France.

"We're calling off the raid," Carlo told him, causing a startled exclamation at the other end. "I thought you'd be the last to know," he added bitterly, and slammed down the phone. Oh, hell, I shouldn't have done that, Carlo thought, and wondered why he had. He picked up the receiver again and asked for a reconnection with Lucas at the Air Ministry. "We were cut off," he lied.

"Sorry about that," Carlo said when Lucas came back on the line. "I'm afraid I'll have to ask your aircrews to stand down."

"That's all right," Lucas replied cheerily. "Postponements will happen."

This isn't a postponement, Carlo nearly said. Instead he said, simply: "Yes."

"Well, cheerio then."

"Cheers," Carlo said, and put the phone down again. He looked up. Thomas, the Scouse teletype operator, was hanging about in the doorway. At first Carlo thought he'd brought another signal; he hadn't.

"Why not come downstairs, Mr. Peat? You'd have some company down there."

217

"Thanks all the same, Thomas. I think I want to be alone."

"Well, there's no 'arm in askin', is there?"

"Later, perhaps. And thanks again, Thomas."

O messenger from the vaults of night, Carlo thought as he watched the teletype operator leave.

Everything had been in the signals, a question of provenance. How had Dorf been able to send all those Bandersnatches without detection?

Carlo had asked almost the same question of the Webers. How was it possible for them to flee Germany without getting caught? Stengel, of course. But the exact nature of the connection between the Standartenführer, Dorf, the Webers, and Kindchen Alberich had escaped Carlo.

The answer was late in coming. It had not arrived until that very night—too late to save Scarr's people—and it came from an astonishing source.

The Kremlin.

Thomas returned after three quarters of an hour. This time he did have a signal, Scarr's second:

> + + + March 14 1945, 0340 Zulu + + + Message begins + + + Have taken out SPELEOLOGICAL RESEARCH UNIT since my 0010 stop FRAÜLEIN redefected stop BANDERSNATCH dead stop JUBJUB BIRD apparently FW 200 KONDOR at HECHINGEN with infant JABBERWOCK stop Am proceeding to snicker-snack stop VORPAL + + + Message ends + + +

"You'd better send the recall," said Carlo Peat.

"Yes, sir. *The mome raths outgrabe.*"

"Who's left downstairs, Thomas?"

"Just the graveyard shift, Mr. Peat. Are you going to come down now?"

"In a minute. I'll have some coffee, then lock up here. I expect there'll be a flurry of signals now."

Thomas retreated from the doorway and Carlo took the cap off the thermos, uncorking the stopper within. The vile black brew tasted rubbery and Carlo's eyes watered as he reread the signal. *Redefected*, he thought, what a coinage.

Abandoning the coffee he picked up the signals from his desk, turned out the light, and locked the door from the outside. In the hallway he noticed light streaming from Harold's half-opened door. He was working late as usual, and Carlo decided to pay him a visit.

Harold looked up, frowning. He said: "Imagine Uncle Joe coming through with that stuff."

"Yes, imagine," Carlo said.

"How's it going?" asked Harold.

"Like this," Carlo said, and showed him Scarr's latest signal. Something like annoyance flickered across Harold's face as he returned the signal, an afterthought. "I say," he said, "you don't think he could possibly succeed, do you?"

"Who?"

"S-s-scarr." Harold frowned again.

"I doubt it."

"Oh, I see." Harold's expression cleared. "You thought I was talking about Stengel."

"Did I?" Carlo said. "I'm going down to signals. Want to come?"

"I have got rather a lot of work to do here," Harold said, with just the slightest hint of recrimination.

"In other words, don't waste my time," Carlo said.

Harold sighed. "Is something the matter?" he asked. "If it's your friends you're worried about," he went on before Carlo could reply, "we could always draft a signal telling them to give up before anyone gets seriously hurt."

"That's already happened," Carlo said. "Dorf is dead."

"Oh, too bad. Before anyone else gets hurt, then."

Carlo said: "Scarr wouldn't obey such an order, and neither would I in his shoes. He wouldn't believe it. We've already sent the recall. I doubt whether he'll believe that, either."

"Well, now you see the wisdom of our policy," said Harold. "We are not answering any more of Scarr's signals."

Moscow was exfiltrating an agent, and Vorpal represented the greatest possible threat to the success of their mission.

Scarr's third signal was waiting for Carlo in the teletype room:

> + + + March 14, 1945, 0350 ZULU + + + Message begins+ + + Herr BERGER from Degussa missing presumed dead stop Request clarification of your apparent OUTGRABE, which I am ignoring stop VORPAL + + + Message ends + + +

"There's no reply, Thomas," Carlo said. The hell with Moscow's agent, he thought, and settled down to wait for his own.

It was 4:50 GMT when Scarr sent his fourth signal, 5:50 local time. Sunrise would be in twenty-five minutes, and the eastern sky was already streaked with red as Scarr's people set off down the Hechingen road.

They kept to the hedgerows, leaving the castle behind. It was here, less than a quarter of a mile from the field's perimeter fence, that luck smiled once again on Johnny Scarr, lucky Johnny Scarr.

Jock stumbled across them in a ditch, a whole stick of canisters that had missed the drop zone. Eagerly, he broke them open. While the others gathered around, the big Scotsman enumerated the contents of each canister: "Concussion grenades, smoke bombs, Sten guns, Lee Enfields. There's enough .303 ammunition here to fight a small war...." His greatest find was a canister packed with a Stokes mortar, still slicked with factory grease, and another containing a dozen mortar bombs.

Johnny Scarr asked Jock to rig the smoke bombs to the concussion grenades. The big Scotsman set to work while Johnny instructed his men: "This is the way it's got to be. We'll split up into two groups: Jock and myself with the bazooka, Charlie and Bony with the mortar. Ian, you'll take a Lee Enfield with the smoke bombs that Jock is rigging to the concussion grenades, as well as a supply of firecrackers. You'll distribute both at suitable intervals around the perimeter—

lighting the fuses and retiring to a safe distance. Sorry, no rubber tanks. Your job is to simulate several real attacks, confusing the enemy and drawing his fire from our two strike groups, while at the same time keeping an eye open for trouble. You'll be a free agent, on your own, and you'd do as well to keep away from the others.

"Charlie, Bony—you'll attack the control tower. Try to get as close as you can, with the mortar at maximum elevation, so that the building will give you some cover. If you can lob just one round into the control deck, then you might be able to put the whole field out of action.

"Jock and I will go after the Kondor with the bazooka. Both groups, for a time, will be in a position to give each other cover fire and support, should one or the other get bogged down. But I'm not reckoning that will happen. Charlie, what do you think?"

"Yers," said Charlie Page, ruminating. "Okay, Johnny. It's a good plan, but Roberts should have more up his armpit than a Lee Enfield."

"Mills bombs, Charlie. He'll have plenty of those."

"What about the timing, Johnny?" asked Roberts, anxiously. "That aircraft will be rolling soon."

"The bazooka is the best antiaircraft weapon we've got," said Johnny Scarr. "The chances are everyone will be watching the aircraft instead of being on the lookout for us. As soon as she starts to roll, that's when we attack. It's the psychological moment, don't you see? The moment of maximum surprise when the defense will be off their guard."

Bony Wilkes said: "What happens if the bomb goes off?"

"It can't, Bony. They won't arm it until they're above their cruising altitude, otherwise it would blow them to pieces as they climbed. They won't be dropping the fuse in until they're well above a thousand meters."

"We should attack it now," Roberts said. "A stationary target."

"One dud round and they know we're here," Johnny Scarr said. "This way we achieve maximum surprise. And there's one other thing, Ian, something you've forgotten. The RAF is attacking at first light."

"Yers," Charlie Page said again. "I like it. If only the frigging RAF is on time."

Johnny Scarr wondered about that, too. He had Bony Wilkes send another signal, requesting confirmation of air cover.

"There's no answer." Bony's refrain was becoming tiresome.

"Keep trying."

Johnny Scarr cajoled and chivvied his people. He'd grumbled at them and with them, sharing their hardships, their hopes, and their fears, sharing also their miserable diet of hardtack, tea, and Benzedrine. He was their armorer, nursemaid, tactician, and conscience—a leader. And in five minutes he had as much equipment, given his numbers, as he could possibly want.

Only a quarter of an hour before he had been on the verge of admitting defeat—before the real battle had been fought. Now his greatest worry was that they would be too late, that the Kondor might be on its way before they could attack Hechingen Airfield. But he did not think so, somehow. The Hun was punctual. If he had a timetable he would keep to it, and that timetable coincided with Vorpal's arrival at the perimeter fence.

In the distance they heard the roar of a starter motor.

Johnny flopped down by the fence. It was triple-depth chain-link fence, electrified, with concrete stanchions and barbed wire looped on top. The ground was wet with slushy snow melting on the asphalt security track outside the fence, which was regularly patrolled by sentries. Johnny could see the tower half a mile away, Dorf's Skorpion in the lee of the tower, and, parked within bazooka range, floodlit, the Kondor—except, of course, it wasn't a Kondor.

Charlie saw it first. He was already on his way, slithering through the slush in the graying light with Bony Wilkes, when suddenly he stopped and swore, glancing back at Johnny Scarr and Jock, jabbing a gloved paw at the bomber. "Look at that frigging plane," he whispered hoarsely over his shoulder. "Look at the tailplane—just look at it! That's not a Kondor; that's a Stirling, a bleeding Short Stirling!"

"We'd better tell London," said Johnny Scarr. There was no doubt in his mind that Charlie Page was right, as there was none in Charlie's that London would not be listening.

The three men waited for Bony to finish transmitting. He looked up at Scarr and shook his head. Johnny gestured at him to abandon the set, which he did, heaping it with slush. Bony felt like one relieved of an enormous burden. Stuff the bloody hump, he thought, as the group scattered, Johnny Scarr and Jock toward the four-engined bomber, Bony and Charlie Page toward the tower.

Bony threw himself down at the fence with Charlie Page, who had the mortar barrel slung to his back. He watched Charlie fiddling with the cutters, a pair of rubber insulators, and a strand of wire. For Christ's sake hurry up, he thought, and froze as Charlie ducked and a Mercedes staff car swung around the side of the tower, its slit beams fanning over the two men at the wire.

No one had seen them. . . . Bony Wilkes, chin resting on his forearms, squinted up underneath the wire. He saw the car doors opening and the Fräulein, in a flying suit, getting in the passenger side, with three men, similarly attired, climbing in behind her.

Roberts crouched in the slush, waiting for the sentry. In the half-light the Englishman might have been a rock, a gray, inanimate thing dropped by some retreating glacier. Only his eyes moved, watching the sentry, whose back was turned, Roberts counting that measured tread, waiting for the jackboot to swing out and turn about, and then he rose, shadowlike, from the earth, swift and supple though encrusted with grenades, the bayonet in his left hand slicing through gray serge, skin, costal cartilages, and the central tendinous muscles of the diaphragm, his right hand clamped over the sentry's mouth, his left changing direction with the bayonet as a man would change gear. The sentry, his aorta severed, died—his mind, still half alive, registering the cool softness of the snow and something, too, of the unyielding earth beneath.

Roberts moved on, svelte, lithe. He had become inhuman, an animal entirely like a machine. He moved on, stringing charges along the chain-link fence, twenty yards from the sentry's body, its blood pinking the melting snow, pausing to light a blue paper fuse, an action that stirred in some dim cortical crevasse Novemberish memories of childish pleasure, memories obliterated by the machine which moved on, scattering, sowing, until—two hundred yards from the tower—the machine's receptors observed the tower door opening, and the woman, framed in the doorway, stepping out into the dim, dawning light, the woman putting her hands into the pockets of her flying suit, the sentry on the other side of the fence turning at the sound of the opening door, neither German woman nor German soldier aware of the machine-danger scuttling toward them, the luminous seconds sweeping away in its mind, a mind brimming with potent memories of humiliation at the hands of this woman.

The machine had decided to ignore her and kill the pilot. Roberts had Stengel lined up in the Lee Enfield's sights, Stengel making a perfect target as he stood behind the Fräulein, framed in the control-tower doorway, the yellow light streaming out from behind him. But then, before he could move a muscle, before the command to execute had been sent, another figure in a flying suit materialized at the foot of the stairs behind the first, and then another. Roberts wavered, paralyzed by indecision as he watched the girl and the three men get into the car. *For God's sake, which one was the pilot?* The machine was fast breaking down, becoming human again. *He would shoot them all.*

He fired at the Fräulein just as the sentry snapped to attention, crossing his line of sight. The sentry pitched forward and Roberts flipped the bolt on the Lee Enfield, holding his fire. He rose, to get a better shot, and as he did so saw a muzzle flash from the car, from the passenger side. Oddly, the flash seemed to expand like the concentric ripples from a stone cast into a pond, filling his consciousness with fire and the roaring of fire.

For a delusive fraction he thought he was at Haigerloch again. Then this delusion passed and he saw that he was in the bunker at Tel Algol. One of the dead Germans was shuffling the cards. Another looked up at him and spoke: *"Willkommen."*

Roberts screamed.

Roberts's charges blew, thunderclaps generating great quantities of smoke around the perimeter fence, what sounded like rapid small-arms fire echoing from all over the map, two shots sounding frighteningly close by as Bony Wilkes heard a scream, a savage, wounded, crazy dying scream, and the staff car sped away toward the waiting plane.

Johnny Scarr heard that scream, too. He watched helplessly from the other side of the fence as the Mercedes sped away, Jock attacking the wire on the opposite side of the tower from Charlie Page.

The Stirling, still illuminated, was for the moment safe: a rocket grenade, with a velocity in excess of the speed of sound, would be deflected by the triple chain-link fence—that, or it would vaporize on contact.

Both men, Jock at the wire and Johnny readying the bazooka, heard a mortar shell fall softly against the side of the control tower and explode. Johnny glanced up at the splintering fall of glass from the tower deck just before the lights went out on Hechingen field. Night-blinded, he blinked away the retinal afterimage of the floodlights. Somewhere a siren whined and died, the field suddenly pulsating with the throaty roar of the Stirling's motors.

In the distance Johnny saw the ground crew struggling to disconnect a fuel line from the bomber. He watched the fuel tanker backing away, the ground crew scattering as the big plane, its engines thundering, began to turn and taxi away from Johnny Scarr, its huge rudder wagging as if in a monumental gesture of insult.

Johnny saw Jock scramble through the wire. He plunged after the big Scotsman, who had disappeared inside the Skorpion. From the tower, machine gun fire and a grenade flash. The pitch of the Stirling's engines rose to a crescendo, screaming across the field, as the huge bomber, encumbered with the dead weight of Kindchen Alberich, began its lumbering take-off run. Jock fired up the Skorpion and popped an overhead hatch. Johnny clambered aboard the roof ladder, lugging the bazooka and the ammo bag after him as Jock brought the Skorpion around in pursuit of the bomber.

It was all Johnny could do to hang on with his one free hand. The vehicle bounced and bucked, several times almost throwing him to

225

the ground, but he managed to crawl over to the hatch and let himself down. Inside, he dropped the grenade, fin first, down the bazooka spout. Johnny Scarr popped up again through the hatch, supporting himself on his elbows, the bazooka propped over his shoulder.

The Stirling's tail wheel was lifting into the air as he fired. At the same moment the tail gunner in the bomber opened fire with the quadruple .303 Browning machine guns. Johnny Scarr ducked inside the hatch to reload.

Bony Wilkes and Charlie Page rushed the control tower. "Cover the doorway!" Charlie roared, dodging around the corner of the building through the open door and bounding up the stairs two at a time. Bony hugged the Sten close to his chest and pressed his back against the concrete wall inside the door. A shot split the air close by, so close that Bony felt the shock wave, the vicious double crack of the sonic wave deflected off the wooden door and reverberating around the walls of his concrete hideaway. A shadow flitted across the door; Bony stepped forward, firing. Upstairs, a door opened and slammed shut, a grenade exploded, the door opened again, and Charlie's Sten chattered. Bony ceased firing at the same time. Silence. Cordite fumes drifted down the stairs, preceded by Charlie Page, who sidled down as if he had been wearing nothing more than carpet slippers on his feet, so quietly that Bony jumped.

"What happened?" whispered Charlie.

"I dunno. I saw someone out there, so I . . ."

"Shh!" The ape rolled his eyes, his nostrils flared. "Where's Roberts?" he whispered again.

"I dunno, Charlie."

"Keep your frigging voice down!"

"I dunno. I heard a shot and a scream out there." Bony jerked his Sten at the entrance. "I dunno."

Charlie cocked his head. "There's no one out there," he said with cold conviction. As he stepped out into the clear air, Charlie breathed in deeply, his chest heaving. All was quiet, all was still outside the control-tower door. Charlie counted bodies—two sentries on the other side of the fence, three Württembergers in a heap by the entrance, Bony's doing, and, close by, near the foot of the fence, Ian Roberts, his sightless eyes looking at a straight flush.

A diamond-patterned bazooka track flared briefly at the other end of the field. The explosion following was insignificant compared with the mounting roar of the Stirling's engines. Charlie listened, transfixed, as the engine noise suddenly dropped to a regular drone above which he and Bony heard the stitching of synchronized Browning machine guns firing in three evenly timed bursts.

Charlie Page threw back his head, watching as the great black beast lumbered into the western sky. It was 6:15 local time, and the Stirling was taking off exactly on schedule.

"Well, Mr. Roberts, you have cashed in your chips," Charlie Page said—to no one in particular. "And it looks like John has missed the bleeding bus. I suppose we had better go and see why. Yers," he said, turning to Bony Wilkes, who was shivering outside the doorway. "Come along, Sergeant Wilkes. Or should I still be calling you Oberfeldwebel Ernst?"

"I dunno," said Bony Wilkes.

Just before he ducked into the Skorpion, Johnny Scarr thought he saw the grenade hit the Stirling amidships. He waited until the machine-gun bullets had ceased drumming on the hull before popping up again with the second round. The firing started again, bullets ricocheting off the hatch cover and ring, one of them catching the bazooka's trigger guard, spinning the weapon out of Johnny Scarr's grip. His hand burned, his eyes filling with tears of pain and frustration as he slumped inside the Skorpion, his hand thrust into his tunic. The bullet, which was spent, had taken the skin off his knuckles; Johnny was sure he'd done a great deal of damage to the Stirling, but he hadn't downed it, and he would have to face Charlie Page.

That was the least of his worries. Johnny Scarr wondered if the plane could reach London. He had never imagined that he could be in this situation, to be alive and yet to have failed.

"A stationary target": Roberts's words haunted him.

London was a stationary target.

Jock swung the Skorpion back around toward the tower. He, too, had seen the rocket grenade strike the plane amidships, and he had wondered if it was a dud round. But he didn't think so, for the Stirling, as it climbed laboriously into the western sky, was trailing smoke.

Trudging across the field, Charlie and Bony saw an old friend bearing down on them, the Skorpion.

Charlie broke to the left, his Sten unslung. Bony sat down. Sit down, a voice in his head commanded. He was played out, and it seemed the most sensible thing to do.

The vehicle halted in front of him and Johnny Scarr stuck his head out of the hatch. "Get up," he said, and Bony Wilkes obeyed this, too.

Charlie sauntered across. He stood, hands on hips before the Skorpion, gazing up at the bazookaless Scarr. "Well, well, well," he mocked, "if it isn't Fliegerkommandant Leckenspeichel. You never know who you're gonna find aboard this ship. What happened to you?"

Johnny told him.

"Save your funny stuff for later," he said, and asked what had happened to Roberts.

Charlie scrambled on board and gave Wilkes a hand up. "He bought it, Johnny," he said. "Over by the fence. I'm sorry."

"We'd better head for the border, Johnny," said Jock from behind the wheel.

Johnny Scarr nodded. He felt only a superabundant weariness, unlike anything he had ever felt before.

He forced himself to think. "Bony, you'd better use the APC radio. See if you can call up London. No, wait. The nearest Allied military unit. There must be somebody out there who's listening."

Carlo Peat had waited an hour for Scarr's fourth signal:

+ + + March 14 1945, 0450 Zulu + + + Message begins + + + Am at HOHENZOLLERN stop Still no clarification of your OUTGRABE stop Will attack JUBJUB BIRD stop VORPAL + + + Message ends + + +

There were two other signals, at ten-minute intervals:

+ + + March 14 1945, 0500 Zulu + + + Message begins + + +
Request confirmation air cover stop VORPAL + + + Message
ends + + +

+ + + March 14 1945, 0510 Zulu + + + Message begins + + +
Correction to my 0340 JUBJUB BIRD not, repeat not FW KONDOR but
SHORT STIRLING repeat JUBJUB BIRD SHORT STIRLING positive stop
Am attacking same stop VORPAL + + + Message ends + + +

Carlo became aware of a presence at his side. It was Thomas.
"Yes, what is it?" he asked.
"Something from the War Office, Mr. Peat. Scarr's people have
opened radio contact with a Yankee military unit near Strasbourg.
Johnny Scarr is sure that he damaged the bomber amidships, but he
doesn't know how seriously. Apparently, he's pinched Dorf's command vehicle and is heading for the Swiss border. The Yanks got a fix
on him about twenty miles north of Schaffhausen. That's all for the
moment, Mr. Peat. I'll keep you posted, of course."
"Oh, good God," said Carlo Peat and picked up the phone again.

30: THE FLIGHT OF THE JUBJUB BIRD

The graveyard shift was long gone when Carlo Peat called the Air Ministry again. He asked, politely, if he could be switched to air traffic control, Strasbourg.

"Isn't that in an American sector, sir?" The girl at the other end sounded faintly scandalized.

"Er, yes. I wish to speak to a General Hoffman. He's expecting me to call."

"That would be General Julius C. Hoffman, sir?"

"Right." For some reason Harland Caisho Peat found American names embarrassing.

"One moment, please . . . Here's your connection now, sir."

Carlo heard the phone ringing.

"Hawfman," a voice answered.

"Oh, good morning, general. London here, Peat speaking. The aircraft you're looking for is a Short Stirling. We think it probable that it's damaged amidships."

"Roger, London. Wanna shoot it down?"

"Oh, I think you'd better leave that to us, sir. It's carrying quite a delicate cargo."

"Alrighty, London. We'll call back when we make contact. Okay?"

"Okay," said Carlo. "Thank you very much, sir."

"You're welcome," Hoffman said, and rang off.

Carlo looked up. Thomas was standing by his desk again.

"I just thought you ought to know," he said, "that we've heard from Scarr again. Stengel and Katherina Weber are on board that aircraft. Roberts and Prentice are dead. The rest are safe and sound."

231

"Thank God, Thomas. Listen, tell Miles Cavendish to get on to Bern. And you'd better alert Channel Air Sea Rescue. And another thing, Thomas. . . ."

"Yes, sir?"

"When General Hoffman calls back, could you record our conversation? For posterity, you know."

"Sure thing, Mr. Peat," Thomas smiled and Carlo watched him disappear into the inner mysteries of the teletype room.

It wasn't posterity Carlo was thinking of. It was himself. Carlo was afraid he would get the blame if Moscow's favorite agent fell into the ocean and was never heard of again. Personally, there was nothing he would have liked better, but he had to think of the consequences.

The phone rang. "Hello?" Carlo answered it before it could ring a second time.

"Hawfman heah. I thought you might like to hear this, London." The line squawked and through the buzz of signal noise and static Carlo heard the female American sector-plotter say: "Tower to Peedee. What vector do you have?"

"Peedee to tower. Two-seven-oh. Angel bearing two-seven-two—port at five o'clock. Estimated altitude three thousand feet. Airspeed two-two-oh. Over."

"Roger, Peedee. Check him out on FOF."

"Wilco, tower. FOF friendly."

"See if you can get his number, Peedee."

"Roger. Uh, airplane is a Royal Air Force Short Stirling on a training mission from High Wycombe. Says he ran into some flak over, uh, Heck—? Heck-someplace or other."

"Read that Hechingen, Peedee. Ask him if he wants clearance for Nancy."

"Wilco, tower. Airplane says he thinks he can make it home to London."

"Roger, Peedee. How's your fuel situation?"

"Hunky-dory, honey."

Oberst Viktor von Wenden gave a sigh of relief as he watched the Thunderbolt waggle its wings and peel off. Now at least he could concentrate on flying his machine, which was none too responsive to the rudder. Von Wenden knew what the problem was. The *Panzerfaust* had torn a gaping hole in the fuselage immediately aft of the starboard wing, bucklig the aircraft floor so that it pinched the control cables under the floor.

"The inboard port motor is overheating," Schneider reported. He was sitting in the copilot's seat, scanning gauges.

Von Wenden grunted. He throttled the engine back, more power to the remaining three solving for the moment the persistent pull to starboard. He found that by planting both feet on the port rudder he could maintain the Stirling on a reasonable heading, though it was flying in a somewhat crabbed fashion with the nose at fifteen degrees to the bearing. Von Wenden checked his fuel gauges, in his head calculating the trade-off between speed and altitude. He had plenty of gas to make it to London, and after that perhaps it really did not matter.

"He's gone, eh, the Yankee?" Rudolf Stengel crawled out of the tunnel that led from the rear turret to the flight deck. He sat down in the navigator's chair, where Schneider should have been.

"Where is Fräulein Weber?" he asked.

"In the bomb bay," said Oberst Viktor von Wenden.

Stengel gazed disconsolately out of the glasshouse at the plane's long shadow rippling across his old battlefields thirty-five hundred feet beneath.

"Can't you fly this thing any higher?" he asked.

"The elevator's jammed." Von Wenden glanced over his shoulder at the Standartenführer and smiled. "We're lucky we ever got off the ground."

"Was someone asking for me?" Katherina's cropped head popped up behind Stengel. "Ach, Rudolf! It's you." She smiled, her teeth too prominent, her face radiant in his presence. He groaned inwardly. What had he done to deserve this, any of it?

Schneider said: "We are lucky to have the Fräulein aboard. There's a problem with the fuses. I'm not sure I could have fixed it myself."

Stengel directed a quizzical look toward Katherina. "Really?" he said.

"It's nothing to worry about," she said. "The fuses are wired to air-detonate the bomb at one thousand meters, which is approximately our present altitude. An electrical branching system activates the TNT detonator, which in turn implodes the hemispheres, causing the bomb to reach immediate criticality."

"Are you telling me that if you arm the bomb now it will explode?" asked Stengel.

Katherina grinned at him and nodded happily. "Unless you can climb to a higher altitude," she shouted from the bomb bay.

Von Wenden shook his head. The plane yawed violently. "Take a look back there," the pilot shouted back.

Katherina turned around, as did Stengel. The Standartenführer felt slightly sick. Chunks of kapok insulation whirled in the howling slipstream. The floor heaved beneath the tunnel like a cakewalk, strips of flayed canvas and severed cables flapping in the gale that roared through the after end of the plane. Stengel realized that he had crawled over a gaping hole in the fuselage floor with nothing but plywood and canvas separating him from eternity. Scarr's round had actually melted the Stirling's skin, which rippled back from the main structural members, the ribs and spars now exposed and flexing ominously. There were two holes under the fuselage, an entry and an exit wound, the latter extending back to the stabilizer. Stengel wondered what was keeping the tail on, and grimaced, his nausea increasing.

To Katherina he said: "What do you propose to do?"

"Recalibrate the pressure fuse," she said.

"Here? Now? Is that possible?"

She nodded again. "I have to get inside the bomb," she said.

"What?"

"I mean I have to open it up. First of all, you'd better take this." Through the hatch she handed up Dorf's Walther, the gun she'd fired from the car, killing Roberts.

Stengel bent over to take it by the barrel, very carefully. "I am glad you trust me, Katherina," he said.

"I am glad you trust me, Rudolf," she said.

"Katherina, why are you doing this? Are you crazy?"

234

This time she shook her head. "As you said, Rudolf, the Herr Oberst is a professional. He will abort the flight if the bomb is improperly armed. And if I can't fix the pressure fuse, the circuits will trigger the TNT detonator as soon as that cylinder is dropped into the panel. So." She shrugged.

Privately, she had another motive that she could not very well admit to publicly.

Curiosity.

"I will help you, Katherina," Stengel volunteered.

Of course, she had expected nothing else.

There was room for only one man, or woman, in the bay, and Katherina had to squirm around the great yellow egg which jostled slightly on the pincerlike bomb-release mountings. She wriggled underneath the bomb, which swayed above her, until she was sitting directly on the bomb bay doors. Katherina reached up to brace herself against Kindchen Alberich's box-shaped fin. It was cold in the bomb bay, yet she left a sweaty print on the yellow-painted steel. She was afraid that the doors might not bear even her weight and knew that if they sprang open she would have nothing to cling to except the bomb.

Stengel, peering down from above, watched her disappear beneath the bomb and heard her call for a cold chisel.

"Where is it?"

"*Wos?*"

"The chisel—where is it?"

"In the toolbox by the hatch."

Stengel got down on his knees and found the chisel. He put his arm and shoulder through the hatch, his arm groping around the curved flank of the bomb to hand Katherina the chisel.

"*Danke,*" she called up cheerily, tracing the welding scar that joined the two hemispheres until she found the panel with its color-coded numerals and the warning:

ACHTUNG!
Z-GERÄT

"I need a hammer," she cried out, sliding the chisel point under the lip of the panel.

Stengel passed her the hammer and heard the chink-chink of her tapping. The bomb swayed a little, and Stengel heard the panel clatter on to the bomb bay doors. Underneath Kindchen Alberich Katherina Weber gazed at a snake's nest of electrical wiring.

"Screwdriver," she called out.

"What on earth are you doing?" Stengel winced as the bomb jiggled again.

"Disconnecting the radar," she answered. "The fuse reads a signal reflected back from the ground. So I'm taking out the whole circuit. Then all I have to do is to alter the barometric setting so that the pressure fuse will detonate at ground level instead of a thousand meters." She was silent for a while. "More or less, anyway," she added.

"What do you mean?" Stengel cried. "More or less than what?"

"Than ground level, *Dümmerling*. Only I can't remember whether the screw turns clockwise or counterclockwise."

"Katherina!"

"It's all right; it turns to the left. There are so many variables, Rudolf. The weather, for one thing. The air pressure at ground level is always changing, and there's no such thing as absolute ground level, you know. Still, we should be accurate to within two or three hundred meters. Hand me the neutron source, will you? That's the red tube."

Stengel swallowed; he had no idea why she was doing this to him.

The hand of Katherina Weber scrawled over the yellow horizon of Kindchen Alberich and opened, clawlike. Stengel surrendered the red tube into its grasp, gingerly. The hand closed and lingered, meditating.

"I have a better idea," Katherina shouted up, worrying Stengel again. "Hand me the pressure fuse—that's the green one." The hand opened again.

"Do you want me to take the other one back?" asked Stengel.

"No, I'll tell you what I'm going to do." The voice of Katherina Weber floated up to him while the aircraft yawed again, the bomb swinging on its mountings. "I'll drop the pressure fuse in first," said Katherina. "That way, if I've miscalculated or made a mistake in the adjustments somewhere, there'll be an explosion—but only the TNT."

"Only TNT? How reassuring!"

"Isn't it?" The hand of Katherina Weber closed over the red and green tubes and disappeared. "If I've slipped up, the bomb will destroy us, you may be sure of that, but we will not be vaporized—there's the difference."

Stengel looked over his shoulder. They had an audience—the navigator-bombardier, Fliegerhauptmann Schneider, anxiously listening from the flight deck.

Stengel shut his eyes. The Stirling shuddered and the Standartenführer's stomach heaved.

"Turbulence," observed Viktor von Wenden from the pilot's chair.

Stengel opened his eyes. Schneider's face was looking down at him from the flight deck. "Everything is correct and in order," he remarked. "The instruments show that Kindchen Alberich is armed."

The Standartenführer blinked. He had seen that face before, in his nightmares, the face of the dead Frenchman floating in *le ravin des morts.*

The delusion was replaced by the head and shoulders of Katherina Weber, toothily grinning. "Give me a hand," she said, and he did.

Stengel hauled her from the hatch, his shirt and tunic jacket, under his flying suit, sticking to his spine between his shoulder blades.

"Thank you, my friend," said Katherina Weber, struggling to her feet and wiping off her hands with a rag from the toolbox. "Thank you."

She was very good, he thought. And very dangerous. All in all, she was too much for Rudolf Stengel.

Things started coming apart over the French coast. A stream of glycol issued from the inner port engine, forming a thin white trail as the droplets condensed.

"What's that?" asked Stengel, in alarm.

"Glycol." Oberst Viktor von Wenden shrugged. "Antifreeze, about the last thing we need at the moment." He raised a finger, pointing: "One o'clock, Spitfires high, two of them."

The Standartenführer made out two specks against the radiant blue light.

"They haven't seen us yet," said Oberst Viktor von Wenden, "but they will if they're looking, with that engine streaming glycol." And then, leaning over in his chair, he pointed down. "The sun's behind us," he observed casually. "See the launch down there? What do you think they are—day trippers?" Oberst Viktor von Wenden smiled.

Stengel gazed down at the sea. The launch was from England, heading toward France, and as it crossed the shadow of the Stirling it turned about ahead of the plane, its wake describing a broad circle in those deceptively placid waters beneath.

"Day trippers," Oberst Viktor von Wenden said complacently. "Ten minutes to Dover, am I right, Schneider?"

"*Jawohl*, Herr Oberst."

"I've done this before, Stengel, many times," the pilot said, "but never with such a cargo." Nor such a plane, thought Stengel as the inner port motor started up an awful racket, the stream of glycol curdling, darkening, gouts of oil pumping from the engine cowling. A red light flashed on the instrument panel. "We have an engine fire," Oberst von Wenden said, using exactly the same tone of voice as he had to remark on the launch. His hand went out to throttle the motor back and feather the great propeller which freewheeled in the airstream, tongues of flame suddenly spurting from the trailing edge of the engine nacelle.

Oberst Viktor von Wenden pulled a toggle on the panel before him. The port wing dipped and great clots of black-fleeced foam erupted from the inner port motor. Von Wenden pulled back the throttles on the mounting between himself and the copilot's seat, and the great plane banked, pluming black smoke.

"*Fräulein, mein Herren*," said Oberst Viktor von Wenden, "you will please put on your parachutes." He took his eyes off the engine to check the altimeter. "Schneider, open the crew door and chuck out the dinghy, will you?"

The navigator-bombardier complied. Stengel helped Katherina on with her parachute and was rewarded with another toothy smile. Von Wenden spoke again, his words lost in the sudden influx of air as the dinghy was sucked through the door.

"What did you say?" Stengel yelled at him.

"I said wait until I bank her again," the pilot shouted back. "Then jump!"

"Do you think you'll make it?" Stengel hollered.

Von Wenden shrugged, and the port wing dipped again. "Now!" he cried.

"After you, Fräulein," said the Standartenführer. He watched her go, then jumped himself.

It was a novel experience for him. Rudolf Stengel, as he floated down, looked forward to a long rest and, after a dip in the ocean, to warm blankets, hot cocoa, the traditional flask of rum. It occurred to him that he had not eaten or slept for many hours. He stretched his long legs and relaxed, surrendering to the novelty of the experience, a tired man but by no means defeated.

He looked down and saw Katherina, already in the water, swimming for the dinghy. Stengel looked up and saw another chute opening above him. Schneider must have got out. A professional, of course. There was no fourth chute, nor did he expect there would be. Von Wenden was earning the diamonds to his Knight's Cross.

Stengel searched the sky for the Stirling. It seemed many miles away, a faint trail of smoke sinking over the white cliffs, the two Spitfires still in attendance. Poor von Wenden. Stengel thought of a hawk mobbed by lesser birds. Beneath him he heard the snarl of a powerful marine engine and saw the launch bucking the waves toward the area where he would splash down. For a moment he was suspended in harness between the mutable air and the icy green depths.

Strong hands would soon be pulling him from the waters.

Soon . . .

Oberst Viktor von Wenden pulled the Stirling around. He glanced at the fire-blackened nacelle on the port wing. The fire had gone out as quickly as it had started. Von Wenden was not particularly surprised. The Stirling was a very durable aircraft, slow and poorly armed, especially vulnerable to attack from beneath, but constructed like a flying tank.

He opened the throttles to clear the white cliffs ahead and pulled back on the control column. The Stirling responded sluggishly, still flying in the same crabbed fashion. But it was still flying, that was the main thing.

The Oberst saw that he had lost a couple of thousand feet in ditching his crew, and he came in very low over those white cliffs. Too low, if he was to have any chance of surviving the blast when he dropped the egg. He listened to the engine note; the three remaining engines thundered harmoniously. Oberst Viktor von Wenden, his feet again planted on the port rudder, set about coaxing the heavy bomber to gain some altitude over the few miles remaining.

He remembered to switch on the "Iffy"—the Identification Friend or Foe—as he had over Strasbourg when the Thunderbolt had been sent up to check him out. One of the Spitfires had moved up close on his port quarter. The pilot was pointing and waving; Oberst Viktor von Wenden waved back, and gave the thumbs-up sign. The Stirling was climbing, slowly, laboriously.

Below, the peaceful rural scene gave way to the southern suburbs of London, a mosaic as unmemorable as any, Hamburg, Cologne, Berlin, Dresden—soon to be part of history.

Oberst Viktor von Wenden was doing his job, and because he took pride in it, he was doing it well.

It was Katherina Weber who hauled him, shivering, from the Channel into the dinghy.

"Ach, what a fish!" She laughed. "What a catch!"

"Katherina," he spluttered. "There is something you should know."

"I know it already, Rudolf," she said.

"I do not think so, Katherina."

"I know everything, Rudolf," she said, with such utter conviction that for a moment he wondered whether it could possibly be true.

Stengel heard the launch snarling through the waves toward them. There was so little time to explain.

"Katherina," he began, "when I joined the Party in 1920, I little thought that—"

"Say no more," she admonished. "I think I can forgive you, Rudolf. After all, we both wanted the same for Germany."

"We did?" Wet, bedraggled, incredulous, he gazed at her. Then he saw that, as usual, she had misunderstood him. "No, no, Katherina," he said. "Not *that* party, the other one."

The launch had cut its motors and had drawn alongside. Its crew were grappling with the dinghy when they were astonished to see one of its occupants pitch the other into the drink, where, bobbing up and down, his head supported by his life jacket, Standartenführer Rudolf Stengel surrendered to his mirth and laughed.

"For God's sake, keep me from that woman," he said in English as the crew fished him out of the sea. "Keep me from her before I die of laughing!"

Oberst Viktor von Wenden flicked on his headset. The Spitfire had requested his flight plan and wanted his unit identification. Von Wenden glanced up at the wing and saw that the Spitfire was no longer there. He would have to say something, before it was too late.

". . . High Wycombe. We were on a training flight and ran into flak over the Black Forest. My crew has bailed out. I can make it back to base," Von Wenden said, and heard the strangely musical twittering of bullets cutting up the underside of the Stirling.

He shoved the control column forward and jammed the throttles wide open. The nose dipped. Von Wenden could see the sinuous river beneath, the two parks, the crossroads, and the buildings alongside the river, the Houses of Parliament. Oberst Viktor von Wenden had flown over this aerial map many times before, yet he had never thought to see it so completely within his grasp, so close it was almost a part of him.

He watched the altimeter unwind, the artificial horizon tilt, the crossroads begin to turn. The motors were shrieking now, and the twittering moved up along the fuselage, cannon fire starring and shattering the glasshouse, steel and perspex splinters scattering through the cabin—and through the body but not yet the mind of Oberst Viktor von Wenden, who wanted to hold on to that map for a little while longer before making it entirely his. He aimed the Stirling like a Stuka for the heart of that cruciform building, the Abbey.

It never occurred to him as he died that he had already suffered the greatest defeat, treason.

The phone rang in the teletype room. "Yes?" Carlo picked it up.

"He's down."

"I heard him. Where?"

"A big piece in Parliament Square. It made quite a hole, quite a hole," Lucas said. "The rest of him splashed into the river. Speaking of which, Dover picked up Stengel, the girl, and the observer. Hello? Are you there?"

"Oh, yes," said Carlo.

"I just thought I'd let you know. Toodle-bye, then."

"Yes," said Carlo. "Thanks. Toodle-bye." He put the phone down and shook his head. "Toodle-bye," he repeated wonderingly.

"Going home are you, Mr. Peat," Thomas grinned at him. "I think it's time to call it a day."

"I have to call in upstairs first, Thomas," he said. "Oh, Thomas?"

"Yes, Mr. Peat; what can I do for you?"

"Nothing—thanks, that's all."

Harold was waiting for him upstairs. "I think you should know," he said, lighting his pipe, "that we've heard from Bern."

"Really?"

"Scarr's people barreled across the Swiss frontier this morning in some sort of armored vehicle. The Swiss are really steamed up about it. Apparently Scarr didn't stop; he just went right through and broke their frontier pole."

"Oh, pity "

"I'll say. The Swiss are demanding indemnification."

"They would," said Carlo. "How much?"

"A hundred pounds."

"That seems rather steep."

"Well, I thought so, too," said Harold, abandoning the effort to light his pipe. "I told them we'd s-s-settle for seventy-five."

"They got Stengel out of the drink, then."

"Yes, and damn Johnny Scarr if he catches pneumonia. I suppose you'll want to talk to him, won't you?"

"Who?"

"Stengel, of course. He's the plum. I'd rather thought of keeping him for myself."

"Oh, you're quite welcome," said Carlo Peat, waving several pieces of paper under Harold's nose. "Quite welcome."

"What are these, Carlo?"

"Scarr's signals," Carlo said, dropping them on the desk next to Harold's pipe and box of matches. "The ones we didn't answer."

EPILOGUE

"Stengel was a Communist, then?" the reporter said.

"Yes, but not in the sense that he believed in great Hegelian machines behind the wings of history. I don't think anyone can have that kind of belief anymore. In anything," Carlo added, looking out across the bay into Lake Lugano. "He joined the Party in 1920 after he got out of the army. Later on, of course, he joined the Nazi Party. That was after the Beerhall Putsch, I believe. Would you care for another sherry, Mr. Johnson?"

"Sure." The reporter was agreeable. "There's one thing I don't understand, though," he said.

"Only one, Mr. Johnson?"

"Well, several, actually." The reporter smiled. "What happened after Scarr's people blew up the pile—wasn't there any contamination?"

"Oh, yes, but very minor, no more than you'd expect from spontaneous fissioning. The pile was never active, Mr. Johnson. So there was nothing like the contamination that occurred at Three Mile Island, say."

The reporter understood. He smiled again, in a wry sort of way. "I'm right in assuming, aren't I," he said, "that Hugo Weber was telling the truth when he said that the German effort was pretty uncoordinated and lacking in direction."

"Yes, until Gerlach's appointment and the move to Haigerloch, but it was too late by then. Fortunately."

"Then why did Hugo Weber kill himself? And why were the documents that Dorf turned over to Balthazar here in Lugano so convincing?"

245

"You must remember that Hugo had nothing to lose. He was dying of leukemia. You should also remember that the whole object of the exercise was to make it look as though Germany really did have the bomb, in order to secure a truce from us so they could turn their armies around and fight the Russians."

"Surely Stengel couldn't have wanted that," the reporter objected.

"Well, he could and he couldn't," said Carlo. "I'll come to Rudolf in a moment, when I've dealt with the documents. In some ways the blueprints were the cleverest part of the whole deception operation, far cleverer than the whole business about the Angel of Death and Hugo's supposed madness. You see, Stengel was actually feeding us our own stuff. Remember, the Russians knew all there was to know about the Manhattan Project, and Stalin wasn't at all surprised when Roosevelt told him of the revolutionary new explosive they were working on. All that Stengel had done was to replace the lettering on the blueprints with technical German, which was enough to make them foreign, and, considering their nature, dynamite, if you'll pardon the pun, Mr. Johnson. So the tubular man was quite right when he said that what the Germans had was as good as *or better than* anything of ours, because his own knowledge wasn't completely up to date; nobody's was. And besides, he was crediting the enemy with his usual technical proficiency under somewhat straitened circumstances. If Degussa could afford to pass on documents like that, there was no telling what they might have up their sleeves. That was Brown's reasoning, anyway, and I can't say, looking back, that I could fault him. You were quite right about his postwar prospects, by the way. The tubular man was farmed out to the World Health Organization."

"What about Dorf?" the reporter asked.

"Dorf was on the board of Degussa and on the letterhead. He was not a technical man, of course, and the documents were supplied by Gisevius at the German Legation in Bern. Dorf had every reason, initially, to believe the blueprints were what they purported to be. Later on, I think he began to have his doubts. Of course, as a German patriot, Dorf wanted to maintain the illusion right down to the wire, which is why he detained Stengel, hoping against hope that he might convince Scarr's people of the bomb's reality. Katherina Weber, too, was similarly motivated, except, unlike Dorf, she knew all along that there was no bomb and that the whole thing was an elaborate hoax. That is why she seized the fuses from Roberts and Prentice when it looked like Vorpal was going to succeed. She even maintained the front on board the aircraft—for obvious reasons. Von Wenden would have turned back if he had discovered he was carrying a dummy. Katherina did splendidly; from what I heard she even managed to scare Stengel a little."

"Well, that answers another question, anyway," the reporter said. "The plane was carrying a dummy."

"Yes, it was a mock-up designed by the ordnance testing division of the Reich Research Council. The bomb had all the ballistic characteristics of the real Kindchen Alberich—if there was going to be a real bomb, which there wasn't, not without the plutonium. By the way, Katherina's playacting wasn't entirely without point. The bomb did have a TNT charge in it—enough to have blown the Stirling out of the sky if she'd slipped up with the fuses. And another thing—this is one of the little accidents of intelligence work that make it so fascinating. When we picked up Dorf's signal to Stengel, *'Die Maschine geht,'* Dorf really believed that the pile had gone critical. Apparently Katz or one of the other technicians made an error in reading the neutron flux. After that, no one was in a hurry to disillusion the Colonel-General. So Dorf's signal, though spurious, was in a sense genuine—a real gift to Stengel. All the other signals—to do with critical paths, explosive rings, and so on—all those were designed to mislead our boffins as much as the people in the Führerbunker. Which brings me to Stengel."

"Yes," said the reporter.

"His task was twofold. On the one hand he had to convince Hitler, on the other, our people. The first task was by far the easiest, psychologically and from the material point of view. This was Hitler's bomb, the dreamchild of a sick fantasy if you like, the last hope of the defeated Führer. It would satisfy his lust for vengeance against the West, who had let him down in the anti-Bolshevik crusade. Materially, the very factor working against the bomb's production—lack of coordination—aided Stengel in his deception. There was no one scientist who could or would deny that Kindchen Alberich was almost ready in March 1945. No one scientist had that kind of information, and it would have taken a very brave man or woman to have gone to Hitler and said, 'Look, the Emperor's naked, the baby has no clothes.' So the lie was generally accepted and encouraged by the people in Hitler's entourage, people like Bormann. This was to be the last and the greatest of the wonder weapons.

"Convincing our people was a good deal more difficult, though of course Stengel had his inside man—Philby—who would debrief him and was generally helpful during the course of the operation, slanting information one way or the other, sitting on this, releasing that—a thousand and one little things all adding up to the big picture. Afterward, for example, we learned all about how Stengel had volunteered for the mission and how, if necessary, he was prepared to use violence to escape from the aircraft, and virtually nothing about the Soviet penetration of the Manhattan Project. So the inside man was a great help to Rudolf, as were the Webers: Hugo as a cover-up we were meant to see through, Katherina playing the part of the virtuous maiden who has decided to tell all. Excellent casting, and Hugo's suicide was the clincher. But I was forgetting your sherry, Mr. Johnson." Carlo stood up to replenish the reporter's glass.

"And the motive?" asked Johnson.

"Obvious, surely." Carlo returned with the reporter's drink. "Stengel gave Germany the one thing she needed most in the spring of 1945: hope, strategic hope. Why *do* you think they kept it up for so long? Because the man at the top was convinced his scientists were going to make him a present of the bomb. A delusion maybe, but a rational delusion. And as long as Germany kept on fighting she would be ruined, utterly ruined, which was entirely in accordance with the policy of Rudolf Stengel's masters in the Kremlin. Cheers, Mr. Johnson."

It made sense. Johnson sipped at his drink, which left a bad taste in his mouth. It wasn't the sherry's fault.

Johnson said: "I'm surprised they would risk their own penetration of the West's atomic secrets by letting their man use those documents."

"Don't be," said Carlo. "They were controlling the investigation as well as the leak. Double security, an absolute master stroke."

Carlo sounded envious, Johnson thought. "Supposing it had been real," he mused. "Hitler's bomb. What then?"

"I wouldn't be talking to you now," Carlo replied.

"Nor me." The story suddenly became a personal thing. Johnson remembered that his mother had been three months pregnant in the spring of 1945.

"Ah," said Carlo.

"What if there had been a separate peace and the Germans had turned their armies around? What then?" asked Johnson, steering around this alarming intrusion of the personal into history.

"The answer's probably the same, at least my part of it." Carlo smiled. "Germany's ruin would have been all the greater. There would have been another war, and war is the catalyst of history. Stengel would have speeded up the dialectic. Who knows really? I can say that the West would have fought the Russians on the Elbe; I think it likely that we would have lost, which is why I said that the answer would have been the same for me. But that is a future that never was."

"Like Hitler's bomb," said Johnson, who suddenly thought of Katherina Weber. It was her death—of cancer, in a Washington, D.C. hospital, that had kindled the reporter's interest in the story, and also the reason Carlo had agreed to see him. "What about Katherina?" he asked. "Did you believe her? Or did you think she was lying to you all the time?"

"I—" Carlo hesitated; the truth had never seemed so evasive or evanescent, a will-o'-the-wisp flickering faintly in the far-off mists of time and memory. "I tried to keep all possibilities in my head at the same time," Carlo answered. "Twice, I came very close to believing her; in fact I would say she had my conditional assent—no, more than that. I don't mean to sound so equivocal, but life is an equivocal sort of business, Mr. Johnson." Carlo smiled again, an equivocal sort of smile. "At least my life has been that way," he added wanly. "The first time," he continued, "the first time was when she said that it was a beautiful thing to believe in the truth, always to be looking for the right way. I knew then, or thought I did, that she was a person who was telling the truth, a person who knows what it is always to be looking for the right way and never to find it. I could have been listening to myself. And, do you know, Mr. Johnson, when she said that you can lie by telling the truth, or just that part of the truth you think people need to know, do you know I think I *was* listening to myself. She was so very clever," said Carlo Peat, lapsing into silence.

"And the other time?" Johnson prompted.

"Oh, that." Carlo frowned. "That was different. It was when I heard the Stirling coming down. I thought, what if? Just for a moment, you know, before the phone rang."

Johnson fleetingly imagined all the permutations of the infinitely possible that must have gone through Carlo's mind. It seemed unlikely they would ever be spelled out.

"So why did you let her go?" Johnson asked.

"Why, Mr. Johnson?" Carlo smiled. "I wanted to see what would happen."

"Philby must have known there was no bomb all the time," said Johnson.

"Yes, just as Stengel knew about the Enigma cipher being broken— illicit knowledge, in both cases. One can use illicit knowledge covertly, but it must never been seen to be used, Mr. Johnson."

"So you wanted to see what would happen?"

"Yes."

Johnson got up, leaving his drink almost untouched, and walked over to the hotel room balcony where he gazed out in silence at the vista along the lakeshore, the hotels, villas, and apartments, the panoply of the Alps. Every other car was a Rolls-Royce, every other car a Mercedes.

Johnson was suddenly bitter. "Look at the bloody world you've left us," he exclaimed, anguished. "Do you think it really made the slightest bit of difference who used the bomb first and against whom?"

"Oh yes, to the Japanese," said Carlo Peat, distressed at such cynicism in one so young. He felt that he had something to explain nevertheless, something to expiate. "You must understand, it's not my world either. After all, I didn't make it," said Carlo Peat, with that irresponsible modesty that comes with age, wondering if the reporter would ever understand him.

Somehow he thought it unlikely, and was surprised when the reporter laughed, such a laugh as Carlo did not like to hear, a laugh that showed his evasions for what they were, his cover all gone and blown, a useless, mangled, broken thing, an apology for life.

"Every man has to make his own bed and lie in it," the reporter said.

MORE FICTION FROM STEIN AND DAY

MORE FICTION FROM STEIN AND DAY

			U.S.	CAN.
8030-7	**SEASON OF THE OWL** Miles Wolff (100)		2.95	3.50
8052-8	**SEIGE** Edwin Corley (50)		3.95	3.95
8148-6	**THE STALIN ACCOUNT** Kenneth Royce (50)		3.95	NCR
8131-1	**STREETS OF GOLD** Evan Hunter (50)		3.95	4.95
8043-9	**THE STUART LEGACY** Robert Kerr (100)		3.50	NCR
8210-5	**THROUGH THE DOOR** Jo Anne Yarus Russell		3.95	4.95
8203-2	**THE TRAP** Kenneth Royce		3.50	4.50
8219-9	**TROIKA** Clive Egelton		3.95	NCR
8069-2	**UNREPENTANT WOMEN** Judith Burnley (100)		3.50	NCR
8137-0	**THE VALUE OF NOTHING** John Weitz (50)		3.95	4.95
8164-8	**WHITE FOR DANGER** David Stevens (100)		3.95	NCR
8098-6	**WOMEN HUNT** Francis Ryck (100)		3.50	4.50